A
VOICE
IN THE
NIGHT

A
VOICE
IN THE
NIGHT

SARAH HAWTHORN

OPEN ROAD

INTEGRATED MEDIA

NEW YORK

ISBN: 978-1-5040-7895-5

This edition published in 2022 by Open Road Integrated Media, Inc.
180 Maiden Lane
New York, NY 10038
www.openroadmedia.com

To Brett, for always believing

A
VOICE
IN THE
NIGHT

NEW YORK

Martin had an annoying habit of leaving his dirty socks in the exact spot he pulled them off: under the dining table, on the sofa, in the bed. That morning they found their way onto the bathroom scales.

'You're a heathen,' Lucie yelled through a mouthful of toothpaste.

'And you're a fucking amazing woman who I love and can't get enough of.' Martin came up behind her and nuzzled his stubble against her neck; teasing and sexy.

'Oh, shut up.' Lucie grabbed a towel, wiped her mouth and wriggled from his grasp. 'You can't charm me with your pseudo-Irish blarney.'

'Sure, I can.' Martin grinned and squirted shaving cream onto his hands. As he slapped it over his face, a blob landed on the end of Lucie's nose. 'See? You're adorable. So adorable, I'm gonna take you for a splendid dinner tonight. Some swanky new bar. Upper West Side? The Village? Your preference, babe.'

'Have you forgotten? You're flying to Florida this afternoon for the rest of the week.' Lucie picked up his socks. 'Your wife's expecting you.' She let her long blonde hair flop forward, hiding her disappointment.

'Change of plan.' With practised speed he whipped a razor over his chin.

'What?' Martin's plans never changed: his wife saw to that. Her professorial work kept her in Boston except for mid-term and semester breaks; in between, she expected to see Martin every other weekend and for designated holidays. The dates were set well in advance so he couldn't wriggle out of his obligations. These new plans had to be last-minute and urgent for him to cancel a long-planned stay at their Miami condo. Odd.

Martin hesitated. 'I'll explain later.' He dried his face and rinsed the razor under the tap. 'I've gotta get to Wall Street by eight-thirty for a meeting with my broker. Book somewhere for tonight. Leave me a message, and I'll meet you there. Make it somewhere special.' He kissed her cheek. 'Bathroom's all yours.'

But it's not, is it? Lucie thought. *The bathroom will never be 'all mine'. Not until you leave your wife. As you've promised.*

She rolled his socks into a ball, threw them in the laundry basket and considered the upside: she no longer faced the prospect of ten lonely days without him.

She called out, 'What's the name of that place we went to on Bleecker?' It was fine for Martin to ask her to choose somewhere, but her budget ran to cheap diners not *New York Times* recommendations, and he was quick to criticise substandard food or service. When he said swanky, he meant five stars.

'I've a better idea—I'll write it down for you.' He sounded distracted, in a hurry to get going. He hated being late.

Naked, she turned on the shower and then leant against the door to the living room. Martin stood at his desk in the window, jacket slung over one shoulder, briefcase at his feet. He put on his wire-rimmed glasses. Began writing. Stopped. Shook his pen. Sighed and lifted the lid from the antique silver inkwell. Unscrewed the pen, held it over the pot and refilled it. His Parker pen. Tortoiseshell. Inherited from his father. Scribbled on the notepad. Put his pen in his shirt breast pocket. Turned and saw her. Grinned. 'You're sure a sight.' He blew her a kiss, picked up his briefcase and disappeared from view. The front door clicked, and he was gone.

An eerie silence descended. Without Martin, the apartment became drained of light and life. She wandered over to the window and ripped the piece of paper from the pad. *Lutèce. Book in my name.* "Wow—it was unlike Martin to take her somewhere so famous, where he'd be sure to bump into someone he knew. Something had happened. With Penelope? Lucie's breath quickened. Had he told her?

She hastily showered and dressed, eager now to leave. She'd buy a coffee and bagel on her way to work. Think about what to wear tonight: something sexy, to make Martin proud. Gosh. Dinner with New York's elite at Lutèce. *Lutèce.*

Caution, ever at her side, reminded her of the rules. In case she'd got it wrong, or on a whim Penelope flew to New York rather than stay alone in Boston, Lucie packed up her overnight bag. She checked around that nothing of hers lurked, but no, the eleventh-floor apartment had that pristine look of male solitude. A pied a terre, he called it, with Penelope nowhere to be seen: no photographs, no clothes in the wardrobe, no make-up in the bathroom. Although the lack of female touches made it easier to pretend Penelope didn't exist, Lucie remained fascinated by this woman who had once upon a time captured Martin's heart.

She double-locked the front door, slung her bag over her shoulder and took the elevator to the lobby, where she smiled good morning to the doorman. Then she exited into a beautiful blue-sky morning and strode down West 72nd towards Broadway and the subway station.

Afterwards, Lucie could only recall that day as a blur. Panic, confusion, fear. Stuck with her legal colleagues in their rarefied Park

Avenue offices, safely away from the mayhem, waiting for news. Everyone knew someone in those towers. Everyone was powerless. Trying to call Martin, but all the phones in Lower Manhattan were jammed. Trying to remember where he had gone. His broker, he'd said. Somewhere around Wall Street. Feeling sick in her stomach, which churned with anxiety. Praying to a god she didn't believe in that he was safe. Surrounded by people in tears, in shock, glued to television screens, unable to comprehend the ghastliness that worsened each minute. Watching, aghast at the jumpers fleeing flames for a certain death below. Sickened when the first tower, swathed in billowing smoke, disappeared forever; and then the second tower folded into itself and slid to the ground. Unable to explain to anyone how frightened she was for her lover—because he was a secret—only able to say she feared for her friends.

All she could do was wait. And hope.

At midday she ventured onto the streets. People swarmed, stunned, distressed, strangers comforting strangers. Sirens screamed. She made her way back to Martin's apartment, in a hurry now. *That's where he'll go. That's where he'll find me.* A cluster of tenants huddled in the lobby, waiting with the doorman. Everyone looked her way, disappointment flooding their faces when they saw only a stranger.

The doorman shook his head. 'No one's up there.' So no Martin, but no Penelope either.

Lucie pressed the elevator call button. 'I'll wait.'

She let herself in with the keys he'd given her. The apartment remained as she'd left it that morning. No shoes tumbled inside the front door. No jacket flung over the back of a dining chair. She turned on the television and watched as day turned to night. She dozed and woke, startled to find herself on the sofa, clutching his t-shirt, until she remembered. On the news, they said thousands had been killed, some companies almost totally wiped out. When she heard the name, 'Cantor Fitzgerald', the firm where his broker worked, she ran to the bathroom and threw up in the sink. He would have been there: the plane had hit the North Tower at 8.46.

Everything went black. She crawled into bed, their bed, where they'd made love, laughed, planned a future together, promised their hearts and souls. She didn't cry, not then. Hours, days went by. A kernel of hope glimmered that maybe he lay in the hospital, bones broken but mind intact. Or pinned under metal. Or helping to find victims. She dared not leave the apartment, in case he came for her; she dared not use his landline, in case he called. The television was her sole companion, but showed only wrenching stories of lost ones, devastation, incomprehension.

A loud knock at the front door roused her, and a thrill of joy kicked inside her. Weak from lack of nourishment, she stumbled down the corridor and, without checking the peephole, opened up.

'You better leave.' The doorman gently squeezed her arm. 'His wife is on her way. Lucky for you, she phoned ahead. Forgot to pack her keys, wanted to check I have a set.'

'Is he . . . Has he. . . ?'

His grip turned firm. 'She told me he's presumed dead, so she's coming to meet the authorities. And see his work colleagues. That's all I know.' With his arm around Lucie, he guided her back into the apartment. She sensed him looking around, taking in her mess. 'Let me help you pack, then I'll clean the place up. You're in no state.'

Too weak to argue, spent of all emotion, Lucie curled up in the corner of the sofa. 'What's your name?'

'Albert. Alby.'

'When will she be here? Penelope?'

'About an hour.' He held out her jacket and bag. 'Keys?'

Lucie took her belongings and scanned the room one last time. 'On the desk. Goodbye, Alby.'

LONDON

PRESENT

A small white envelope lay facedown on the mat, where it had fallen through the letterbox. Briefcase under one arm and laden with groceries, Lucie picked it up, bottom-bumped the front door shut, paused to drop the letter and her keys on the hall table, and stomped down the passageway to the kitchen. She was still furious with Charles Fensham-Smith for undermining her by making her look a fool in front of that arsehole client: a belligerent Greek bigamist with nine children, who failed to understand the advantages of using a condom. Or the workings of British law.

She tossed her shopping bags on the scrubbed pine table alongside a half-finished bottle of New Zealand pinot noir. Muttering profanities that would have turned Charles F-S's pompous English ears bright pink, she unloaded three bottles of mineral water, an assortment of fruit and a tub of yogurt into the fridge. She took a glass from the cupboard above the sink and slammed it on the counter. 'Fucking stuffed shirt, double-barrelled, up himself know-it-all.'

Swearing only fuelled her aggravation. So what if he was senior partner? He had no right to hijack her meeting, contradict her client advice and freeze her out when she spoke. He'd allowed the back-and-forth arguments to drag on for three tedious hours until well past seven o'clock—no doubt to jack up the firm's billables—and afterwards expected her to join him for a cosy nip of whisky. Standing in the doorway of his office, jacketless with tie loosened, he'd jangled the ice in his tumbler with an air of arrogant expectancy. 'We make a good team, my dear,' he'd had the gall to say, accompanied by that supercilious smile that made her want to hit him. Except as the new kid on the block she had to swallow her pride or sacrifice the promised pot of gold: equity partner in a prestigious British law firm. She needed a majority of the partners' votes, and Charles wielded political influence among his peers.

Glass of wine in hand, she made her way upstairs to get ready for dinner. It was pointless being angry or frustrated with Charles. A dyed-in-the-wool English snob, doubtless he viewed her as a rookie Australian colonial. She'd prove herself, and he'd back off.

Winding her hair into a messy bun, she went in search of her leather jacket and a pair of loafers. Jonathan hadn't struck her as the kind of guy to overdress for; he'd probably take her somewhere casual. And if he was the type who liked a stroll after dinner, she'd prefer to be wearing appropriate footwear.

She glanced at her watch: eight-fifteen. Twenty minutes to relax before she went in search of a cab. She took a long sip of wine, headed downstairs and saw the letter on the hall table. Probably a bill or a circular—nothing interesting came via snail mail anymore. She picked it up and went to the living room. The streetlights from the mews cast a dull glow across the room, and she switched on the art deco sconces either side of the fireplace. With her legs up on the delicate blue-and-green striped sofa, she selected *Don Carlo* from her playlist, and turned the envelope this way, then that.

No stamp, and blank of her name and address, it must have been hand-delivered. A note from a neighbour? An invitation? She turned it over, flicked her finger under the flap, then withdrew and unfolded the single sheet of paper. The neat, unfamiliar handwriting seemed to bounce off the page.

At last, I've found you. A shock, I'm sure. But in time, I'll explain.

Martin

Martin? She mentally ran through her list of contacts. Perhaps someone reaching out, having heard she'd moved to London. If so, why not message her via Facebook? Or LinkedIn? Twitter, Instagram? She'd touched base with a few old friends who'd ended up in England and received vague promises to 'catch up soon', but they all had families now who kept them occupied with pursuits in which she had little interest.

A shiver ran through her. There was something ominous about the short, sharp sentences. She checked the envelope again; nothing suggested it was intended for her, and yet *I've found you . . . A shock . . .* implied she was the intended recipient. Hand-delivery was a bit creepy—if it was meant for her, then the sender knew where she lived.

The more she examined the note, the more intrigued she became. She'd only been in London a few weeks, and so far she'd made acquaintances, not friends. The neighbours remained aloof, limiting communication to a small nod or muttered greeting. There was no one she could imagine going to the effort of popping such a message through her letterbox.

Someone in the office? A new colleague, too shy to make a direct appeal to her? She snorted at the idea. Lawyers were renowned for not mincing words. Still, some junior associate, overawed by her seniority, might be testing her willingness to be approached. A pretty strange way to go about it, though.

The orchestra swelled to crescendo, and Jonas Kaufmann's flawless tenor burst into the living room. As she re-read the note, the melodic strains of the opera took her back to another time, another place. In New York, once upon a time, she'd loved a man called Martin. Martin Cornish. But those days were long gone, and Martin long dead. Corpses buried under rubble, reduced to ashes, didn't write letters.

She folded the note. If it was important, the sender would contact her again.

There was another alternative, of course: the letter wasn't meant for her. She tucked the sheet of paper back into the envelope. It could have been intended for the previous tenant, the sender not knowing they'd moved away. If she didn't hear from this Martin again soon, next time she passed the letting agent's office she'd drop it in. Right now she needed to apply a slick of lipstick and make her way to Southwark.

Tonight was her first real date with Jonathan. They'd known each other a few weeks and so far shared an occasional coffee, breakfast or lunch, always somewhere close by her office. Lucie's working day left little time for breaks, so she appreciated his understanding that when she said she could only spare ten minutes, she meant it. She found him good company. Intelligent and well read, more a listener than a talker, he plied her with questions about her area of law, her political views, authors she favoured. Never anything all that personal. Extracting information about him had proved a challenge, but she put it down to English reticence and figured with a glass or two of wine he'd loosen up.

They'd first met at Two Hens, her favourite place for an early morning coffee. Books lined the walls, tables with mismatched chairs wobbled on the uneven floor, and in places the ceiling beams were so low she had to duck her head. She revelled in the ambience created by the cafe's eclectic clientele of barristers, journalists, actors and random drop-ins, and she found it conducive to preparing for the day's onslaught of client issues.

Jonathan had disturbed her peace by asking if he could share her table. When she'd replied, 'I'd rather you didn't,' to her bemusement he'd guffawed: a hearty, slightly insincere, somewhat nervous explosion. 'Oh, jolly good. I like your honesty,' he said, and proceeded to tap something on his phone before shrugging out of a crumpled linen jacket and squeezing his lanky body into the narrow space opposite her.

As they shook hands and exchanged names—how British, she had to stifle a laugh, they were only sharing a space for their coffee cups—she scanned his face. Boyish. Attractive. Youngish. Younger than her, anyway. Early thirties, maybe. His eyes had an intelligent glint, but his smile was unsettling. Knowing. It jolted her.

'Aussie, eh?' he asked, and she flicked a glance to her laptop, hoping he'd get the hint.

Undeterred, he carried on. 'I recognised the accent. A dinky-di.'

'Lucie, actually.'

He frowned and thumbed his phone screen. 'Ah.' Then roared with laughter as he got the joke. 'Oh, good one. Lucie, not Di.' And laughed again—a genuine one this time, a boom of glee.

Despite herself, she laughed too.

'I'm guessing you're an accountant or a banker,' he said.

She kept her head down. 'Lawyer.' She mentally kicked herself for answering, but she couldn't have this annoying stranger believe she filed tax returns for a living. The sin of pride wasn't attractive, but hell, she'd slaved for years to make it into a top-tier firm, so some amount of boasting was justified. 'Charnbrook and Henley.'

'Impressive.'

The antique cuckoo clock on the wall above Jonathan's head chirruped nine o'clock, catching her attention. She stood and buttoned her Armani jacket.

'Are you leaving already?' Jonathan ran his fingers through his rumpled hair and affected a look of perplexed dismay. 'But we've only just met.' He chuckled at his cliché. 'I'll call you.'

Lucie had been surprised he'd followed through. They didn't have much in common, as far as she could fathom. And he must be a good ten, fifteen years younger than her, which she found flattering but mystifying. Still, he was a serious young man, which gave him an aura of maturity—somewhat belied by the way he kept checking his phone, with bitten-down fingernails.

As she paid off the cab and crossed the road to Geronimo, a small restaurant tucked down a side lane off Bermondsey Street, she mused about what he'd be like in bed. Would he be voracious, taking her on the carpet or the kitchen table? Or slow and gentle, savouring every part of her? In all likelihood, she'd find out later that night.

Geronimo sported a distressed, industrial design with exposed brick walls and polished concrete floors, but also a log fire to warm the cool autumn night. Her kind of place: out of the way, intimate, character-filled.

While she read the limited menu, Jonathan ordered a Californian merlot, but not before checking out its credentials on his phone. After reading the label, he waved away the waiter, unscrewed the top and poured a small amount into his glass. He swirled the blood-red liquid, took a deep sniff, sipped and lifted his eyes to heaven as he tasted. 'Elements of black cherry. Well balanced. You'll like it.' He filled Lucie's glass, then his. 'This wine always reminds me of that film *Sideways*. Did you see it?'

'With the guy who pronounced it "murr-low"?'

They laughed. 'That's the one.'

That was a good segue into learning more about Jonathan. 'Do you know America?' she asked.

He chewed on the side of his thumb, considering. 'Not really. And you?'

'I spent some time in New York.'

'Oh?'

'After I left uni. I did some more study there, and interned. A long time ago:' She returned her attention to the menu. 'Shall we order?'

'I nearly went there a couple of years back,' said Jonathan, signalling to the waiter. 'Sondra Radvanovsky was performing.'

That captured her attention—not many men she knew held an interest in opera. 'I saw her *Norma*. She was sublime.'

'Radvanovsky.' Jonathan looked up from studying the menu. 'Awesome. So you were recently back in New York?'

Lucie laughed. 'Sadly, no. It was a live performance at the movies in Sydney. But we—I—did see Pavarotti in *Aida* at the Met.' Martin had paid a small fortune for the tickets. 'That was truly memorable.' A disconcerting sensation ran through her. Odd to be reminded of Martin twice in one evening.

'I'm beyond envious. What a legend.'

Lucie nodded. Before Jonathan could ask more about New York, she switched subjects. 'Do you travel for work?'

He sipped his wine. 'I tell you what . . . Come with me to *Falstaff* next week. I've got tickets. I'd be honoured if you'd accompany me. Bryn Terfel's singing.'

This was the moment when a mild flirtation and nice friendship could turn awkward. She found it almost irresistible, the idea of being courted and wooed . . . except she didn't want her life hijacked by a romantic entanglement with an intense young man who might become a nuisance. A date at the opera, in her experience, was an invitation that came with expectations. It smacked of potential coupledom.

'That sounds marvellous, but I—'

'Excellent.' He snapped closed the menu. 'I'll text you the details. Shall we do share plates?'

She shook herself—what was she thinking? A night at the opera by no means constituted a declaration of undying love. She really needed to stop fearing being trapped in another relationship. 'Perfect. You choose.'

Jonathan signalled to the waiter again. 'We'll have one of everything.'

'That was easy,' Lucie said with a laugh.

He topped up her glass. 'Tell me about growing up in Sydney.'

Where to begin? 'I was pretty fortunate. My parents were comfortably off and managed to stay together until my sister and I finished school.'

'What happened?'

'With my parents? Dad had a midlife crisis, bought a Harley-Davidson and disappeared across the Nullarbor desert—well, maybe not the Nullarbor but into the outback. Came home and told Mum he'd had enough of Australia, he wanted to live in Asia. She basically said fine but he'd be on his own. As far as I know, he now lives on a beach somewhere with his Thai bride.' She'd not heard from him in months. His erratic unreliability had worsened since he'd left her mum and gone troppo. Finding himself, he called it; in the process, he misplaced everyone else.

'And your mother?'

'Funny, really. She threw herself into good works, and now we hardly see or hear from her because she spends so much of her time volunteering. Nepal, Ethiopia—wherever she thinks she can make a difference. The stupid thing is, since she's now hardly ever in Australia, she and Dad probably could have worked things out and stayed together. I don't think either is that happy.' The arrival of zucchini puffs, calamari and seared artichokes saved Lucie from further explanation. 'As for my sister Zoe, she's happily married with twin boys, loves being at home baking cakes, and works as a hotel receptionist.' Lucie envied Zoe, who had met and married her childhood sweetheart and never looked back, never questioned her choices.

'How were you at school?' Jonathan prompted.

'A bit of a rebel. Always in trouble. But I was smart too, so I got away with it most of the time. I only got suspended once.' For smoking marijuana: she'd stolen some of her dad's stash. 'I really enjoyed school. All the sport, the thrill of learning new things, the challenge of working hard enough to get into law at Sydney uni. But most of all, the friendships.' Especially with Em, her partner in crime. They were still there for each other whenever they needed to share their ups and downs. Em, the rule breaker, the girl who had taught her about mascara and tampons, and introduced her to skinny-leg jeans. 'Enough about me. How were your schooldays?'

He looked askance at her. 'I loathed school.'

Such a blunt admission wasn't what she'd expected, and she experienced a prick of guilt at gushing about her own happy memories. But as Jonathan had offered up virtually no information about himself to date, this sudden about-turn intrigued her. 'How come?'

He fiddled with the pepper grinder. 'I'm a bit of a loner, I suppose. I don't make friends easily. I was never one of the crowd.'

A lonely boy, suffering on the edges of other children's gangs. 'What about sport?'

'Not my thing. I was a geeky little guy. Skinny. Glasses. Not athletic.'

'How did you get out of it?' In Sydney, everyone played sport at school; it was non-negotiable.

He shrugged. 'I'd do anything to avoid team games—and as for cadet camp, I hated all that trudging through forests and sleeping in wet tents.'

His forlorn look made Lucie want to throw her arms around

him. 'Yes, I can see the lack of appeal. Especially given the English climate.'

He gave her a cheeky glance. 'I got very good at feigning illness and sprained ankles. And volunteering for library duty.'

'So you were more of an indoors type?'

'Back then, I can definitely say, I preferred books to people. Well, there was one boy, but his parents moved him to another school.'

'What about your parents? Didn't they worry about you?'

He focused on serving the calamari. 'If they did, I never knew. And I never said anything. I mean, what would have been the point? It was my "normal", if you like.' He sat up straighter and exhaled. 'I had a good education, but I was glad to leave school and start to make my own decisions. No more teachers dictating what I did and when.'

Lucie couldn't understand how his parents had been so ignorant and uncaring of his solitary state. 'Tell me about your family.'

His face closed down. 'I've no siblings, and as for my mother and father—they're a bit reclusive.'

'Reclusive?'

'Yes.'

'And?.'

'That's all.'

At least this helped explain their lack of empathy for his paucity of friends. 'What did you do when you left school?'

'I went to Cambridge,' he said, perking up. 'Did an arts degree and joined a few societies. Life got a whole lot better.'

'You've never said what you do for a living, other than some part-time study. How do you pay the bills?'

He lowered his eyes and bit his lip. 'It's embarrassing . . . I inherited a lot of money. I go to uni classes sometimes, engineering and industrial design. You know.' He sounded a little vague. 'I have lots of ideas. I sketch them.' He examined his bitten finger-nails. 'Let's not talk about me.'

'What about girlfriends, then? You've never mentioned anyone.'

'No, I haven't.'

'Haven't what? Got one, or had any?'

He shifted in his seat. 'Don't be daft.'

Lucie inwardly sighed. What was it with English guys? So stitched up. If she had her breezy Australian way, she'd get him to loosen up over time, learn to trust her—and stop that anxious habit of biting his nails.

'And you?' he asked, obviously trying to sound casual.

'Almost divorced.'

He gave her a questioning look.

'We separated more than a year ago. It's just a matter of the final paperwork now.'

He clearly expected more, and she shifted uneasily. Months later, her guilt hadn't lessened; the pain she'd caused, the gap-ing hole she'd ripped in David's life, still haunted her. No matter that their wrenching separation had been long overdue—David had been blind to the inevitable. He'd explained away their con-stant bickering, awkward bedtime embraces and public pretence of happy togetherness as a phase, a blip in their commitment. For her, after years of unhappiness, it was time to draw a line. For him, their vows were unbreakable: for richer, for poorer; for better, for worse.

'Our marriage lost its way.' She splayed her hands. 'He wanted a wife who'd give him children and be content to play home-maker, and that wasn't me. I became more ambitious, he became more stuck in his ways.' She wouldn't tell Jonathan more: the ghastly fallout, the toxic combination of David's pride and anger. Instead she put on a bright smile. 'Shall we order dessert?'

Jonathan took the hint, and the conversation shifted to Brexit and Trumpism.

* * *

After dinner, he ordered an Uber and insisted on accompanying her home. To her surprise he told the driver to wait, and walked her to the door. 'Thank you for a wonderful evening,' he said. He gave her a gentlemanly peck on the cheek, and she experienced a tick of bafflement, a nudge of pique at his reticence.

'Come in,' she said. 'I've a bottle of champagne chilling.'

He seemed taken aback. 'But the taxi—'

'Pay him off.' She put her key in the lock and pushed open the door. Her cat slunk out of the shadows and, with a swish of his tail, slipped into the house.

Lucie turned to see Jonathan checking his phone as he walked down the hall towards her. 'Just making sure the driver only charged me one way.' He looked sheepish, as if she might think him penny-pinching, and bent to stroke the cat. 'What's her name?'

'Him. Trim.'

'Odd name.'

'A nod to Matthew Flinders' cat. He sailed around Australia back in the early 1800s, and Trim was his fearless and loyal companion.'

She'd acquired Trim on impulse, the British Blue she'd always craved but never got around to owning. His sleek appearance and elegant affection enchanted her—if only she could exhibit such restrained hauteur when it mattered.

She retrieved a bottle of Bollinger from the fridge. 'Let's open this.'

Jonathan nodded his approval. He accepted the bottle and two flutes from Lucie, then followed her into the tiny living room. 'Very nice,' he murmured, as he circled the space. 'Comfortable. Feminine.'

Perhaps not the place for a bodice-ripping seduction. 'Let's go upstairs,' Lucie said.

His eyes widened, and she took his hand. Clammy. Nerves?

Once in her bedroom, he sidled towards the bathroom. 'Why don't you undress while I, um, open this?'

It wasn't quite the arousing foreplay she had imagined. But she stripped down to her silk underwear—ivory, lacy—and arranged herself on the bed. Waited. One, two, three minutes. At last she heard the cork pop, and he appeared naked in the doorway, his penis flaccid, holding up two flutes of sparkling liquid and the bottle. Quick as a whippet, he passed her the champagne, turned his back, edged into the bed and covered his body with the duvet.

Side by side—him in the bed, her on top of it—they said an awkward 'cheers'.

Lucie took a couple of large sips. 'Mm. Delicious.' She made to put her glass down, but he picked up the bottle.

'Have a top-up.' Without waiting for her answer, he filled both flutes to the brim, taking his time. 'You must always pour at an angle, slowly. It helps preserve the tiny bubbles, which in turn improves the flavour.'

Lucie couldn't think of a suitable riposte, and they drank in a silence broken only by Jonathan's appreciative sighs. She figured he must be really anxious. Or shy. *If I don't get this show on the road, we'll end up drinking the whole bottle and be too pissed to screw.* She sat up and pulled her camisole over her head, giving him a full view of her breasts. Before he could protest, she took his glass and leant across him, brushing her nipples against his chest. He gave a sharp intake of breath, and she smiled as she placed their drinks on the bedside table.

Straddling him, she took his face between her hands. When she bent to kiss him, he moved his head away and slipped from under her. 'Let's do this my way,' he said.

His bed manners reflected his character: considered, patient and unhurried. He seemed disinterested in his pleasure, want-ing to explore every part of her. Whenever she tried to touch him, he pushed her away. 'You'll get your turn,' he whispered, then took her breast in his mouth. At last, he thrust himself into her and came almost at once, silently clutching her to his chest. 'Sorry, sorry.' He rolled off her and went to the bathroom. She heard a running tap before he returned, towel in hand. 'Clean yourself up.'

He'd already put on his boxers. Was he ashamed of himself, or had his childhood shyness lingered into adulthood? She sat up, pulled on her dressing-gown and watched while, with shaking hands, he refreshed their champagne. Whatever, he had a cute factor. She relaxed against the pillows and took a long sip of the refreshing bubbles. It may not have been the shag of the century, but she reckoned Jonathan could be moulded—once he got over his nerves.

NEW YORK

EARLY 2001

Lucie stretched her arms and scanned the long row of tightly jammed-in desks. Paralegals and interns, heads bowed, pored over paperwork. No one said much; they were all too busy being determined to out-do each other. She checked the clock at the far end of the office: 5.25. In theory, five more minutes and she could leave for the day. In practice, no one left at quitting time, not if they wanted to keep their job or stand any chance of a pay rise—let alone a promotion.

The pile of files in her in-tray never seemed to lessen, just a constant flow of depositions to redact. The cases she got dumped with weren't even interesting. Such was the lot of the intern, the lowest rung on the corporate ladder, her boredom occasionally relieved by making coffee or witnessing documents. Had she really studied four years of law in Sydney and another at Columbia to be treated like a worthless idiot, a drone?

She peered around the side of her desk to see whose attention she could catch. When the clock eventually ticked over to seven o'clock—the unspoken, acceptable, hour to depart—she hoped someone would be up for a drink or a quick bite. Her roommate, Jocelyn, had signalled she was off to see a baseball game with her latest boyfriend, another New Zealander she'd met at an Irish pub on St Patrick's Day. Knowing Jocelyn, she'd haul him back to their tiny Soho apartment and noisily bonk him half the night.

'*Lucie.*' The voice boomed from the far end of the room, and she swung around to see Chester Lockstein Jr, portly and commanding, with his ubiquitous unlit oversized cigar clenched between his teeth, hands on hips and legs astride. He beckoned to her. 'My office. Now. Bring a pen. And pad.'

Of all the partners, Chester was her favourite. Blunt and no-nonsense, you knew where you stood with him—he told you straight if you messed up, and slapped you on the back for a job well done. His attitude made a refreshing change from most lawyers with their whopping great egos that jockeyed with self-importance, who treated anyone their junior with contempt.

Before she had a chance to shut the door behind her, Chester barked instructions. 'Sit. Take notes. Only when I say so.'

A man stood up, buttoned his jacket and held out his hand to her. 'Chester may have no manners, but allow me to introduce myself. Martin Cornish.' Was that a Brooklyn or a New Jersey accent? She still had trouble telling the difference.

Chester chuckled. 'Always the charmer, eh, Mart?'

Lucie shook hands, then took a seat at the corner table. The two men sat in armchairs, and Chester gave forth on the intricacies of trust funds. Martin leant forward, frowning with concentration, here and there interrupting for clarification. With his lean frame, he was the type of man who wore a suit well. Who clearly worked out at the gym. Round, metal-rimmed spectacles added a touch of gravitas. Late thirties, Lucie surmised, his dark hair just beginning to silver at the edges. Good-looking in a chiselled, tidy way.

For more than an hour, she waited to take a note. Finally, Chester said, 'That'll be all.'

'Geez, you're a jerk,' said Martin. 'Why'd you get the poor gal in here for nothing?'

'Back-up. In case.'

Martin grinned at her and turned back to Chester. 'Wanna ticket for *Eugene Onegin* tonight, Ches?'

'No can do, Mart. Other plans.' Chester tapped the side of his nose. 'Take Lucie, she's new in town. Time she saw more of the Big A than the inside of her paralegal's cubicle.'

'What d'you say, Lucie? Are you game?'

She hovered in the doorway; she had no idea what *Eugene Onegin* was. But anything would be better than playing third wheel, albeit on the other side of Jocelyn's thin bedroom wall.

Martin tipped his head. 'Say yes. Please?'

His smile radiated charm. How could she refuse?

When she realised that Martin was taking her to an opera, to endure hours of screeching and high-pitched wailing, Lucie almost backed out—but his delighted amusement when he cottoned on to her confusion made her determined to enjoy the experience. And she didn't need to be the butt of Chester's jokes, if he discovered her ignorance.

'You're gonna love it.' Martin led the way to their seats and handed her the program. 'You can bone up on the story. It's all in here.'

Walking into the stalls of the Metropolitan Opera House in the Lincoln Center, she felt grand and important and insignificant, all at the same time. Women swathed in expensive gowns and perfume, on the arms of men in evening dress, mingled among city slickers and others in less formal attire. Straight from the office in a black dress and knee-high boots, Lucie faded into the crowd, but being with Martin, who squired her with urbane confidence, gave her a glow of pride.

As they sat side by side in Row C, she became conscious of his shoulder against hers, and the sensation made it hard to absorb the program notes and digest the plot. Her eyes glazed across the words, aware only of his warmth, not wanting him to shift away, and she yearned to touch him. He leant closer. 'Sit back and enjoy. The story is incidental to the music and the singing.'

'Whose seat have I taken?'

'No one's. I always buy two tickets.'

'I thought . . . maybe—'

'My wife? No way. Penelope's taste runs to the plebeian. Broadway musicals. Pop.'

She'd known he was married; he made no secret of it, wearing a gold band on his ring finger. But to hear her name—*Penelope*— and learn she had no interest in joining her husband, gave Lucie an idiotic thrill. 'What's she doing tonight?'

'No idea. We lead separate lives. Me here, Penelope in Boston. I guess it's a matter of time before we legalise the whole situation.'

The lights dimmed. Silence descended, broken by a few rustles of anticipation.

Martin placed a hand on Lucie's arm. 'Look to your left. You'll see the conductor enter.'

In a daze, she applauded as the conductor took a bow, turned his back to the audience, and raised his baton. As the first haunting violin strains filled the auditorium, she let the music wash over her. She felt drenched in a sense of belonging. Of arriving. Of having come to a place she didn't know she'd been looking for. Martin's wife appeared to be a mere background character who played no obvious part in his life, a troublesome shadow soon to be dealt with. So there was no harm being done.

LONDON

Lucie woke long before dawn, a few minutes until six. She lay in bed musing over Charles F-S's presumptive behaviour and plotting how to circumvent a clash of wills. In order to achieve the promotion she craved, she needed to act accordingly: not bitchy or sullen or complaining, but in a way that commanded respect. She had to win Charles over and gain his unbridled trust.

They'd got off on the wrong foot from the get-go when she'd chosen to hot desk, despite being entitled to her own office. Charles, who'd fought long and hard for this concession, had been dismayed. 'I'm a stranger here,' she'd explained. 'If I switch around, I'll get to know people quicker and pick up on cultural differences.' In truth, she didn't fancy being shut away behind a closed door after almost two decades working in an open-plan environment. Still, her rejection of a private space didn't justify Charles treating her like an underling.

This new role was more than a job to her: it fulfilled a dream, from all those years ago in New York, to one day reach the pinnacle of her career and play among the big boys. A dream derailed by 9/11 and all that had followed. So when Charles Fensham-Smith—from Charnbrook and Henley, no less—had emailed to say he'd been forwarded her LinkedIn profile and wished to discuss an opening at the firm, she took it as a sign. She would be a salaried partner initially, with Charles F-S dangling the carrot of full equity partner if her performance was up to snuff—that meant being a 'good egg', he said in their Skype interview.

She didn't need to think it over. The time had come to cleanse her life of all its debris, start afresh, take a chance. That night, she told David she'd made the decision to end their marriage, resign as partner at the mid-tier Sydney law firm and move overseas. What she hadn't revealed to Jonathan over dinner was how when David realised he couldn't change her mind, he became petty and bitter. His tears and recriminations that she'd ruined his life left her bruised with his hatred: his phone calls to friends, ranting about her cruelty; emails to work colleagues, telling them never to trust her; text messages repeatedly accusing her of infidelity. After working out her one year's notice, she was relieved to be in London.

She flung herself back onto the pillows. 'Be honest, Lucie.'

Arching her spine, she stared up at the pressed metal ceiling with its pattern of thorns entwined with roses. In two years she'd hit forty-five. Impossible to fathom; in her head, she'd barely passed the milestone of thirty. And she didn't intend to allow another decade to drift by, with life taking her up a series of blind alleys. She vowed to stay true to her ambition and let nothing block her path: career first. If her billings skyrocketed, Charles would be hard-pressed to ignore her contribution. For the time being, any Jonathans in her life would be relegated to the sidelines, a fun distraction.

Whatever happened, she wasn't going to relinquish a stint in London and all that went with it. This charming cottage in Fulham, for example, was a far cry from her post-separation, twelfth-floor two-bedder on the fringes of downtown Sydney, which had boasted a faulty lift, erratic air conditioning and

paper-thin walls. It was worth the heart-stopping rent to tot-
ter along the uneven ancient cobblestones of Bellings Mews
to her shiny black front door with its brass handle. The novelty—the delight—of stepping over the threshold into the tiny
one-up one-down, with its antique furnishings, Laura Ashley
and William Morris chintz, and wall-to-wall deep pile carpet,
captivated her every time.

At six-thirty she rose, pulled on leggings and a hoodie, folded
a black dress and jacket into her backpack, and jogged up the
mews. The streetlights glistened off the damp cobblestones—even
with the end of daylight saving, it would be dark for another half-
hour. This early there'd be few pedestrians to block her path, and
if she ran all the way, she'd be at the office in less than an hour, in
time to prepare for her first meeting over a cup of coffee at Two
Hens. Charles had given her a new client—an old schoolfriend
of his—and she intended to blow him away with her detailed
advice and documentation. The story was as old as the hills:
Peregrine Smythe, divorced from his wife, alienated by his adult
children, had met his 'dream woman' (Charles's description,
not hers). The girl was twenty-five and a croupier at the Empire
Casino. Charles had cautioned his friend to tie up his consider-
able wealth, then passed the brief to Lucie. 'Make it airtight,'
he'd said.

She pounded along Kings Road, legs pumping and mind
jumping, past sleeping boutiques, delis and eateries. Charles, she
realised, took pains to avoid clients with any potential for conflict
or failure; he had a deep-seated need to be admired and congratu-
lated. Although it might stick in her craw, she'd feed his ego and
become indispensable—but on her terms. Charles would learn
she wasn't to be messed with.

Charnbrook and Henley's head office was situated in the heart
of the City of London, close to Inns of Court, in a handsome
red-brick Georgian building. Every time Lucie stepped through

its imposing panelled door, she took pleasure in the perfect architectural proportions, grid windows and soaring ceilings. Today, however, she sprinted up the steps and through the foyer without acknowledging her impressive surrounds.

The on-duty security officer waved her through. 'You look like a woman on a mission.' He held open the lift door. *Mission possible*, she thought, buoyed by a surge of adrenalin from her run.

At level six, Lucie stepped into a grand space where artful period interior design disguised space-age technology. She walked across the plush, pure-wool, chocolate-coloured carpet, past the oversized mahogany reception desk—devoid of clutter aside from an elaborately curlicued silver bowl—and a setting of uncomfortable Queen Anne visitor chairs.

In the staff cloakroom she showered, changed, and swapped her trainers for sensible black court shoes, which she kept on the rack alongside a pair of black stilettos. She'd don the high heels later, for her meeting; their height would give her an aura of power.

Late on Friday afternoon, Charles F-S strode through the office. Without pausing to engage in conversation, he passed between desks, enunciating strident opinions of his underlings' performances.

'Excellent summing-up, Brett. His Honour told me he thinks you'll go far.'

'Billings down this week, Sophie. Not good enough.'

'Joshua, mediation date still not set? Get onto their side.'

When he reached Lucie, he propped his elbows on her workstation, leant down and lowered his voice. 'Perry's in shock.'

She peered over her computer. Her meeting with Charles's old school pal had gone much as she'd expected: Peregrine, blustering and defensive, blamed his wife for their costly divorce; his new girlfriend—'the only bright star in a dark night'—had apparently saved his soul. He'd nodded a lot and said little while Lucie had gone through the draft prenup. If he'd been surprised by the terms, it hadn't been evident.

'How so?' she asked.

'Put it this way, Lucinda, you had the desired effect.' He raised one eyebrow, which along with his covert tone parodied a comedy spy.

'You make it sound like a conspiracy. I merely did as you asked to ensure he won't get fleeced a second time.'

Charles snorted. 'Ha. Better than that—listening to you slice and dice his assets spooked him. Good old Perry is having second thoughts. Asked me if I thought he was being foolish.'

'And what did you say?' It amused her to think of Charles in the guise of a marriage counsellor.

He dipped his head, checking from side to side he wouldn't be overheard, and spoke in a whisper. 'Play the field. It's safer.' He straightened up and moved towards his office, talking in a loud voice over his shoulder. 'Quick result. Well done. I'll find more little cases like this for you.' He smirked. 'Until you've built up your profile.'

Lucie bit back a testy response. Charles's habit of damning with faint praise infuriated her, but she wouldn't engage in his power games.

She ignored the giggles of the associates seated behind her, doubtless thrilled to have someone else the butt of Charles's barbs, and went back to checking her week's invoices. By six o'clock, all done, she switched off her computer. For once she planned to take an early mark and join Kristy for a drink at The Tipperary.

Kristy, with her blunt approach to all life's problems, was Lucie's favourite person at Charnbrook and Henley. The receptionist was only twenty-something, but she seemed all-seeing and all-knowing, and Lucie often sought her out for her wise, no-nonsense attitude. She could be relied upon to put office politics in perspective, voice what no one else dared say, and maintain everyone's respect. Even Charles F-S reined in his imperious manner and snide criticisms around her—a good receptionist was hard to replace.

Cosy with dark wood panelling and plaid carpet, the pub's decor was a far cry from the steel-and-chrome, cavernous designer bars favoured by Sydneysiders. Here, Friday night drinkers jostled in the tiny space for the publican's attention before spilling out onto the pavement clutching pints of Guinness. At home they'd be braying over exotic cocktails, yelling to be heard above high-decibel music.

Lucie ordered a gin and tonic and edged her way outside, glad of her cashmere coat. The locals seemed anaesthetised to the wintry weather—women in lightweight dresses and some men in shirtsleeves. She felt cold looking at them.

Behind a group of heehawing barristers, she spotted Kristy talking to a guy in a tight-fitting blue suit. The receptionist held her body erect and appeared ill at ease—unusual for Kristy, always full of sass.

'Hi,' said Lucie, am I interrupting?'

Kristy spun round, relief flooding her features. 'You're kidding me, aren't you? I've just been telling Alan about you, and now here you are.'

Lucie glanced at her companion. Tall, blond, floppy fringe. Confident. Sexy—and knew it. He reminded her of someone, but she couldn't think who.

'G'day.' He lifted his beer mug and laughed. 'You see, I know Aussie-speak.'

'Alan's in mergers and acquisitions,' offered Kristy.

The last person Lucie wanted to talk to was another lawyer, especially one who found it clever to mimic her accent. 'Pleased to meet you.' She raised a questioning eyebrow at Kristy.

'At Moores Bank.'

'Oh—I'm sorry. I thought you might be with Charnbrook.'

Alan laughed again. 'Sorry I'm a banker, or sorry I'm not a colleague?'

A burst of guffawing from the barristers muffled his next words, but Lucie thought he'd said he provided advice, and something about offshore investments in the Canary Islands. Or Canada? She registered him as 'a type', pleased with himself, a smart aleck. A smart Alan.

Kristy fiddled with her hair braids. 'Will you excuse me a mo? Need the ladies. Hold my drink?'

Stuck with Kristy's sparkling wine and trapped with Alan, Lucie could see no way out. She covered the sticky pause by sipping her gin and looking down at his shiny leather Oxfords, which appeared a size too big, perhaps because of the long pointed toes. A throwback to winklepickers.

'What's so funny?'

Oh dear, she must have grinned. 'Your shoes are an unusual shape.'

'I got them in New York last week.'

The mention of New York sent her off balance, as it always did. Always would.

She covered her distraction with the first thing that came into her head. 'A shopping spree?'

'Business. I—' He caught her tease in time, and flicked her a look. Startling blue eyes shimmered with amusement and another emotion, which he made no effort to disguise: lust. It pierced her armour. He kept staring at her, this man who repelled and excited her, and it was as though he could read her mind.

She shifted under his gaze. 'Where are you from?' He had an accent she couldn't quite place.

'East End. Hackney.'

She pulled a face, and they both laughed.

'You're right. I'm not a cockney boy—grew up in South Africa, moved to California in my teens, came to London about five years ago.' He sounded bored, rattling off his history. 'And you, which part of Australia are you from?'

'Sydney.' Lucie sipped her gin. 'Not far from Bondi,' she added, before he asked—everyone did, as if Bondi Beach was the only Sydney landmark worth acknowledging. Or the only one they'd ever heard of, besides the Opera House and Harbour Bridge.

'So, that's the niceties done,' he said. 'Tell me about the real you. Your secrets. Your desires.'

She had a pulsating urge to reach out and touch him. He'd caught her off kilter—and knew it. *I want to fuck you.* She fumbled for a witticism, a way to lower the temperature, but her mouth was dry and words wouldn't come. *I want to fuck you.*

A girl, tipsy and giggling, knocked Lucie's elbow, spilling her drink.

'Hey, careful.' Alan took Kristy's wine from Lucie's hand. 'You're shaking.' He leant down and whispered in her ear. 'Shall we go?'

It was too soon, much too soon, for a close encounter. But Lucie's breasts swelled under her jacket, and her nipples hardened. 'What about Kristy?'

He nibbled her earlobe. 'A threesome? If you like . . .'

She gasped.

He put Kristy's champagne flute in his empty beer mug and took Lucie's glass from her. 'Your place or mine?'

They never made it to the bedroom. Or even up the stairs. As soon as Lucie closed her front door, Alan grabbed her from behind and pushed her skirt above her thighs, grinding into her until she could no longer cope with the agony of it, the feel of his wool suit rubbing her buttocks and his hand groping through her knickers.

She turned around, unbuckled his trousers and tugged them down in one sharp movement. He pushed her against the wall, her head at a painful angle, banging against the side of the gilt mirror. He felt in his pocket for a condom, rolled it over his cock, pushed aside her pants and entered her without a word. They grunted in animal unison, and in seconds it was over. Breathing heavily, she slumped against the wall.

He pulled out of her. 'Where's the bathroom?'

She gestured along the hallway, wondering how fast she could get rid of him. Wondering why she found him attractive. Wondering, already, how soon she could have him again.

She straightened her clothes and went to the kitchen. In the fridge she ignored the remains of a bottle of wine and took out mineral water. She didn't want to encourage him; there was something dangerous about a man she'd have sex with after knowing him less than an hour. And they'd not even kissed.

'White wine for me.' He came up behind her and took her breasts in his hands. Another shock of longing bruised her. He ran his hands down her hips. 'I'm starving. Anything in that fridge?'

'Eggs. A couple of apples.' Plus the remains of a takeaway, best chucked in the bin.

'Move over. I'll make us an apple omelette.'

'Serious?'

He took a pink-and-blue floral apron from the hook on the back of the door. 'Pretty.' He slipped it over his head. 'You whisk the eggs, I'll slice the apples.'

Masculine and efficient in Lucie's pinny, he chopped and hummed. To an outsider, the two of them would have looked the epitome of domestic harmony, not strangers bonded by a quick shag. The scenario rendered her speechless, unsure what kind of conversation to pursue; it seemed too late for small talk, and yet what else was there?

'Is that your cat?' Alan pointed an accusatory chopping knife at Trim, who had slunk into the kitchen, looking for food. 'Can you get it out of here?'

Had she heard right? 'It's his house, too.'

'Cats should stay in the wild where they belong. Useless animals, if you ask me.'

'I didn't.' She reined back another sharp comment. 'And he has every right to stay.'

'I'm allergic.'

Lucie suppressed a ripple of irritation—everyone was allergic nowadays; gluten, nuts, pollen. As if to make his point, Alan sneezed and pulled out a handkerchief, while Trim encircled Lucie's ankles in purring figures of eight. 'I'll shut him in the living room,' she said.

'Good idea.'

She picked Trim up and carried him out. 'Not for long,' she whispered in his ear. 'Just this once.'

Alan scraped the apples off the chopping board into a pan of sizzling butter. 'Why did you look so startled when I mentioned New York?'

'Envy, I suppose.' A little white lie.

'Do you know it?'

'I lived there for about two years, before I moved back to Sydney in '02.'

'Why did you leave?'

She reeled off the answer she'd used so often, she almost believed it. 'Career going nowhere. I decided there'd be more opportunities back home.' *Me going nowhere,* she thought.

'Then you were there for 9/11?' The unavoidable question.

She bent down to take plates from the cupboard. 'A bad business.'

'For me it's been good for business.' He slid her omelette onto a plate. 'Harsh but true.'

Almost twenty years—of course there'd be winners and losers. But that didn't make her like it any better. Or him.

They sat in silence at the table, Alan shovelling down his food, a man who took his pleasures quickly, while Lucie savoured the unexpectedly delicious mixture of sweet and salty. Still chewing the last bite, he dropped his fork on his plate and sat back, stretching his arms behind his head to rest it against his hands. 'Eat up.' He looked at his watch. 'I have to get up early, go home and pack. Plane to catch.'

'Oh?'

'Chicago. I'll be gone for a week. But I'd like to fuck you again before I go—leave you something to remember me by.'

His words sent a shockwave of desire through her. And something else she couldn't quite catch: a shadowy memory, disconcerting.

In one movement he pushed back his chair and reached to stroke between her legs. 'C'mon.'

Her body tremored under his touch. God, how she'd missed animal, unfettered sex. She turned to him, and he pressed his lips to hers, gentle at first and then harder, until she could bear it no longer. They tumbled up the stairs, devouring each other, raking at their clothes.

Half undressed, they fell onto the bed. She arched beneath the heat and hardness of his body and grasped his head, pulling him down between her legs. His tongue, rough against her skin, brought her to a frenzied orgasm—and again, until she cried out for him to stop. In a daze, she lay back, shorn of breath, while he fumbled in his discarded trousers' pocket for a condom.

This time he thrust into her with agonising slowness, stopping and starting. She clawed at his buttocks, rising to meet his rhythm, trembling when he paused to look at her, grinning at her desperation, before pushing deeper. At last, he threw his head back and gave a loud grunt.

They lay, their sweat mingled, in a brief state of exhaustion.

'You're a sexy bitch,' he said. 'Set your alarm for five, would you?' He rolled from the bed, pulled off the rest of his clothes—shirt, vest, socks—and went to the bathroom. She heard running water, gargling, the toilet flush.

Staring at the mess of his clothes on the floor, she wished he'd leave now. She didn't want his body in her bed in the morning, awkward goodbyes and fake promises.

He stood in the doorway, waiting to be noticed, showing off toned muscles, an erect penis. 'Do you have any condoms?'

She shook her head, caught unawares.

'What fun.' His grin, boyish and cunning, made her ache. 'A night of pure pleasure and invention awaits. I hope you're up for it.'

Her eyes drifting over his nakedness, she was struck by his boldness and lack of guile. So what if she hardly knew him—wasn't this what everyone did? Wasn't it what she had done, long ago, before she'd met David?

She stretched out an arm. 'Come here. Let's find out.'

LONDON

When she didn't head to Europe for the weekend—galleries in Paris, ruins in Rome, beaches in Croatia—Lucie followed a routine on Saturdays. An hour's intensive exercise with her personal trainer, Sonya, followed by a reward coffee. Home by midmorning and then chores, errands or me-time. If Lucie had no evening plans, she'd check emails and FaceTime or Skype with her sister and Em, whenever they could spare a few minutes of their Saturday mornings in between kids' sport (Zoe) and hangover recovery (Em). Lucie made a point of avoiding her briefcase, a trap too many of her colleagues were lured into. No matter how urgent the client business, a day's rest made her more productive.

Built like an Amazonian warrior, Sonya kept Lucie fit by forcing her desk-bound body to run, lift weights and perform press-ups. They'd met a few weeks earlier after Lucie, spent from a five-mile run around Battersea Park, recovered her breath and did leg stretches on a bench. They got chatting, and when Lucie admitted her propensity for laziness, Sonya offered her personal training services. Their arrangement had worked well ever since: while Lucie groaned and grunted, Sonya regaled her with updates from the week's celebrity news—Hollywood divorces, scandals, the latest royal family dramas.

After a brutal session that Saturday, Sonya handed Lucie a towel. 'Here, wipe off with this. I'll grab us a coffee.' She walked across the lawn past groups of fitness freaks doing cardio work-outs, leaving Lucie to dry away the shimmer of sweat on her skin. For a moment she turned her face to the weak English sun, soaking up its meagre warmth; on days like this, she missed Sydney's perennial blue skies more than when it rained.

She jogged to the exit where Sonya waited with two take-away cups. 'You're getting much fitter. I hope there's a bloke who appreciates all this work.'

A twinge of guilt assailed Lucie. 'One. Possibly two.'

'Ooh, do tell.'

Lucie had no one else in London to confide in, and Sonya, with her toned muscles and striking Slavic looks, was a woman who'd attract a lot of attention. Surely she wouldn't disapprove. 'Do you have a partner?'

Sonya's face hardened. 'I gave men up. These days I prefer the company of birds—the feathered variety.'

Lucie laughed. 'I'd never have taken you for a birdwatcher.'

'I'm not, I just have a couple of canaries.'

Lucie suppressed a shudder. Domestic birds had terrified her since childhood, when a neighbour's cockatoo had bitten the top of her head. 'I'm more a cat lover.'

'Each to her own.' Sonya slurped the froth off the top of her coffee. 'C'mon. 'Fess up about these men of yours, I'm all ears.'

'Have you ever dated a younger guy?'

'How much younger?'

'I'm not sure—ten, twelve years?'

'So he's, like, thirty-ish?'

Lucie shrugged. 'I've always preferred men my own age, or older. Going out with a younger one seems . . . oh, weird, I suppose.'

'Get over yourself. Do you like him?'

'He's easy company. We've been to the opera, and he takes me to galleries, museums. A friendship, I'd say.'

'With benefits?'

'A few.' Jonathan seemed ambivalent about sex; most times after an evening out, he either dropped her home or saw her into a cab. Which, considering her workload, suited her fine—she didn't need late nights and broken sleep. He only ever stayed over at her invitation, and the sex was passable.

'And the other guy?'

'A high-flyer, work obsessed, travels a lot. Conversation was ho-hum, but the sex was next level. Though it's been two weeks since I heard from him. A one-night stand, I guess.'

Sonya flexed her rock-hard biceps. 'That's the way it goes with a fuck buddy, darling. He'll get in touch when he has the itch.'

Back home, Lucie couldn't get those words out of her head: *fuck buddy*. Could she do this? Would a stimulating bedmate compensate for the lack of decent conversation? Ten years of failing at marriage with David had persuaded her she'd be better off on her own, and the novelty of being single hadn't yet evaporated. Work kept her busy, but a woman had needs . . .

She stripped off her gym gear, showered and decided she'd earned a quiet day cloistered with a book. Ignoring the pile of pristine new release bestsellers next to the bed, she chose to reread *Tess of the D'Urbervilles*. To take advantage of the unexpected sunshine, she brought Thomas Hardy onto the tiny Juliet balcony that overlooked the mews. Not much traffic ventured down the narrow cobblestone laneway—vehicles were barred except delivery and taxi services, and those of residents who garaged them in the converted stables—promising her an undisturbed few hours. Wrapped in a chunky cardigan and sitting with her socked feet on the iron railing, she buried herself in nineteenth-century rural England.

The front doorbell rang out, harsh and assertive. Shaken from fictional Wessex, she peered over the balcony but could only see a man's back. She hurried downstairs and shouted through the door, 'Who's there?'

'Package for Miss Wilkinson.' The confident voice held a note of impatience.

She frowned—she wasn't expecting a delivery. 'Just a minute,' she said, unlocking the door.

A young man in a Top Couriers uniform held a rectangular box. She signed for it, gave him two one-pound coins, and took the package upstairs.

She tore off the brown wrapping. A shoebox: Manolo Blahnik. She lifted the lid and pushed aside the tissue paper, expecting— oh, well, she really didn't know what to expect. Legal papers, perhaps; Charles F-S's idea of a prank.

Lucie's jaw dropped. A pair of the most exquisite shoes she'd ever seen, tissue nestling in their toes, glimmered up at her: slender stilettos in layered shades of red, stitched with delicate brocade, oozing lush indulgence. She stroked the satin, feeling the ripples where embroidery met fabric. A cruel error, she thought, and picked up the wrapping paper. Her name and address were clearly printed, no sender's details.

She checked for a card stuck to the paper or tucked into the box, then slipped her hand into the neatly folded, soft velour bag. It was intended to envelop her shoes—*her shoes!*—whenever they rested, weary after evenings of walking red carpets or dancing at balls. Her fingers found a small envelope, and her heart beat a little faster as she pulled out a white card with typewritten words: *Beautiful feet deserve to walk in splendour.* Unsigned.

A white bolt of memory, searing hot, flashed through her like lightning. Another time . . . another pair of shoes . . . a love note . . . a promise.

She slammed the lid down on the box and sat, shaken, on the bed. The last time anyone had given her shoes was twenty years ago. Red stilettos then too. She glanced towards the wardrobe where they were hidden on the bottom shelf, stowed in their box, with Martin's card—*For you, my forever love*—and one of his t-shirts, the only thing she had of his. She'd clung to it during her darkest, most painful days, praying he would rise from the ashes and stumble home. Those shoes always lived with her, still in their box, like a talisman. She never wore them, rarely looked at them.

She emptied this new box and turned its wrapping inside out, but did not find a consignment note. Had the shoes come from an online store, there would have been paperwork, so whoever had sent them must have made the purchase in-store and placed the note inside the bag.

Was it a mistake of some sort? She rang Top Couriers to see if they'd registered the name and origin of the sender. They had nothing in their records, and the girl she spoke to was adamant whoever booked delivery had specified Lucie's full name and address.

Then she phoned the Manolo Blahnik store in Burlington Arcade, but a harried assistant couldn't help her. 'They could have been bought from any of our stores or stockists. You could try contacting our online shop. If the buyer checked out as a guest, you'll need the receipt to make an exchange.'

'I don't want an exchange—I want to know who purchased them.'

Lucie could almost hear the shrug of shoulders down the phone. 'I doubt we can provide that information. Privacy concerns. Apologies, madam.'

There seemed little doubt they were intended for her, even down to the correct size. But what could the giver hope to gain by remaining anonymous? She wondered if they were somehow linked to that strange note pushed under her door: *At last, I've found you. A shock, I'm sure. But in time, I'll explain. Martin.* Was someone playing games with her? Yet the shoes were addressed to her, whereas the note's envelope had been blank. It was still in the drawer of the hall table; she had forgotten to give it to the letting agent.

She repacked the shoes, pondering how to proceed. If anyone would have an opinion, it would be her old friend Em. Lunchtime in London was late Friday night in Sydney, but not too late to Facetime.

Em picked up almost straightaway. Lucie roared with laughter when the video appeared: a charcoal-coloured clay mask covered Em's plump face, and a green polka-dot shower cap hid her hair. She wore what appeared to be a pink towelling bathrobe.

'Very fetching,' said Lucie. 'Another action-packed Friday night, I see.'

'I'm off to Singapore tomorrow.'

'Junket?'

Em snickered. 'Conference, darling. Five hundred shrinks.'

'Well, you're dressed for it.'

'This is just the pre-prep. Some very powerful dudes will be there, and who knows what might transpire?' Em made no secret of her preference for short-term romances with men of high IQ— not for her a life of nappies and weekly supermarket shops. 'I can give you ten minutes,' she said, 'then I have to wash off this volcanic residue. What's happening?'

'Weird shit. I'm trying not to get antsy, or overanalyse what's probably nothing, but . . .'

'Go on.'

Lucie explained about the note and the shoes, while Em nodded, um-ed and ah-ed.

'Thoughts?' Lucie asked when she'd finished.

'Either it's someone you know or a creepy stranger—if the note and shoes are linked, that is, and they've both come from someone called Martin.'

'Or pretending to be.'

'I suppose so.' Em frowned. 'But let's leave aside the note, which was probably put in the wrong letterbox. The shoes are another matter. Anyone spring to mind?'

'A few candidates, but I can't think for what reason. My boss, Charles, likes to keep me on my toes, and he's always suggesting an after-hours drink, so he might have a thing going for me. And he'd have no trouble getting my shoe size, as we all leave our outdoor shoes in the staff cloakroom.' Even as she said it, the notion seemed ridiculous—Charles would surely never go to such devious lengths. 'Then there's Jonathan, the quiet guy I told you about. He told me he's independently wealthy, meaning he could afford Manolos. So far he's not been the present-giving type, though.'

'What about that super-bonk?'

'Alan?' Lucie giggled. 'At a stretch, maybe. A late apology for loving and leaving me then never getting in touch? Unlikely.'

'Someone you don't know, or met in passing? Have you noticed unusual activity on your social media?'

Lucie shook her head.

'Or a new client, that could be it—a divorcee who has his sights on you?'

'Hm, maybe, but no one comes to mind.' Lucie paused. 'The most obvious person is David. Since we split, he's become so unlike the man I believed I knew so well. Maybe he's followed me to England, wanting to check out his *theory* that I left him for someone else. Or perhaps it's his warped way of trying to get me back.'

'Okay,' said Em slowly. 'Talk me through the logic.'

Lucie took a deep breath. 'When I asked David—or rather, *told* him I wanted a divorce—he went into lockdown. Wouldn't discuss it. The next day this huge bouquet arrived at work, no note, obviously from him. I'm not sure what he expected—that

I'd rush into his arms and say, "Thank you for the roses, I've made a huge mistake"?'

'Manolos aren't roses.'

'Exactly. And David isn't known for his imagination.' Lucie pushed her hair back from her forehead. What she was about to say sounded a bit mad. 'Remember Martin Cornish, all those years ago in New York? He gave me red Manolos. David knows that. And that I loved Martin very deeply.'

'A copycat crime?' Em raised her eyebrows, cracking her face-mask into thin crevices.

'An ill-considered way of getting to my heart, more like.' When they'd met in the mid-2000s, she'd told David how she never thought she'd get over Martin, and David had been sweetly caring. How horrible if he'd turned that information into a psychological weapon, or a stupid plan to get her back. 'Maybe he figured if Martin had won me over with shoes, he'd repeat the trick.'

'Darling, if that's the case, it sounds like he's gone down a rabbit hole. He could be depressed. If he's drinking—or snorting—his erratic behaviour might turn dangerous, so my advice is don't engage. At all.'

'What should I do?'

'Talk to your sister. Zoe stays in touch with David, doesn't she? See if she can find out what he's up to, his state of mind. Whether he's gone overseas—or found a new woman. Don't jump to conclusions.'

Lucie nodded uncertainly. Speaking to Em hadn't quietened her fears, only made them seem more real. 'I can't bear feeling I'm not in control. You know how I get,'

'Yes, I do. So hear me, and hear me good: alcohol and sleeping pills aren't the answer. That didn't bring Martin back, and it didn't stop David behaving like an imbecile, it just scrambled your brain. Keep a clear head, don't let your imagination go off half-cocked, and keep up the workouts.'

Lucie bit her lip, not keen on being scolded. 'Okay, Mother Teresa.'

Em laughed. 'Anything else?'

'What about the Manolos?'

'Who cares who gave them to you? They want it to be a secret, so have respect. Wear those fabulous shoes and enjoy. Now buzz off, I've got to cleanse and pack.' She blew Lucie a kiss and ended the video chat.

Seized by a sense of urgency, Lucie got up and went straight to the wardrobe. She took out the box she hadn't opened in a long time and extracted the contents from their drawstring bag. These shoes were a paler red. The soles were scratched, and the material across the toes was creased. She slipped them on, still a perfect fit. A shadow of the past caught her unawares—laughing in Martin's arms as he spun her around—and she put the shoes away before memories and regrets could take hold. She squared her shoulders as she replaced the box in the wardrobe, with the new pair on top.

It must be coincidence, sheer coincidence. Eventually, someone would own up—who wouldn't want to take credit for such a generous gift? Just in case, she'd ask if Zoe could find out more about David's movements; the idea of him stalking her around London seemed fantastical, but best to be safe and prepared for a visit. Meanwhile, by subtle means she'd try to find out if one of the others was behind this.

NEW YORK

2001

At dawn, they made glorious, sleepy love. Their bodies pressed together, Martin breathed, 'Happy quarter century,' into her ear when she came, exploding in tiny fireworks. She held him close, his warmth wrapped around her, and felt him fill her with his longing until he collapsed in her arms. 'Beautiful, beautiful, Lucie,' he murmured.

Sated, she lay in his king-size bed, transported to that other world where her head left her body and floated on a sea of passion.

Then he slid off her and lightly spanked her bottom. 'Stay there. I've got a surprise.' He pulled on his navy silk robe and strode purposefully out of the room. Lucie drew up the bed-clothes; outside it was blisteringly hot, but the air con had cooled the apartment to a fridge-like state. She hummed *Summertime* and turned one eye to the alarm clock: almost seven.

Martin returned, swinging a bag. 'Here you go.'

Lucie sat up. As soon as she saw the iconic brown bag, with *medium brown bag* emblazoned across the front, she knew. *'Bloomingdales!'* she squealed.

He perched beside her. 'I figure you can guess what's inside.' He kissed the top of her head.

She could guess—kind of. But she held her breath in case she was wrong. She didn't want to be disappointed . . . Whatever he gave her would be special . . . It wouldn't matter if it was a book, or something practical like a sandwich-maker . . . but *please, please, please,* she prayed.

Inside, an oblong box. Gift-wrapped. Tied with an extravagant silver bow. 'Oh, Martin.'

His grin was pleased. 'Go on.'

She slowly pulled open the ribbon. The wrapping fell away. A plain white shoebox. Printed on top: *MANOLO BLAHNIK.* She exhaled a breath of amazement.

Martin put his arms around her and rested his chin on her shoulder. 'Aren't you gonna open it?' he asked with a laugh.

'Yes, yes, yes.' She lifted the lid, separated the tissue paper and stared in awe. 'The red stilettos. Wow.' They'd caught her eye weeks ago, during a stroll along Third Avenue. She'd tugged on Martin's elbow—they never held hands, not in public—exclaiming how she'd never seen anything quite so exquisite. 'How wonderful to be rich and famous,' she'd said. He'd left her ogling them in Bloomingdale's window display, and when she'd caught up to him, he'd dismissed her interest: 'Your feet are prettiest naked.'

Now he hugged her. 'What were you expecting?'

Taking his face in both hands, she kissed him. 'Not this.'

'Y'know that saying, "head over heels in love"? That's me, feet first. That day we met up at the Rainbow Room and I saw you on that bar stool, your very ordinary work shoe dangling from your high-arched foot, I knew.'

'Knew what?' she teased.

'That I was crazy in love, and one fine day I was gonna whisk you away and marry you.'

Her jaw, literally, dropped.

'Ha, that shut you up, didn't it?' Martin released her and jumped off the bed. 'Time to get dressed, babe.'

A stupid grin on her face, she listened to the shower and Martin's tuneless effort at a rousing *Nessun dorma*. She was twenty-five, and the man of her dreams, her girlish fantasies, the love of her life, would one day be all hers. She rubbed the shoes against her face, pushed aside the bedclothes and slipped them on. While Martin's enthusiastic tenor hit an offbeat crescendo, she skipped around the living room like a twelve year old.

No matter what other gifts she received today, they'd shrink to nothing compared to this. A red-letter day in all senses: Martin had as good as promised to leave his wife to be with her. Until then she'd hug her luck and keep her perfect future secret, tucked inside her heart to cherish while she waited for him to be free.

LONDON

Kristy, usually perky and smart behind Charnbrook and Henley's mahogany reception desk, looked sulky today. 'You've got an admirer.' With a stage magician's flourish, she handed Lucie an oblong box encased by an enormous gold ribbon, labelled *White's Florist.*

Lucie paled. Not another anonymous offering—it was too much to handle.

'Well go on, open it.' Kristy's mass of beaded braids jiggled as she leant forward, wide-eyed, and tapped the box. 'Card first.'

Reluctantly, Lucie opened the small envelope and read the message. *Back Thursday. Dinner Friday? Alan.* The words shouted at her in large loopy letters, a childlike scribble—not his writing, though, but the florist's. She lifted the lid to reveal a dozen long-stemmed yellow tulips laid with precision on orange tissue paper, expensive and over the top. She seesawed between feeling flattered and annoyed: he couldn't buy her with a bunch of flowers after two weeks of nothing. She flipped over the card. No phone number, no way to cancel or make an excuse. Arrogant sod.

'Wow.' Kristy sounded sour. 'Someone's keen. Nice one.'

Lucie pocketed the card. She didn't know what had gone down between Kristy and Alan, but the normally bright receptionist had shown little enthusiasm for him when she'd introduced them at The Tipperary; in fact, she'd been eager to get away. Lucie's instincts told her to keep shtum.

'A thank you. From a client.' She turned towards the rows of desks. 'I need to get going,'

'What about the flowers?' Kristy called after her.

'Oh . . . You keep them.' A flashback came of Alan, hands on hips, flaunting his manhood at her. She owed Kristy. 'There's no room on my workstation. You enjoy them.'

As Lucie made a beeline to her desk, the pieces fell into place. Of course the shoes had come from Alan, his way of courting her. He must be one of those shopaholic guys—with a predilection for shoes. He'd bought his dandyish leather brogues when he was last in New York, and when he'd stayed at her place he could easily have found out her shoe size. The flowers were simply another flamboyant gesture. Unbidden, a memory flashed of Alan sucking her toes before tracing his tongue along her calf to her thigh, and higher . . .

Charles called out as she swung past his office. 'A minute, Lucinda.'

She snapped from her reverie. With a client teleconference in a quarter of an hour, the last thing she needed right now was a tete-a-tete with Charles. 'It better be quick.'

He gestured to the informal seating arrangement in the corner. She took one of the leather bucket chairs and rolled up her shirtsleeves, as he smoothed back his thinning hair, unbuttoned his jacket and sat opposite. He pinched the creases in his trousers and laid his hands on his thighs, giving her a taut smile; then he glanced down at her feet, let his eyes travel to her face and slapped his knees. 'I trust you enjoyed a restful weekend break, Lucinda, because I'm giving you more responsibility.' He spoke with the air of a king bestowing a great honour. 'I'm passing you most of Jack's clients.'

Jack Hindmarsh was a respected partner who specialised in custody disputes. This must mean some sort of promotion, a recognition of her efforts.

'Has he resigned?' Lucie asked.

'Good lord, no. People don't resign from Charnbrook and Henley.' Charles tweaked his cuffs. 'Poor bugger broke his neck skiing. In Whistler. It's doubtful he'll walk again. But his chances of returning to work are good, albeit in a wheelchair.'

'How dreadful,' she murmured. 'His family must be devastated.'

'Yes. Terrible business.' Charles sighed an insincere sigh. 'But life must go on. Clients attended to and all that. Jack wouldn't want it any other way.'

Charles's trite summation of Jack's feelings irritated her, and also made her wonder if pushing his cases onto her desk wasn't a reward but a test of her true capability, to see if she buckled under pressure. And that flick of attention to her feet—to see if she wore red stilettos? At work? She covered a breaking smile with her hand. Nope, definitely more Alan's style.

'Thank you, Charles.' She stood. 'I assume you'll allocate extra resources to assist me.'

He looked startled. 'Well, I . . . Budgets, you know . . .' He waved a hand in the air. 'Speak to Kristy.'

Jack managed a topnotch list. She'd gain new skills and knowledge, and add some impressive cases to her CV. Most importantly, she'd make good contacts among some of London's leading barristers. The additional workload would be worthwhile—even if it meant sacrifices.

The late afternoon meeting drained Lucie's emotional reservoir. It took all her powers of concentration to remain detached and focus on the issue at hand. The tearful mother, married to a Saudi man and desperate to get her children, three boys under seven, back from her husband's clutches, stood little chance. They both knew it. An English wife had no rights in Riyadh, and any claims of kidnapping would go ignored.

It was almost six o'clock when Lucie walked Grace Shalhoub to the lift, promising to do everything in her power but knowing she couldn't do more than go through pointless motions.

The lift doors slid to a silent close, and Lucie breathed a deep sigh. All she wanted was to pick up a takeaway, and veg out in front of the TV, but she still had to go through Jack's files and sort any urgent matters for that week. And she needed to catch Kristy before she left for the day, to put in her ambit claim for another junior associate on her team.

Kristy glared at her, stony-faced, as Lucie passed through reception. The yellow tulips splayed from a crystal vase on her desk, a sunny slash of colour amid the brown-hued leather furniture and oak-panelled walls.

'Can I run through a couple of things?' Lucie asked.

Kristy reached for a pad and pen. 'Shoot.'

'Can you assign me a junior or two? I need to spread the load of Jack's work.'

'Good luck with that.' Kristy flicked back her perfect black braids. 'I can try, but that lot are mostly work-shy. They'll all claim no extra capacity.'

'Hire someone, then?'

'You kidding? Charles has a moratorium on head count.'

Lucie groaned. No wonder her colleagues showed little envy that she'd inherited the extra—albeit prestigious—work. 'Surely someone would want the chance to expand their portfolio?'

'Nah. They're just glad to dodge the bullets.' Kristy pushed back her chair. 'That all?'

'Is something up?' Kristy had barely spoken to her since they'd gone for that drink at The Tipperary, and Lucie figured she was pissed off at her for leaving without a word. She should make amends. 'Look, about the other night—'

Kristy stared at her. 'It's fine.'

'No, it's not. You were nice enough to invite me, and I left—'

'I said. It's fine.' Kristy buttoned her coat and slung her bag across her body. 'I left *you,* actually, with that dick Alan. I should be apologising, not you.'

So that was it. 'God. Sorry. Were you. . . ? Was he. . . ?' Her face grew warm.

'He's awful. I was glad to escape.'

Lucie couldn't help herself. 'Why awful?' Although she thought she knew.

'Did you go home with him?'

'No, of course not.' The lie dropped before she had a chance to tell the truth.

Kristy's taut shoulders relaxed. 'We dated. I really liked him.' She shrugged. 'But then he dumped me, in a text. Christ—a text.'

Lucie grimaced. 'What a tosser.' Her mind flashed to Alan, strong hands lifting her up and down, up and down. *Ride me, baby. Harder.* Always wanting more.

'I'm over it. You're welcome to him.'

'I don't think—'

Kristy put her hands on her hips. 'I introduced you because he asked me to.'

'Whaaat?' Had she heard right? Alan had deliberately staked her out?

'That night at the pub. I tried to get of rid him, said I was meeting someone. He wanted to know who. I thought for a moment he was actually jealous, that he assumed I must be hooking up with some bloke. When I explained who you were, he got all interested. Said he had some legal shit you might be able to help with.'

The switchboard lit up, and Kristy took the call, her tone brisk and efficient. She gave Lucie a friendly but dismissive wave: conversation over.

Lucie and Alan hadn't talked about anything of a legal nature. She stroked a tulip petal. How on earth could she tell Kristy that Alan was making major overtures in her direction? After this uncomfortable chat, the sooner she put the kibosh on more sex with him, the better. Totally inappropriate, not good form. Better to stick with Jonathan: friendship without demands. When Alan contacted her to firm up dinner details, she'd thank him for the flowers and that would be that.

After collecting her trainers from the cloakroom, she made her way back to her desk to fetch her coat and bag. She shovelled the stack of Jack's files into her briefcase. She'd have that takeaway after all, and read the files in the peace of her living room.

Charles stepped from his office, holding a glass of whisky. 'Nasty situation, my dear. English women can be so naive about what it means to marry a Muslim.'

Lucie glared at him. 'She fell in love. She believed in him. They met at University of St Andrews, years ago, and by all accounts had a happy marriage. This is a family dispute, not of her husband's making. You really shouldn't broadcast such sweeping opinions.'

He affected a pout. 'Quite, quite. Like to discuss the options?'

'Not Grace Shalhoub's options. But I would appreciate you considering some sort of solution for handling Jack's clients.'

'Speak to Kristy.'

'She stonewalled me. So tonight I'm going to investigate and prioritise what's on Jack's plate, and I'll have some *options* to you tomorrow.'

'Jolly good. Leave them on my desk.' He lifted his glass. 'Fancy a drink?'

'Thanks, but I'm not a whisky drinker.' She kicked off her heels and changed into her walking shoes.

'I've got gin?'

'Another time. Unlike you, I'm heading home to a few hours more work.' She kept her head down, focused on tying her laces.

'I suppose they must be practical, but I much prefer to see a woman in heels.'

Lucie groaned. If she had a drink with Charles, her loosened tongue might tell him he'd just behaved like a chauvinistic throwback to the 1980s. Instead, she threw a look that caused Charles, not known for his tact and sensibility, to back into his office.

The texts began on Thursday, before his plane took off from JFK. *I'm taking you to La Famiglia. Sexy food.* And another: *Not before we share an appetiser at your place.* Followed by: *Expect me at 6. Hungry. Greedy.* Signed off with suggestive emojis.

She should cancel, say no, tell him he was a jerk for not mentioning he'd dated Kristy—but Lucie found the promise of another rendezvous impossible to pass up. Especially when the texts kept coming: passionate, dirty, exhilarating.

By the time Alan arrived to take her for dinner, Lucie had worked herself into quite a state. Should she wear the red stilettos? Would he expect it? With careful deliberation, she chose an outfit that wouldn't match the shoes, opting for beige slacks and a white button-down shirt with a chocolate sweater. Then she pulled on tan lace-ups.

Trim squawked with displeasure when, despite her earlier promise, she shut him in the living room again. 'Sorry, buddy.'

As she opened the door, she watched Alan's face, but he never looked at her feet. No mention was made as she poured them each a drink. He pressed against her and fondled her breasts while she stood at the kitchen bench and sliced a lemon. 'Let's take our drinks to bed,' he murmured in her ear, unbuckling her belt.

She nudged him away, then handed him his vodka and tonic. 'Thank you for the shoes, but I can't accept them.'

'What shoes?' Alan cocked his head.

She grimaced. 'Stop being ridiculous, I know they're from you.'

'I don't know what you're talking about.' His expression gave nothing away.

Had she got it wrong? 'Well, no one else would've sent them,' she said, uncertain.

'You must have an admirer.' He kept his voice light. 'Someone at the office. Or a client.'

'Why are you pretending they weren't from you?' How juvenile. What did he hope to gain?

He clenched and unclenched his left fist. 'Because they *weren't* from me. And as they weren't, that leaves someone else. What's so special about them?'

'Nothing. Nothing special.' She didn't want to make this an issue. 'It must have been a mistake.' He obviously wasn't going to own up to it—or could he be telling the truth?

'However . . .' He put their drinks on the counter. 'I do have a little something for you.' He undid the top button of her slacks and pulled down the zipper, letting them fall to the ground, keeping his eyes fixed on hers. His hand slid into her knickers, and she gasped. 'You horny witch.'

Grabbing the back of her head, he bruised her lips with fervid kisses. She yanked at his trousers, and he lifted her onto the counter, fumbling in his jacket pocket. He sucked on her ear, then in one swift movement entered her, pounding her until she screamed out, again and again. Throwing back his head, he groaned before collapsing against her with a roar of laugher.

His breathing slowed. 'That was just a taster. Later, I'll show you how much I really missed you.'

Lucie straightened her clothes and excused herself. Upstairs, she stared in the bathroom mirror at her flushed face, disturbed by her loss of control. More disturbingly, now they'd had sex she wasn't overenthusiastic at the idea of dinner together. Having taken her pleasure, she'd be happy to see him out the door, then settle in for the night with a good book.

She sprayed on perfume, reapplied lipstick and said to her reflection, 'Fuck buddy.'

She drank too much that night, laughed too loud and talked incessantly. Each glass of wine—an excellent Tempranillo—improved her opinion of Alan. He let her rave on, ordered Caprese salad and a platter of mixed pasta, and served them both while she regaled him with stories of growing up in Sydney's elite eastern suburbs, which only made her schoolgirl self sound like a spoilt, entitled little snob.

'You never answered my question.' Alan pointed his fork at her.

He was right to interrupt her—she'd been carrying on, talking about people and places of no relevance to him. *He's really rather sweet,* she thought, *listening to me babble on and smiling as if he's interested.* 'Remind me.'

'Whether there's someone in your life.'

A convenient question. 'There is, as a matter of fact.'

'No one in particular, though? If there were, you wouldn't be screwing me, would you?'

Point taken. 'We share similar interests. Opera. Exhibitions. Exploring London.'

'How very cultural.' Alan grinned. 'What about the sex?'

'None of your business.'

'Gotcha.' He sat back and crossed his arms. 'So, out of ten? Would you put him at a six?'

'I'm not playing.' She flicked her serviette at him.

'Fine, be coy. I don't care who you sleep with—it's not my place to monopolise you when I travel all the time.'

'And get up to who knows what.'

'Yeah. That's right.' He reached into his breast pocket and brought out a thin oblong box. 'For you.'

Lucie frowned. 'Why?'

He was laughing. 'I saw it. Thought of you.' He uncurled his fingers and dropped the box on the tabletop. Cappuccino-coloured, it was decorated with an oval circle slashed by a pen. A Parker pen. 'Being a lawyer, you're always signing things. Figured you'd enjoy it.' He sat back, looking pleased with himself.

Lucie opened the box. A ballpoint. Chrome. It could join the others scattered between her desk, briefcase, handbag, hall table. 'Thank you. Just what I needed.'

She tapped the pen. Did Alan want to impress her? A bottom-of-the-range Parker didn't compare to top-of-the-line Manolos. Her theory about his largesse dissipated, replaced by a less attractive alternative. 'What were you doing in Chicago?'

'The usual. Clients. A conference. Caught up with some pals.'

As she'd suspected. She twirled the pen under his nose. 'Nice delegate gift.'

Lowering his eyes, he pulled down the corners of his mouth and pouted. 'Oh, what a naughty boy I am. You caught me out.' He gave a twinkling smile. 'You'll have to punish me later. The more it hurts, the more I promise I'll do better next time.'

Next time? 'Alan . . . don't get me wrong, but I'm not in the market for anything serious. You don't need to give me things. I wouldn't know how to reciprocate and . . .' How could she say she wasn't that interested in him as a boyfriend? 'Let's have some fun. That's all.'

'My kind of gal.' He winked. 'I'll get the bill.'

She reached across the table to put her hand on his arm. 'Let's go Dutch. I insist.'

A spark of understanding lit his expression. 'You got it.'

LONDON

PRESENT

It had been a gruelling week. Aside from constant roadblocks in her efforts to retrieve Grace Shalhoub's children from Saudi Arabia, Lucie battled with the marital woes of the Greek bigamist, Charles's schoolmate, a drug-addicted rock musician, and an aspiring politician. On top of which, Charles showed no inclination towards giving her additional support. Kristy shrugged, when yet again Lucie asked how soon she'd get an extra pair of hands, and said, 'It's on the agenda.' Which was as good as saying the matter was shelved for a week or more. So Lucie continued to arrive and depart Bouverie Street in the pitch-dark; a mole, burrowing in an underground nest.

This evening she'd made an exception, as Jonathan had tickets for *Othello.* He'd offered to try for a refund, but she'd refused: all work and no play was not why she'd come to London.

When she met him in the theatre foyer, she could see he'd made a big effort. But compared to how he came across in his usual casual wear, he looked like a nerd. He'd combed down his hair; he wore a suit that landed uncomfortably on his tall frame, along with a badly knotted tie. She wanted to ruffle him up. Instead, she muttered, 'You look posh,' and they took their seats.

The lights went down, and the music wafted through the auditorium. Lucie's eyelids fluttered, and to keep from nodding off she clenched her fists, digging her fingernails into her palms. At interval, she refused a glass of wine, opting for a black coffee. After the final ovation, her head spinning with fatigue, they exited into Covent Garden where a cold drizzle dampened the air.

Jonathan took her arm. 'I've booked a table at Frenchie. It's not far.'

'Oh, but I . . .' With longing, she eyed the black cabs drawing up kerbside beyond the security bollards. She'd been awake since 5 A.M. and yearned for her bed.

'Come on,' he said, 'it's Friday night. You don't have to get up tomorrow.'

She did a quick calculation. Sonya had cancelled their usual Saturday morning session, and Jonathan had been generous enough to buy dress circle tickets. To refuse dinner would be rude. Then there was the matter of the shoes. She'd avoided asking him in a text or over the phone. It was delicate—she didn't want to offend him, but if he had sent them she wanted to read his body language, his expression, and try to understand why.

The brasserie buzzed with a post-theatre crowd, hungry and chatty, exchanging loud opinions of *The Mousetrap, Harry Potter* and *Mamma Mia!* Lucie and Jonathan shared foie gras, smoked eel and banoffee pie. The food and a couple of glasses of wine perked her up, and his enthusiastic critique of *Othello* against other productions was illuminating.

'I'll find out when it's on next at Stratford.' He pulled out his phone. 'It would be interesting to compare the play to the opera, so soon after seeing Verdi's interpretation.'

Lucie had never been to Stratford-upon-Avon, the home of Shakespeare. 'It would be great to see *anything* there. It's not far, is it? We could get a train.'

Jonathan rubbed the back of his neck. 'We'd have to stay the night. It's a two and a half hour journey from Marylebone.'

'It sounds like you go there a lot.'

The waiter brought their coffees, and Jonathan gestured for the bill. 'I used to. Not anymore.'

'Is that where you grew up?'

He looked up from his phone, startled. 'No. Why would you ask that?'

'You never said.'

'We went on school trips.'

'That must have been fun.' What a stupid thing to say: it would have been awful to be the odd boy out, the one who sat by himself on the coach trip, pretending not to care. Lucie recalled a girl at school no one ever wanted to sit next to—until the day she brought her new puppy to class, and her popularity soared. Shameful to think of it now.

He stared at a spot above her head. 'It was a highlight, going to the theatre. I could lose myself.'

She struggled to know what to say. His childhood had been very different to hers, and she didn't want to make thoughtless comparisons. 'Did you only go with the school?'

'Sometimes my mother took me. As a special treat, for my birthday or a good exam result.'

'Do you see much of your family?'

He concentrated on stirring milk froth into his coffee. 'No.'

'Do you get on?'

'No.'

'So you don't still live at home?'

'No.' He sucked his spoon clean, 'What's with the inquisition?'

'Only that you've never invited me to your place. I thought maybe you lived with your parents, or had unlikeable flatmates.'

'You can come back tonight, if you like.'

Did she? She hadn't prepared by bringing a toothbrush, spare underwear or make-up remover. At her age, slumming it held little appeal. On the other hand, she was curious. And too exhausted to do much more than pass out, wherever she laid her head. 'Sure, why not?'

Jonathan folded his napkin. 'Good. Great.' He pushed back his chair.

'But first, there's something I need to ask you.'

A look of guilt passed over his face. 'Oh?'

'A strange thing happened last weekend. I received a package, a gift. But there was no card with it. Sorry, it's rather tricky, but I need to ask—was it from you?' She clasped her hands together, palms damp. Ridiculous. Because if they had come from him . . .

His demeanour relaxed. 'Lucie, why would I send you something and not tell you? Why not give it to you in person? Perhaps it was some sort of mix-up.'

'Yes, that must be it.' She scanned his face.

He grabbed his phone and jumped up. 'Wait there while I go to the gents and pay the bill.'

She watched him cross the bistro to the waiter's station, a little surprised he'd exhibited no further curiosity. Didn't he want to know what she'd received? This was probably another example of English reticence to intrude where not invited, and thereby risk rebuff. And, as it turned out, he hadn't been holding back on taking her to his flat—he'd been waiting for her to ask. One day she'd figure out the English and their funny notions of etiquette.

He returned after a few minutes, carrying her coat. 'Let's get going.'

They bundled into a cab and headed towards Victoria. In Pimlico, the driver pulled up outside an imposing four-storey terrace. So, not a student hangout in a dodgy area; in fact, somewhere rather smart. Jonathan led her up the path to the front door, and she stood back while he shielded a keypad with his hand and punched in the code.

In the second-floor flat, he ushered her into a living room devoid of any personality. The walls were white, their sterility relieved by a few bland abstracts and a large flat-screen TV. White shutters disguised the windows, and the black-and-chrome furnishings would have been more at home in a corporate office. Two silver candlesticks—no candles—on the mantelpiece were the only decoration.

'Nightcap?' Jonathan asked.

The idea of sitting on one of the stiff black leather sofas didn't appeal. 'Bed,' she said, pulling off her raincoat. 'Can I get a glass of water?'

He nodded and pointed to the hallway. 'Bedroom's down there. Feel free to wear my t-shirt.'

On the way, she poked her head into the all-white kitchen. It boasted a breakfast bar, chrome bar stools, and benchtops empty except for a stainless steel kettle and toaster. The bedroom—white sheets, black bedside tables—had doors to an ensuite and a walk-in wardrobe. A grey t-shirt lay perfectly folded on the left-hand pillow. In the bathroom, a mug with a toothbrush and razor stood beside small bottles of shampoo and conditioner in a neat line on the glass shelf over the basin. White towels graced a heated rail.

She wasn't surprised by any of this: it was typical of Jonathan's pedantic ways to keep his apartment pristine.

She rubbed her teeth with toothpaste, tugged off her clothes and slid between the starched sheets. The mattress was hard—did he suffer from a bad back? He'd never mentioned it. Within moments, as she drifted into delicious sleep, he slipped in beside her and pressed his hand between her legs. He insistently worked to arouse her, but she couldn't drum up the enthusiasm. The apartment was too sterile, too impersonal; she had no place here. 'No, no.' She pushed him away, and he immediately obeyed.

'I thought that's what you wanted.' He sounded hurt—puzzled, even.

'I do. Of course I do. Just not tonight. I'm tired.' Her last coherent thought was never, ever to come here again. *My place from now on,* she vowed.

She woke with the light, her head fuzzy, mouth stale and dry. Confused at facing white window blinds rather than pretty floral drapes, she took a moment to orient herself. In the bleak morning, her opinion of Jonathan's flat hadn't altered. Beside her, he snored to an erratic beat. There was no way she'd get back to sleep, so she rolled over, keen to escape and return to the cosiness of the mews cottage.

He stirred, pressing his hand to her thigh. 'Come here,' he murmured, and pulled her closer.

She ran her tongue around the inside of her teeth and felt the beginnings of a headache throb at her temples. 'I can't—I've got a gym session,' she lied.

He nuzzled an unpleasant, stubbly cheek against her neck. 'Are you sure?'

Lucie hesitated. Had she told him about Sonya cancelling? 'It's a regular date.'

'Ah.' He flipped onto his back. 'Take a shower, and I'll make coffee and toast.'

'Shower, yes. Breakfast, no.' She edged out of the bed.

'I knew you wouldn't like it here. I don't have the feminine touch.'

About to demur, she realised he'd handed her the perfect get-out-of-jail-free card. 'Well, I do like being surrounded by my own things. If that's okay with you?'

'Sure. I like your place.'

Relieved, she popped a kiss on his forehead. 'But I'm so glad I've seen where you live.'

*   *   *

After parting from Jonathan at Victoria Station, Lucie caught the Tube, grocery shopped, and decided to turn her lie to Jonathan into truth: in lieu of a workout, she'd head home, change into her tracksuit then go for a run. She needed to blast away her hangover, along with the cobwebs of being shuttered in Charnbrook and Henley's offices all week. A small amount of exercise meant she'd suffer less at Sonya's next session. She could hear the trainer's stern exhortations: *Faster, girl. And again. One more time. And again . . .*

Soon she was jogging towards Hammersmith. Yesterday's cruel sleet had dissipated, leaving damp pavements and a cloudy sky. When she reached the river, she pounded along the towpath before retracing her steps to face the inevitable: a mound of files that would keep her occupied for the rest of the weekend.

The day flew by, punctuated by several trips to the coffee machine and a dinner delivery from Uber Eats. A little after ten, she pushed aside the pile of papers yet to be dealt with and opened a bottle of red Burgundy. Her brain seethed, trying to frame an irrefutable argument to Charles about why and how he should fast-track her staffing requirements. In less than an hour, she drank the whole bottle. Satisfied she'd fall into an induced slumber, she went to bed.

Surrounded by black night, an insistent ringtone pulled her from a deep sleep. In the darkness she fumbled on the bedside table for her phone, and inwardly swore. She'd forgotten to abide by her own rule: put the phone on silent at the weekend and let clients go to voicemail. Admittedly, calls at unsociable hours tended to be from Australia—someone who forgot about the time difference or was unaware she now lived in London.

'Go away,' she mumbled into the phone. 'It's the middle of the night.' She kept her head buried in her pillow, holding on to sleep.

A voice, male. American? 'Lucie, that you?'

The voice had a strange ring of familiarity. One she'd heard recently. Or remembered. Which was it? Her befuddled brain gradually cleared. 'Alan?'

'No Lucie. It's me. Martin.' *Martin.*

Martin? Was this a joke? And yet as that thought hit her, years flooded away, a tidal wave in retreat. Only one person had such a distinctive accent: that deep, fast-paced New York twang with an undertone of warmth and humour about to bubble to the surface. A voice she could no longer remember but nevertheless recognised in an instant.

But it couldn't be.

She whispered, 'Martin?' Her heart thumped in noisy staccato against her chest.

'Don't be scared, Lucie. This is hard. I tried to warn you. My note. The shoes.'

Sweat dripped between her breasts. She sat up and turned on the bedside lamp. Her body shook, and her head felt heavy from lack of sleep and too much alcohol. The dull electric light seeping through the room pulled her back to reality. *Don't be a fool,* she told herself, *Martin's dead.* 'Who is this?'

'Lucie, stay calm. I'm not dead.' His voice drawled, skipping consonants, soft and distinct in her ear.

'It's not possi—'

'Listen to me. I did a terrible thing, and for twenty years I've been praying for forgiveness. Hoping for this day. It wasn't planned—I just saw a way out, and took it.'

Her eardrums thrummed. She stared at the paisley curtains, which twitched on a breath of night wind. *No, no, no.* 'David, is this you? Your idea of getting back at me?' Did her ex believe he could throw back the hurt she'd caused him, send her spiralling into the same destructive sorrow he'd experienced?

'It's a lot. I get that. You go back to sleep. I'll call again.'

'Martin?'

'One more thing: don't tell anyone. Not till you gimme a chance to explain. Please.'

The line went dead.

The phone lay, an innocent object, clutched in her hand. She looked at the last call received: *No Caller ID*. She went to the bathroom, took a couple of Panadol and put her phone on silent.

Flashes of the past, distorted and distressing, flickered in her troubled brain. The horror of Ground Zero, where weeks later the dust still swirled with the ashes of the dead and the smouldering remains of those monuments to US trade dominance. Reading the hundreds of messages, cries of help to find lost ones, pinned to makeshift fencing barriers. Weeping for Martin. Unable to compute the incomprehensible.

Sleep eluded her. She got out of bed, wrapped her duvet around her shoulders and went downstairs. She poured a brandy. And a second one. The burning liquid numbed her feverish mind, but it didn't soften the shock. Trim curled on her lap, and she stroked his smooth fur, soothed by his purring presence, while she wrestled for perspective.

There was no way Martin Cornish had telephoned. She must have got confused, heard a phone ringing and muddled everything up. A dream, that was all.

Or someone determined to fuck with her, big time. Who else but David would be so vengeful? But even he seemed a far-fetched culprit. However much pain he was in, what could he hope to achieve by raking up the past? He knew how much she'd loved Martin. She'd wept and wept the night she'd told David about her first true love; how, for a short time—an hour or two before the planes hit, plunging her life and those of so many others into grief and darkness—she'd been giddy with excitement, certain he planned to tell her he'd at last left his wife. David would know how much this masquerade would screw her up, so if he had decided to play this dirty trick, even more reason not to engage with him. Follow Em's advice, wait to hear from her sister.

Slightly drunk, Lucie returned to bed and lay awake until dawn began to filter through the drapes. Finally she fell asleep, comatose until her alarm penetrated her weary head. She took herself to the bathroom. As she splashed cold water over her face, the call in the night came back to her. In daylight, it seemed more surreal; so, too, the notion the caller might be David. For starters, it was laughable he could assume an American accent.

What if it was true?

She shook her head at her reflection, tightened her dressing-gown, dried her hands and hung up the towel. *Get a grip, Lucie.* She swallowed hard. Hearing his voice, so close and recognisable, had challenged the reality of his death.

She grabbed her phone, punched in her passcode and checked the log of received calls. There were now three: one from her cousin in Hobart, asking if she was coming home for Christmas, and two from No Caller ID, neither with a voicemail message. As her rational mind reiterated, those two calls had to be from overseas. Probably her father, notorious for keeping his number ex-directory in a vain fight against telemarketers. Or one of those call centres, selling her internet services, or a scammer, trying to extract her bank details.

What if it was true?

Tangible reminders of Martin were scant. That last day in his apartment she hadn't thought to pack any of his personal items for keepsakes: his razor or aftershave or cufflinks. All she had were the red shoes and his t-shirt, which she'd been wearing when she'd been bundled out of his apartment. Later, she'd railed at herself for being so cavalier. Certain of their future together, she had never planned memories for a life on her own.

She had no photos of him: once, for fun, she'd tried to drag him into a Passport Photo booth, but he'd pulled away. 'Best not,' he'd said, ever anxious to leave no trace of their affair. Even after 9/11, his mugshot was never one of those published online or in the newspapers.

While she would send long, rambling letters to his New York apartment when he went to Boston to be with Penelope, he never risked anything—not a postcard, or hastily scribbled note: *Could you put washing in dryer if you're back before me?* or shopping lists: *Milk, butter, eggs, gin, candles.* Her stomach tightened. There was one thing: the birthday note he'd written. *For you, my forever love.* She could compare it to that first note. *At last, I've found you. A shock, I'm sure. But in time, I'll explain. Martin.* See if the handwriting matched.

She scrabbled in the bottom of her wardrobe and pulled out the shoebox; flung aside the lid and shook the shoes from the bag. She rummaged inside, peering into the toes, but there was no white card. Martin's t-shirt was in the base of the box, but no note poked out; she shook the garment open, but nothing emerged. She rocked back on her heels. Surely she'd kept that card. She *knew* she had. She looked again—nothing.

She opened up the second box, with the new shoes. Just the typewritten note in there: *Beautiful feet deserve to walk in splendour.*

Horrified at her carelessness, she realised one of her last links to Martin—five words inked with his tortoiseshell Parker pen on a neat white card—must have got mixed up with the wrapping around the new Manolos, and she'd thrown it away. She let out a growl of frustration. What the hell was going on?

NEW YORK

SEPTEMBER 2001

For a few days after 9/11, Martin's voicemail message was Lucie's last remaining link to him, a lifeline: 'You've called the cell phone of Martin Cornish. I'm sorry, I'm either in a meeting or unable to take your call. Please leave a message after the beep, and I'll call you straight back.'

Again and again she called—willing him to pick up, praying that somehow the sheer force of her love would get through to him. Whether he lay deep in the rubble of Ground Zero or wandered the streets of Manhattan dazed from shock, she needed to hear his voice. He was invincible, wasn't he? He couldn't be gone.

Three days later, his cell phone no longer diverted to voicemail, and all she got was an impersonal voice advising, 'The number you have reached is no longer in working order. If you feel you have reached this number in error, please try again.' The phone's battery had finally died. And, she began to accept, so had he.

But his monotonous, impersonal message was seared into her memory. With the passage of years, she lost the ability to conjure his face but could never erase the last words she had heard him speak: *I'll call you straight back.*

LONDON

PRESENT

Autumn morphed into winter, and work became her salvation, a ballast against fruitless speculation and miserable weather. Charles F-S continued to be a superior pain in the arse, treating her with mild disdain or insincere flattery, which her colleagues assured her was de rigueur. She stopped asking him for help with her extra workload: it only made her sound a petulant nag, and the request was better coming from Kristy. What would be, would be.

A couple of times, Kristy rescued her from corporate embarrassment. When she overslept and missed an early morning meeting, the receptionist took the blame, citing a diary clash. Another time, when she neglected to file a court order on time, Kristy sweet-talked the clerk into an extension. She brushed off Lucie's slip-ups with a cheerful, 'That's what I'm here to fix.' But it was Lucie's fault; her mind kept wandering elsewhere—*Don't be scared, Lucie . . . I'm not dead.*

She tried to be mindful of Em's advice: keep fit and stay off the booze. The former was easier than the latter. Sonya kept her to a strict regime, setting relentless targets. 'You can't be taking all your exercise horizontally,' she said. 'We need to keep that butt cute.' Unspoken: *For your fuck buddy.* Sonya didn't probe, and Lucie didn't offer that she'd only heard from Alan in a crude text: *I'll be back for more soon.* She hadn't replied.

As for Jonathan, she suspected his feelings about their relationship ran far deeper than hers, but it suited her. When she explained that her workload, training schedule and need for personal space only allowed time for them to meet one evening a week, she expected him to push back, but he gave a solemn nod and said, 'I understand.' In a perverse way, this made him more appealing. He became more of a challenge—or, at least, less of a pushover. As long as he remained happy with the status quo, he provided the perfect balance between work and play.

Time at home, when she wasn't working to a deadline, allowed her to savour the pile of books by her bed, or chat with Em. Anything to keep from fretting about that blasted phone call. Sometimes she found her eyes wandering to her mobile, checking the screen. She double-locked her front door and took solace in Trim, who stayed close, his uncanny cat's antenna alert to her jumpy moods.

Solace, too, came in the few glasses of wine she indulged in every night. Better than relying on sleeping pills, she reckoned.

With the double-lined curtains drawn to keep the night out and the warmth in, Lucie felt safe cocooned amid their floral luxury. Nothing bad could touch her in such a pretty winter garden. She topped up her glass, leant her head against the back of the armchair and put her feet on the tapestry footstool. Amy Winehouse crooned, croaky and raw, through the speakers. Trim washed his paws with diligent, quiet concentration.

Her phone rang, and her body jolted from the moment of peace. FaceTime. Her sister, Zoe, sprang into view, sporting sunglasses perched on her head and a strappy top.

Lucie sank back into the chair. 'Hey there.'

'Hi, lovely. Aha. Wine time, I see. Lucky you. Me, I'm about to run the twins to school.'

'Aren't they a bit old for the mummy bus?'

'Feels safer—less oddballs and drug pushers.' Zoe dreaded the day when her boys grew out of needing their mother; they were her whole life. But it wasn't Lucie's place to lecture her about the sin of mollycoddling.

'What's up?' Lucie asked.

'I got hold of David last night.'

Lucie sat up straighten 'And?'

''Fraid there's not much to report. He was pretty nasty . . . vitriolic, you might say. Said he was fed up seeing my calls on his phone, and he answered purely so he could tell me to stop harassing him.'

'But you and David always got on so well. I don't get—'

'He was drunk. Angry drunk. I got the impression the alcohol fuelled his decision to call me back. When I tried to find out if he'd been in touch with you, he began ranting. Said he wanted nothing to do with you, or your family. He thinks we all—Jake and me, Mum—turned you against him. He even used the word "conspiracy". And that obviously you'd been having an affair, and we all knew and hid it from him.'

'Jeez.'

'I asked if he'd taken some time out, been on a holiday, and he snapped. Said his whereabouts were none of my business. So there you have it. Maybe he *is* the one sending you weird shit. To be frank, I'm worried about him. No one we know has seen anything of him, and I think he's gone into a self-pitying downward spiral, probably depression. I feel kind of responsible.'

'Because you were his sister-in-law?'

'Yes. No. Look, I like him. I thought of him, still do, as a friend. I should have recognised the signs, made a bigger effort after you split.' She paused. 'It's hard to believe he'd hurt you like this.'

'I agree. But he's said some pretty awful things about me.'

'That's all talk, justifying himself, not a premeditated plan.'

'Yes . . . I suppose—'

'Sorry, lovely, got to run. Boys are waiting. Chat soon, eh?'

Lucie stared at the blank screen. She hadn't told Zoe about the late-night phone call. Why not? Surely Lucie wasn't going to be hamstrung by those parting words: *Don't tell anyone. Not till you gimme a chance to explain.* Was she?

One evening in early December, after tossing two loads of washing into the dryer, Lucie perched at the kitchen counter and opened her laptop to catch up on personal emails. A brief note from her mother asked what she'd like for Christmas, warning Lucie to reply soon as she was heading off to help build a school in Nepal and could be away for months. Lucie smiled. Her mother was a complex woman: one minute she adhered to strictures ingrained from childhood, such as remembering birthdays, always sending thankyou letters, never discussing sex, religion or money; the next, she threw aside her twinsets and pearls for kaftans and espadrilles to live a simple, charitable life, away from modern distractions.

Christmas was only a few weeks away. Except for those two years in New York, Lucie had always spent the holiday with family in Sydney—parents, sister, nephews, extended family dropping by, and friends or strays invited to join the melee. David had adored their Christmases and insisted on dressing up as Santa. With a pillow stuffed under a red felt jacket and a cottonwool beard flaking from his chin, he'd handed out gifts to the delight of the young ones and the amusement of their elders. What a turnaround this year, with the family all fragmented now—Lucie in London, her parents on other continents, David in a black hole—leaving only Zoe to keep the traditions going.

Lucie scanned the remaining emails: credit card statement, electricity bill, numerous special offers from online stores, a reminder to buy coffee pods. And another, alerting her to a message on LinkedIn from an Everett Black. Curious, she logged on to her account.

Hi Lucie

Forgive me tracking you down this way. You probably don't remember me, but we met a couple of times around 2000—I was sent over from Sydney to NYC on work experience (nice gig!). Thing is, plans are afoot for a celebration of Lockstein Feltermann's hundred-year anniversary. Sydney is to be the Ideation for Asia-Pacific employees, past and present. New York for northern hemisphere folk. I see from your LinkedIn you're a lawyer in London these days so with fingers crossed, I'm hoping this may be an excuse to get you back here, rather than to the NY shindig—tentatively early Feb TBC. Hope to hear from you— my email below!

Everett Black

Lucie stared at the screen. The name rang no bells, but it had been two decades ago. She'd only worked at Lockstein's for a couple of years, and although a fellow Aussie might have stood out, the large communal office had been an international airport of interns, trainees and paralegals passing through.

Checking his profile, she noted he now worked with Jackson Bright, one of Sydney's largest law firms, which had swallowed up the New York firm some years ago. *The fruit doesn't fall far from the tree,* she mused. Not many of her contemporaries had stayed so loyal to their earliest employer. Everett advertised his role as 'Regional Head of Practice, Dispute Resolution. A handsome, fresh-faced man. His eyes held unwavering warmth, and a smile played at the edges of his mouth as if he were trying not to laugh at a joke from the photographer. She supposed he'd be her age, but he looked much younger.

It seemed pointless to attend this mass gathering of lawyers she no longer knew or cared about, and she tapped out a quick email from her personal address.

Hey Everett

Thanks for reaching out to me. Yup, I'm in UK. I'll diarise the dates but put me down as a 'doubtful'. Sorry, I don't remember you.

Lucie

She pinged off her reply and considered what to request from her mother—something lightweight to avoid huge postage? In the end she provided a list of books. Her mum was pretty tech savvy but, just in case, Lucie reminded her to order and send direct from an online store.

About to close her laptop, she saw Everett had already replied.

Awww Lucie, that's a shame but I hope you make it. Scarred you don't remember me. I had a bit of a crush on you—even asked you on a date one time. Standing by the water cooler on Level 15. Ring bells? You refused, obviously. I was that extra-tall guy, with aspirations in criminal law. I played in the inter-firm cricket match (not many candidates, they scrabbled a team from expats). I guess it was a long shot that you might harbour regrets for turning me down all those years ago . . . Everett

Lucie laughed out loud.

Everett . . . a lot of people hung out at that water cooler! I still don't recall you but there's a vague blur entering my consciousness the more I try. Did you possibly go on to represent Australia at cricket? Lucie

His reply pinged.

Flattered you're trying to remember me, Lucie. As for my cricket career, I'd love to claim I made it as an international cap, but in reality I never made it farther than the local oval on Sundays. The only cricket I play these days is with my boys in the back garden. How about you? How come you left New York? What happened to get you to London?

Although she was tempted to pursue the chat, at that moment the washing machine beeped. Time to sort the drying. She typed out a short message:

Gotta go. Will respond when time permits.

She flipped down the lid of her laptop. Of course she didn't recall him—in those days, she would have turned down a date with George Clooney. Back then, she'd only had eyes for Martin.

After those first emails, Everett and Lucie corresponded regularly, some days conversing back and forth if they caught each other at the same time: mornings for him, evenings for her. His appetite for delving into myriad subjects was refreshing, along with his interest in her opinions and raw honesty about his own situation. She learnt he'd got divorced several years ago, and he and his ex had two sons in their early teens. He told Lucie: *Wendy said life was too short to be buried in domesticity and ran off to Queensland with her toy-boy yoga teacher, taking our kids with her. That was what really hurt. She never seemed to think I deserved any choice in the matter.* He'd recently split up with his partner of three years, citing a lack of commitment on both sides: *When push came to shove, neither of us wanted to change our lives enough to accommodate the other.*

She told him about David: how she had struggled to make the marriage work, hanging on way past its due date, and her relief when they'd separated. She surprised herself by telling Everett about losing Martin—*the one love of my life*—but not about the pretender posing as his ghost. When Everett didn't judge her for having an affair with a married man, she grew emboldened and admitted to marrying second best. *I persuaded myself David ticked enough boxes,* she wrote. *And for a while he did, until I realised I didn't love him enough to have children with him, and eventually my small affection for him diminished into despair and I became afraid if I didn't leave him, we'd end up hating each other.*

When Everett asked if she was seeing anyone, she said yes but gave no details about Jonathan—or her guilty pleasure, Alan.

Once they'd caught up on the basics, they spoke about everything from international politics, books they were reading and jokes they'd heard, to global terrorism, climate change and the power of celebrity. His banter was witty and offbeat.

Maybe it was the freedom that came from writing rather than speaking, but Lucie found herself looking forward to chatting with Everett and began checking her personal inbox daily. It wasn't surprising their correspondence was so relaxing and easy; after all, they came from the same town, both were lawyers, and they'd even worked for the same firm. No wonder they had lots in common. He was funny, too.

And he kept her mind from wandering to darker places. Alone at home, she was often confronted by an edginess as she waited for the phone to ring, or for another unexpected occurrence to catch her off-guard.

LONDON

PRESENT

Attending Charnbrook and Henley's Christmas party was non-negotiable. A garish poster, pinned up by Charles F-S's executive assistant, announced it would be employees only: *No spouses, please!* Lucie thought it a bit churlish of Charles. Everyone had worked hard all year, and too often their partners took on the domestic burden when long hours made home and parenting duties difficult—the least the firm could do was thank them with a slap-up dinner and lashings of French bubbly.

Kristy dismissed this in her usual blunt way. 'F-S avoids all social contact with his wife wherever possible. In the old days, he'd also have hoped for a bit of bottom pinching behind the filing cabinets. That was before #metoo. This year, F-S will have to satisfy himself with tasteful flirting. He's also too stingy to chuck out freebies.'

Despite this, Lucie felt a twinge of relief she couldn't invite anyone. She'd been to enough Friday night work drinks to know how noisy and outrageous a group of alpha male and female lawyers could get, especially when fuelled by alcohol (and more). And she liked keeping her private life private; lawyers were notorious gossips.

* * *

When Lucie made her entrance into the splashy Canary Wharf warehouse, she dazzled in a gossamer-fine chiffon and silk dress that fell in pale crimson, soft pink and ivory layers. She'd piled her hair into a stylish, deceptively casual chignon, warmed her bare shoulders with a white faux-fur bolero, and slipped on the red stilettos.

Kristy—standing by the door, clipboard in hand as she ticked off the guests—let out a screech at the sight. 'Oh my God, those are to die for!' Her eyes fixed on Lucie's shoes. 'Seriously, are they Manolo Blahniks? Woo hoo. Leave them to me in your will.'

Charles, in standard black tie, appeared with a glass of champagne. 'Well my heavens, Miss Wilkinson, don't you look fine.' He gave her a once-over. 'Such elegant shoes.'

She slid off her bolero. 'Stop it, Charles, you're making me feel like a racehorse under inspection.'

He held out his hand. 'May I have this dance?'

She hesitated, mindful of Kristy's tart heads up. 'Delighted,' she said. It wouldn't do to brush him off. Besides, surely he'd know better than to make a fool of himself with her.

Almost sixty, he still cut an imposing figure, and Lucie knew they looked quite a pair as he spun her onto the dance floor. They boogied and jived to a few classic hits before she begged to be allowed a drink. While he fetched a flute of Moet, several colleagues buzzed around, chummier than they'd ever been in the office. Chat flowed as easily as the champagne, and for the first time since her arrival in London, she felt like one of the clan.

Towards midnight the music slowed, and Charles asked for another dance. She smiled, allowing her mellow self to be led onto the dance floor. Around them, interdepartmental friendships had formed rapidly, judging by the number of cosy couples who swayed to Frank Sinatra's 'My Way.'

'You're quite the revelation, Lucinda,' Charles said close to her ear.

Moving her head away, she raised her voice. 'Lucie. Please.'

'Ah. Australian informality.' He barked out a laugh. 'You're a refreshing addition to the office. A delight.'

She kept her tone light. 'Professionally speaking, I hope.'

'Indeed.' He pulled her a little closer. 'And from my personal point of view.'

She said nothing; perhaps he'd get the hint and change the subject.

'We, should, ah, get to know each other better, don't you think?'

It seemed Kristy, as usual, was spot on. 'Not really, Charles.' Lucie jabbed a stiletto heel onto his patent leather dress shoe. 'Not a good idea.'

He winced, his hand beginning to sweat into the back of her dress.

'Let's sit this out,' she said, easing out of his embrace.

He took her elbow and led her to their table. 'I can help you, Lucie.' He patted the side of his nose with his index finger. 'You know. Career advancement.'

She frowned at him. Had she missed a trick somewhere? Was Charles a chancer, or had he been building up to this? No, he was just an unhappily married man who'd drunk too much. Best she left before the situation turned difficult.

He dipped his head and took her hand. For a horrible moment, she thought he might kiss it, but instead he leant in and whispered in her ear, 'I know a little about you.' His breath came in unpleasant puffs. She tried to pull back, but he held firm and lowered his voice further. 'Martin Cornish.'

Had she heard him right? She spun to face him, aware of curious heads turning in their direction. 'What on earth are you saying?' she hissed. 'Are you drunk?'

He released his grip. 'Maybe a little,' he admitted. 'An attractive woman can have that effect.'

She picked up her bolero. 'This is my cue to exit.'

How did he know about Martin? She wanted to have it out with him, there and then, but this wasn't the place—surrounded by colleagues, emotions heightened by alcohol. Best to remain dignified, confront him in private.

'Oh, but you haven't let me finish. Because you and I, Lucinda, as I've said before, make a good team. We could be a great team. Both on and off the playing field, if you get my meaning.' When she opened her mouth, he held up a hand. 'Don't be rash. Think it over. I know you don't have qualms about, er, friendships with married men.'

'Let's stop this right now, Charles, before you embarrass us both any further.'

Her words appeared to hit home—or at least land in a part of his brain that recognised he'd overstepped the line. 'Yes, of course. Foolish of me. Mea culpa. Apologies.' He cleared his throat, brushed down his immaculate trousers, and signalled Kristy to come over. 'Could you find Lucinda a taxi, please?'

In the cab, her heart rate gradually returned to normal, and she tried to prevent her imagination getting out of control. But it was hard not to make connections—if Charles knew of Martin, he must also be responsible for teasing her with shadowy hints of her lover's survival. Or it could be a weird coincidence. Maybe, somehow, Martin's name had come up in a reference check. Maybe Charles knew Chester, her old boss in New York; they'd be about the same age. Maybe he'd even known Martin. Come to think of it, she didn't know much about Charles's past; she'd assumed, given he came across as so parochial and old-school Etonian, he'd never ventured beyond British shores.

She stretched out her legs and contemplated the pointed red toes peeking from under her dress. Because of his frugal nature, she couldn't credit Charles with lashing out on expensive Manolos.

It was almost one o'clock when the cab dropped her off. She spotted a note pinned to her front door, and her panic level escalated. She looked up and down the mews, but all remained quiet except for some Christmas revellers a couple of streets over on Fulham Broadway.

She scrunched the note in her hand and entered the house. With trepidation, she leant against the front door, read the note and exhaled. A neighbour called Mabel wrote that she'd put out a bowl of water for Trim and would be delighted to feed him whenever Lucie required help. Thank God, nothing sinister—but how stupid to frighten her like that. What was the woman thinking?

Appalled at her reaction, Lucie kicked off her shoes, sat on the bottom stair and gave herself a stern talking-to. She must keep a clear head, not get rattled by the slightest thing. Tomorrow she'd find a quiet moment to talk to Charles. Tonight she'd check that all the doors and windows were secure, and take a sleeping pill with a large glass of brandy.

All day, Charles avoided coming anywhere near her desk. When she caught his eye, he bustled, shamefaced, into his office. The majority of staff abandoned their workstations early, too hungover to focus on complex legal problems. Lucie, jittery and overstimulated from too many coffees, waited until only a couple of diligent juniors remained.

She didn't knock but stood in the doorway, arms crossed, until Charles looked up. Ah.' He shuffled the papers on his desk, hemmed and hawed, and went to the drinks cabinet. 'Whisky? Gin?'

'It's not a social call.' She closed the door.

His hand a little unsteady, Charles poured a large measure into a crystal tumbler. 'I rather need this.'

She perched on the arm of the leather sofa, not wanting to settle in or remain standing. 'Setting aside for a moment the woeful inappropriateness of your behaviour last night, I've a few questions for you. I'd appreciate honest answers.'

'Of course, Lucinda. By all means.' He took a gulp of whisky and sat back behind his desk. 'First, let me say, I think you probably misunderstood.' Avoiding her gaze, he waved his glass in the air. 'The noise. Dancing too close. Too many drinks. You know how it is.'

She ignored him. 'What do you know about Martin Cornish?'

Charles shifted in his chair. 'Nothing. I shouldn't have said—'

'Did you know him?'

'No, no. Foolish of me to mention him. Please forget it.'

'Did Chester Lockstein mention him?'

'I don't recognise that name.'

Lucie hesitated—aside from both men being lawyers, why would he know Chester? Surely Charles wouldn't have bothered checking an internship reference from the turn of the century. 'Maybe you met him on one of your New York trips.'

'This may surprise you, but I've never set foot in America. I'm a Europe man.' An anti-Brexiteer, to boot.

'Perhaps you met Martin here in London.'

'I don't recall him.'

'Then who put you up to this?'

Charles twirled the tumbler in his hands. 'Surely it's not important? As I said, a misunderstanding.'

She drummed her fingers on her thigh. 'Did you call me in the middle of the night?'

'Good grief.' He blanched. 'Whatever next, Lucinda? I don't make it my habit to call colleagues at unsociable hours.'

His reaction was as she'd expected: denial of any wrongdoing, obfuscation and making light of her concerns. All the same, he *had* murmured Martin Cornish's name in her ear—and he hadn't denied it. Somehow he'd learnt of their affair, and not many people knew about that time in her life. Those who did would be unlikely to recall Martin's surname.

Smoothing down her skirt, she stood. She had some thinking to do, but first she had to let Charles know he hadn't got off scot-free. 'If there's ever a repeat of your behaviour last night, I'll report you to the Law Society.' His expression of dismay gave her a smidgeon of satisfaction. 'And if you change your mind on revealing how you gained information about my private life, I'd appreciate knowing.' With that, she turned on her heel.

Lucie settled at the dining table with a strong gin and tonic, and a blank notepad in front of her. Since she'd walked out of Charles's office, a stream of questions and theories had been tormenting her. She needed to get everything down on paper, sift through and see if something obvious jumped out.

There were two stark alternatives. She wrote: *1. Alive. 2. Dead.*

If—*if*—Martin hadn't been killed in 9/11 and had somehow escaped detection this long, what had caused him to come out of hiding and find her? If she accepted what he had said on the phone, then he would explain in his own time. But another call wouldn't satisfy her or make the words more credible—she'd have to see Martin in the flesh, hear from his own mouth what had occurred. If he'd remained underground for almost two decades, any amount of searching for him on the internet or via any other means would be pointless. He couldn't have had some miracle recovery from a coma, or he'd have been identified at the time, and she'd have known.

The second option was that Martin had indeed died in 9/11, and someone wanted her to believe otherwise. For what purpose? And who? The most likely reason was some form of revenge. Because of their affair? Or a belief that she was responsible for an unknown injury, such as a financial loss? She scrambled to come up with anything plausible. The best way forward, she decided, was to look at possible culprits and see if she could fathom a motive. At least one thing was certain: the voice belonged to a man.

With Charles uppermost in her mind, she jotted down his name, and listed how he could be linked to Martin. In terms of age, they were contemporaries, separated only by two or three years. Old friends? Or enemies, perhaps from a business deal gone sour. Or . . . could they be related? Not brothers—Martin always said he was an only child. A cousin? She flirted with the notion that Charles *was* Martin incognito, having undergone extensive facial surgery, and sighed at her silliness. This was real life, not a science-fiction novel.

She drained her gin and wandered into the kitchen. As she rinsed the glass, she recalled Charles saying he'd recruited her because someone had suggested he look at her LinkedIn profile. Could that be a lie? If true, who had recommended her?

She put down a bowl of food for Trim and returned to the dining table, considering who, aside from Charles, would be in a position to make calls, send her gifts, know where she lived. Lots of people, she realised: her neighbours, everyone in the office, anyone who cared to comb through her social media and mentions of her on Google. A successful lawyer couldn't live like a mushroom, in the dark, unseen.

Perhaps Jack Hindmarsh, resentful she'd made a success of his workload, wanted to prevent her usurping his top dog status while he lay immobile in hospital. She scoffed at the idea: every ounce of his energy was focused on his recovery. And besides, she had received the note and shoes before his accident.

What about Jonathan? Quirky, bright, always a gentleman. Thoughtful, kind, generous. Too good to be true? They'd met by chance at Two Hens. Could it have been a set-up? Pretty hard to pull off, but not impossible. And why?

Of course, one person with a reason to take revenge on her was Martin's wife. Maybe he hadn't been as discreet as he'd led

Lucie to believe, and Penelope had found one of Lucie's letters to him. If only she could remember what she'd written in them, but it was too long ago now to conjure those details. What if, eaten up by years of hatred, Penelope had decided to come after Lucie, somehow posing as her dead husband? Lucie dismissed the idea as impossible and berated herself for going on another ludicrous flight of fancy.

She took a wineglass and a bottle of Australian shiraz from the drinks cabinet, then poured a hefty serving.

David—it always circled back to David. He knew more about her history than anyone besides Zoe and Em. Maybe he'd never believed her reassurances that she'd long got Martin out of her system; maybe he didn't care, he just wanted to spook her. If only Zoe had been able to see him face to face. Might he talk to Em? But if this game-playing wasn't his doing, Lucie didn't want to add to his long list of grievances against her.

She couldn't shake an uneasy feeling about Alan. He'd made a point of asking Kristy to introduce them, and he spent his time flitting between cities, or so he said. He could be anywhere. What if he was somehow related to Martin? She'd never asked his age but put him at late thirties, early forties. Why would he be doing this? Could his family have some grudge against Martin? Unpaid debts? Could Martin have slept with Alan's mother? What if Alan was an illegitimate kid Martin had fathered and known nothing of?

Lucie added one last option: *Mr X.* It was possible a stranger was doing this, someone she'd met in passing and unwittingly offended. A stalker. A shadow with malignant intent.

She scanned her phone contacts. She might not be able to work out what was going on, but she could sure as hell take measures to protect herself.

Sonya sounded out of breath. 'Hi. Sorry, I was working out. How are you?'

Lucie hesitated, not wanting to share too much with Sonya; it would invite curiosity. 'I've been putting in way too many hours, and coming home in the dark.'

'Are you about to cancel our sessions?'

'No, quite the opposite. I'm hoping you can squeeze in an extra hour or two for me. I'd like to get lessons in self-defence.'

'Any reason?'

'Yeah . . . there's been a couple of incidents around Fulham lately. This mews is quiet, an easy place for someone to lurk. I figure I should be on the alert.'

'Sensible lady. I've a pretty busy schedule but could do Sunday afternoons.'

'Can we fit one in before Christmas?'

'Sure. See you Sunday at three. I'll come to your place—we can run through some strategies to keep you safe indoors, and I'll scout the mews.'

The tension dropped from Lucie's shoulders; she felt she'd taken back some control. After her call with Sonya, she googled *capsicum spray.* Turned out it was illegal, so she ordered two cans of what was just called self-defence spray.

LONDON

PRESENT

Lucie worked up until Christmas Eve, by which time the staff had thinned out. Only those who didn't want to eat into annual leave, or whom Charles decreed essential, remained. The chatter revolved around parties, getting home to family, gift-wrapping, and recipes for ham, turkey, pudding. A week stretched ahead with the office closed, the enforced holiday embraced by everyone except Lucie. Her plans extended as far as a daily exercise routine, reading books and getting some decent sleep. Then she might take off to northern Europe for a few days if she could get a last-minute hotel. Tallinn appealed, or Helsinki—maybe she could spend a night or two in each.

Kristy dropped a pile of folders oh Lucie's workstation. 'I'm off. Train to Gran's.'

'Hang on a mo.' Lucie opened her top drawer and handed Kristy a square package, wrapped and ribboned. 'For you, as a thankyou for all you do.'

'Aw, thanks.' She tucked the parcel under her arm. 'I'll save it for Christmas Day. What are you up to?'

Charles sidled up behind Kristy. 'I trust you won't be on your own, Lucinda?'

Lucie examined their enquiring faces: genuine interest, or nosey parkers? 'No, no. I'll be busy.'

'Enjoy. See you next Thursday. Kristy blew her a kiss and hurried off.

Charles leant over the workstation and lowered his voice. 'My, ah, wife and I would be delighted if you'd join us on Christmas morning after church. A sherry or two?'

She couldn't think of anything she'd like less. 'That's awfully kind, Charles, but I've planned a big day with a group of old friends.'

It was the same excuse she'd given Jonathan, when he'd asked. He hadn't really been listening, his thumbs agitating his phone screen. Without lifting his head, he'd said, 'Come with me, instead. I'm sure my mother and father would welcome another person.' Lucie couldn't believe it—an invitation to meet his parents, whom he rarely spoke of? She'd thanked him before making her apologies, relieved not to be cornered into time with his family, enduring a sticky afternoon of polite chitchat. Pink spots had flared on his cheeks, and he'd resumed his typing.

Now Charles made a palaver of checking his watch. 'Goodness, five-thirty already. I must get home.'

'Me too.' She had a date with Alan at Claridge's for cocktails before he caught the Caledonian Sleeper to Inverness. He was heading to a house party at some laird's castle owned by a client, an institutional investor. It brought to mind snow, kilts, bagpipes and whisky. He hadn't invited her, and she suspected there was a wee Scottish lass in the glens to keep him entertained. Or else he'd taken offence at Lucie's recent string of excuses not to be alone with him—until she sorted the Martin mystery, it felt safer.

The exterior of Claridge's gleamed, resplendent with sparkling fir trees and life-sized toy soldiers. Lucie gasped in delight: this was how she imagined a fairytale Christmas in London.

Inside, firs freckled with fake snow dotted the lobby and public corridors, turning the hotel into a forest of frost. Dominat-
ing the foyer stood the most beautiful Christmas tree she'd
ever seen, topped with a golden crown and decorated with red
and gold baubles, twinkling fairy lights, and stilettos made of
gingerbread.

At the base of the grand sweeping staircase, Alan stood grinning beside a red train that had a golden sign above its entry:
Loubi Express. He waved her over. 'Your carriage awaits.'

'What the—?'

He took her hand. 'God knows how I managed it, but I've got
us a table and ordered a bottle of Laurent-Perrier. Step aboard.'
She followed him through an arched entryway into an exquisite
carriage. Red decor from carpet to ceiling. Cosy booths, lamplit
tables, red floral displays. Red-and-gold velvet-trimmed curtains.

A waiter approached them, uniformed in a white shirt, black
waistcoat and flat black cap. 'This way, sir, madam. I'm your cocktail conductor.' He gestured to the far corner booth, where a table
was set with red linen and crystal glasses.

Alan laughed. 'Your face is a treat.'

'I've never seen anything like it. It's amazing—a fairyland.'
'Nothing like this in Australia, eh?'

'No way. Back home it's prawns on the barbie, speedos and
full-blast air conditioning.' She pulled out her phone. 'This may
be a bit tacky, but do you think I could take a photo?'

Their cocktail conductor finished pouring their drinks and
whipped away her phone. 'Allow me.' He took one of her and
Alan smiling across the table, and she took a couple more of the
carriage to send home.

Christmas by herself didn't seem so lonely anymore. 'Thank
you for this,' she told Alan. 'Very thoughtful.'

He winked. 'If I had more time, I'd've booked us a room.'

That familiar tug between her thighs. 'This is better.'

'Cock teaser.'

Canapés arrived, along with the waiter's longwinded explanation of the ingredients. Conversation moved to the mundane, stuttering between the weather, TV shows and news headlines. Alan didn't ask how she planned to spend the next day, and she didn't ask how long he'd be in Scotland. Without sex to bind them, they struggled to connect.

Just before eight-thirty, he pulled a box from his pocket, wrapped in Harrods paper. 'I forgot . . . I bought you this, but I gotta go or I'll miss my train. Put it in your bag and open it tomorrow.'

'I'm so embarrassed, I didn't get you—'

He flashed his credit card to the passing conductor and asked for their coats. 'It's a small insurance policy.'

Lucie stared at the package, intrigued. A sex toy? From Harrods? Hardly. Or was this Alan showing his hand as her tormentor. She hovered, unsure whether to take it.

He leapt up. 'C'mon. Let's go.'

She pushed the box into her handbag.

Waking up alone on a raw, dark English morning struck Lucie as a strange way to start Christmas Day, rather than bright sunshine and the promise of a swim before breakfast. She peeped between the curtains, hoping—childishly, she knew—for snow, but London could only manage a sleet-like drizzle. A stab of guilt pierced her as she thought of David on the other side of the world; despite his hostility, she hoped he'd had somewhere to go, someone to share the day with.

Trim at her heels, she pottered downstairs in bedsocks, made a strong black coffee and turned on her laptop. Several e-cards and Christmas circulars from friends waited to be opened, including one she read straightaway.

Yuletide greetings from Down Under . . . sweltering in 35
deg heat here. Took kids to Bondi this morning. Watched
the surf lifesavers in their Santa hats. Barbecued bugs and
yabbies. Hope there's lots of nice things under your tree.
There's nothing like an English Christmas—log fire, gluhwein, reindeer, snow sleighs. Keep cosy and warm. Best,
Everett

Hearing from him gave her a ridiculous thrill. She glanced at the
carriage clock and did a quick mental calculation: it was about
9 P.M. in Sydney. She'd reply in the morning and maybe, if she
timed it right, he'd be online at the same time. Right now, she
wanted to open her presents and phone her family to say thanks
before they were all too tipsy to make sense.

Even after she drew back the curtains, a gloom filled the living room. She turned on sidelights, lit the gas-flame heater and
played Handel's *Messiah.* A choir of five hundred exquisite voices
boomed from the speakers in glorious harmony, and surrounded
by a small pile of gifts, her spirits lifted. Feet tucked up on the
sofa, she opened a cream pashmina from Zoe; the requested books
from her mother; soaps and body lotion from Kristy; a cashmere
scarf from Em; a batik beach wrap from her dad; and a set of tea
towels and oven gloves from her nephews.

Last, she unwrapped the Harrods package. Alan hadn't
bothered to include a card with the navy-blue box. Inside was
a Longines watch, handsome and expensive, its large round face
on a gold bracelet. She sat back against the cushions. 'Wow,' she
murmured.

From the speakers, the words 'He was despised' cut the air, the
alto soprano's voice firm, decisive.

She stroked the watch face. There was something familiar
about it. Someone she knew had one like it, she supposed. A picture flicked into her mind: a washstand, a watch, an arm reaching

around her to strap it on his wrist. Martin—he had owned a gold watch. A Longines? She couldn't recall. Maybe it had been a Patek Philippe. Or Cartier. On a black leather strap. The more she tried to conjure the image, the hazier it became.

Disquieted, she pulled her cardigan around her shoulders and went to check the front door locks. A few shags, and Alan had given her glamorous, exclusive Christmas drinks at the classiest place in London, topped off by an expensive gift. Who did that? In her book, someone creepy. She pulled a bottle of brandy from the drinks cabinet and half-filled a balloon glass.

Her phone rang, and she jumped. It was just Zoe. No longer in the mood to chat to her drunk, happy family, she ignored it. They'd assume she'd gone off to some jolly gathering. She drank the brandy, nestled Trim to her chest and curled into a ball.

Images of unsolicited gifts circled, teasing her. The watch. That Parker pen, similar to Martins. Almost identical red stilettos. Deliberate or coincidental?

She got up and paced the living room. Drew the curtains against the outside world and prying eyes of passers-by. She muted the music, listening for strange sounds in the house; the tick of the clock, the whirr of the fridge. Then she turned the volume up louder.

As a distraction, she re-read Everett's email, which gave her an idea. She googled *gluhwein* but as she had none of the ingredients, poured another brandy.

Dear Everett

I was so happy to get your email. Life's all shit and upside down here. It's been a miserable fucking Christmas so far and it's not even lunchtime yet. Someone's trying to send me crazy.

She deleted the draft. Not a good idea. *Write drunk, edit sober,* some famous writer had wisely said.

The *Hallelujah* chorus swelled in joyous rapture. She scrunched up all the wrapping paper, put it in the kitchen bin and poured another drink.

Lucie picked up on the third ring, her mouth dry. Her head was pounding as she opened one eye. A mellow glow filled the room; she'd fallen asleep with the bedside light on and a half-drunk glass of brandy on the bedside table. The clock showed 10.25 P.M.

'Merry Christmas.' A male voice, American. 'I hope it's not too late.' Not Alan's smooth, buttery Californian accent but another—clipped, efficient.

Bleary, she raised herself onto one elbow. 'You've got the wrong number.' Her chest tightened.

'Don't hang up. It's me, Martin.'

'No, it's not. You're dead.' Her voice was strangled, high-pitched, as she struggled for air. 'Why are you doing this to me?'

'It's not a trick, I promise. Will you let me tell you?'

It sounded like him. Her memory of him. *You've called the cell phone of Martin Cornish. I'm sorry . . .*

She gripped the phone, weighing the options. She could press the red icon, cut him off. That wouldn't solve the mystery, though, and she'd lie awake, waiting for another call.

'Yeah, it's a tough one,' he said. 'Let me talk. Hear me out.'

Trim stretched, moved up the bed and turned circles before lying on Lucie's stomach, purring softly. She stayed silent, too afraid to speak to a ghost—or an imposter.

'I'll take that as a yes. You gotta understand, it was spur of the moment. I looked up at those buildings exploding, people screaming. And I ran—escaped. My chance to leave everything behind. I guess I wasn't thinking straight.'

She tried to picture Martin, her Martin, abandoning his life. 'Where did you go?'

'Better you don't know. Safer.'

'For you?'

'And for you.'

Her head cleared: this must be a con. 'It's ridiculous. You couldn't simply disappear. Someone would know.'

'Lucie, sweetheart, don't you see? I always loved you. Never stopped. So many times I wanted to contact you, but I didn't dare.'

'Why? What had you done?' Her voice rose in anxious staccato.

'Leave that for now. I want you to believe this is me. I know you moved on. Got married and divorced—'

'How? Have you been following me?' As she asked, she realised all he needed was access to her Facebook account, or one of her close friend's. Even David's.

'Sweetheart, I want us to get to know each other again.'

'It's all in the past.' She wavered, shocked at giving him even a mote of credence.

'It's never been over for me. I always knew one day I'd come back for you. Now's our time. Trust me, I'm free. You know it's me, don't you?'

'Where are you?' She looked around the room and pulled Trim closer. Was he in the street below? Hovering, waiting to pounce?

'I'm here,' he said. 'But I'm a different man.'

'What do you mean?'

'I'll—' The line went dead.

She checked the number. No Caller ID again, the bastard.

The whole thing was preposterous. Trim in her arms, she went to the window and opened the balcony door. Barefoot, she stepped out and looked up and down the mews. No one in the shadows. A few glimpses of light between drawn curtains.

Sounds in the distance, cars and sirens. She went back inside, shivering, feet hardened to ice.

Armed with a mug of hot chocolate, Lucie returned to bed, expecting sleep to be elusive until she'd calmed her jittery mind. By 3 A.M., still wide awake, she'd conjured no believable explanation for the man's behaviour. But as long as she let him call the shots, she'd be a sitting duck. She had to be proactive, seek answers, not wait at his pleasure, terrified to trust any men friends or be on her own. To get to the bottom of this, she needed to go to New York City.

One thing was certain: the man stalking her couldn't be Martin Cornish. People didn't disappear in literal puffs of smoke then rise like phoenixes. And the Martin she'd known had always called her 'babe', not 'sweetheart'. But whoever it was knew a lot about her time with him.

She checked her diary. Charnbrook and Henley would be closed until mid-next week. In New York, however, Christmas holidays didn't cause a business hiatus, with most white-collar workers back at their desks after Boxing Day. If she got a flight tomorrow, she'd have a week in Manhattan. Enough time to retrace the past—and enjoy a break, spoil herself, make the most of a few days away from the office.

In the morning she booked flights and a hotel, and texted Sonya to cancel next week's training sessions. She phoned her elderly neighbour, Mabel, who said she'd be delighted to feed Trim. Lastly, she emailed Kristy to let her know she'd be away, and how to deal with any urgent client matters. As an afterthought, she explained where she kept a spare set of house keys, in case of emergency.

NEW YORK

2001

Lucie and Martin sat at the bar in the Rainbow Room, at the top of Rockefeller Plaza, sipping daiquiris like any normal couple. She was perched on a bar stool, legs crossed, shoe dangling from her foot. Around them the room buzzed with energetic conversations: New Yorkers completing business deals, office workers winding down with a cocktail, people on dates, friends catching up on news.

'Perfection.' Martin stroked the tip of his shoe up the length of her calf. 'This is that moment.'

Lucie gave him a quizzical look. 'It is?'

He nodded to her foot. 'The moment when everything changes. When life spins on its axis and all the chips are thrown in the air.'

'That's a mangled mess of mixed metaphors.'

He laughed. 'And that's an array of alliteration.' A man's bulk moved between them. Martin's head jerked up, and in an instant he moved his shoe. 'Brian.' He stood. 'Good to see you.'

Brian towered over them, the height of a basketball player and the width of a sumo wrestler. He wasn't looking at Martin at all. 'And who might this be?'

As if he'd rehearsed for this moment, Martin didn't miss a beat. 'Lucie Wilkinson from Lockstein Feltermann, my attorneys. Lucie, meet my old friend, Brian Jessop.' He slapped Brian on the back. 'Forgive me, buddy, but Lucie only has a few minutes to spare, and we have to finalise a couple of contract clauses. I'll call you, eh? Lunch?'

A smirk appeared in the corner of Brian's mouth. 'Sure. You got it.' He sloped off, but not before he gave Lucie a backwards glance.

Martin slipped back onto his stool. 'Sorry about that.'

'How do you know Brian?'

'We play squash together.' He straightened and buttoned his jacket in an effort, Lucie supposed, to look professional. 'Sorry, it was a mistake coming here. If you don't mind, could you look like you're taking notes?'

So far, she hadn't met any of his friends or colleagues. He couldn't afford the scandal, he said, nor did he want her tainted by the label of 'the other woman'. It meant she'd never seen him through the filter of someone else's relationship with him; hadn't had a chance to discover how he socialised with friends, or learn things about him he'd never otherwise reveal.

She propped a notepad on the counter and waved a pen in the air for the benefit of Brian. 'You better ask me some complex questions. Play this for real.'

Martin grinned. 'Tell me something I don't know about you.'

'Like what?'

'Your all-time favourite book.'

'*Anna Karenina,*' she said without hesitation.

'No? That's crazy. Me too.' He laughed, his eyes crinkling at the edges, and she spilled over with longing for him. 'I guess it makes sense.'

'How so?'

'We both enjoyed reading about an affair so much, it became a self-fulfilling prophecy.'

She'd never asked him if she was his first extramarital dalliance, and while she itched to know, she dreaded discovering a parade of lovelies before her. 'Your turn. If you had the chance to live somewhere else, where would it be?'

'That's easy—Oxford in England, for sure. Gee, what a great old town. I went over for a conference, couldn't get over the place. The history, the buildings, the weight of learned forebears. If I had my time over, I'd be born British and go to that university. It even smells of old age.'

Lucie giggled. 'Can you judge a city by its aroma?'

'Sure you can. Think about Manhattan in summer: that quintessential smell of food, garbage and people. Riches mixed with poverty.'

'Sydney smells of sunshine and blue skies.'

'Is that where you'd go?'

She shook her head. 'Not yet.' There were too many places on her bucket list to explore before she returned home. 'First I want to do a stint in London. Imagine being a hop flight from so many amazing places, like Venice, Paris, Geneva . . . Although if I got in with a big international firm, I'd try for a posting in Asia—Hong Kong, Singapore, even Tokyo.'

Martin fell silent. 'I forget how young you are.'

'We could travel together.'

'Holidays, yeah. Not quite the same, is it?' He stroked her hand under the table. 'Tell you what, I promise I'll take you to England some day, and we'll explore those cobbled streets, churches and cute villages.'

Was he hinting at being closer to leaving Penelope. 'Does that mean—?'

He pressed his index finger against her lips. 'Ssh. Don't let's wreck the evening.'

'Be careful.' She looked over his shoulder, but there was no sign of Brian. 'I think your friend has left.'

'Good. Let's order.' He snapped his fingers at the barman. 'Menu, please.'

Dinner out—*anywhere* out—was a rarity. And the mention of an overseas trip. Surely, *surely*, their time was coming. She bit back a smile. Patience. She needed patience.

'You happy for me to choose?' He pulled his glasses from his breast pocket and perused the menu. She marvelled at how his face altered from cheeky to professional when his eyes went behind those classic circular frames. 'Anything you don't eat?'

'Oysters.'

'Anything else?'

'Tofu. Rice pudding. You?'

'Thousand Island dressing.'

'You're limiting our choices here.'

'Babe, as long as I get to have you for dessert, I'll be a satisfied man.'

Lucie touched pen to paper. 'I'll make a note of that, Mr Cornish.'

NEW YORK

PRESENT

The Algonquin Hotel didn't disappoint with its lush Edwardian styling and sumptuous lobby filled with potted plants and leather sofas. All the time Lucie had lived in New York she'd never paid a visit, and she took a moment to explore the Round Table Restaurant and the Blue Bar, imagining Dorothy Parker holding court and the literati who'd debated and partied there for more than a century.

As befitted a hotel for writers, her small, elegant room had a work desk beneath a black-and-white photograph of 1920s New York. After showering then changing into a pair of warmer slacks, multilayered tops and fur-lined boots, Lucie headed onto West 44th. The wind whistled up the street, and she tamed her hair into a makeshift knot. She stood on the sidewalk, tugged on gloves, and gazed up at the towering buildings. The years dropped away, taking her back to the turn of the century, her life ahead of her, in love with Mr Right, and planning a glittering future where anything was possible and everything an adventure.

She made her first priority a visit to Ground Zero, although she dreaded reliving it all. And the significance of the day wasn't lost on her: it would have been Martin's fifty-eighth birthday. *Serendipity.*

The bus dropped her in Church Street, where the breeze had whipped into fierce gusts. Her hair escaped from its scrunchie, and she rummaged in her bag for a woollen beret. Swallowing hard, she walked across the forecourt of the World Trade Center Memorial to where once the North Tower had dominated. She struggled to summon up one hundred-ten storeys rising into the sky, filled with people going about their business, earning a living, arguing, doing deals. This hole in the ground, walled and lined with charcoal stone, obliterated all signs mankind had ever inhabited here, except for the names carved in relentless lines.

As she looked into the depths of the building's footprint, water streaming down its carcass into a pool, it seemed laughable that Martin had somehow escaped the carnage. And even if he had, she'd still lost him. He'd vanished from the lives of everyone who knew him. To conjure wild theories about him behaving in a cowardly or shameful way seemed outrageous—and disrespectful. All who had died here deserved to be remembered as heroes. She wrapped her coat tighter around her body and gave herself up to this moment: at last she had a place to mourn him, pray for him, say her final farewell.

Around her, adults and children—some in reverence, others out of curiosity—circled the vast memorial, their faces bleak and strained. Conversation was muted, peppered by murmured sadness at the loss of a pregnant mother, a first responder, a flight captain. Lucie edged her slow way among the sombre visitors, along three sides of the former building, until she saw his name: *Martin Franklin Cornish*. She traced her gloved finger over each letter, etched in bronze into the stonework.

A white rose stood vibrant and tall, fitting perfectly into a small hole next to the *M*. Odd. Had someone been here earlier to say a prayer and pay their respects? She stroked the petals, which fluttered in the brisk wind coming off the Hudson. Then her tears flowed; not just for her loss, but for all of them. At Ground Zero, the ghosts lived on.

A voice—female, nasal—dragged her from her reverie. 'They do it for everyone. The rose.'

Lucie wiped away stinging tears with the elbow of her coat, and turned to the small, pale-faced woman next to her. 'Oh?'

'The authorities. They place a rose in those holes on their birthdays. Remembering the dead. God knows how long they'll keep doing it.' She nodded at the rows of names. 'Friend?'

Lucie wished she'd go away, not wanting to share this moment—not with a stranger, not with anyone. Giving a polite nod, Lucie turned back to the memorial.

'Sorry.' The woman moved off. Then stopped. 'Normally there's water fountains—too windy today.'

'I prefer it this way.' Lucie didn't know why she said it. After all, she'd never been here before. Well, not since they'd gouged out the charred remains and turned a place of terror and destruction into this permanent tribute to lost lives. She pretended to study name upon name upon name.

'Bye, then.' Finally the woman moved on, and Lucie returned her focus to Martin. But the moment was broken.

She stared over at the museum and shuddered. Living through those days was enough; she didn't need to see relics neatly labelled for public consumption. The smell of ash, the stink of fear, the hundreds of *Have you seen?* posters stuck on wire fencing would stay in her memory forever.

She took the white rose from its holder, heard a sharp intake of breath from a man standing beside her, and pushed the flower into the buttonhole of her coat's lapel. At least she could take this small—very small—part of Martin with her. She'd press the petals between the pages of *Anna Karenina*, one last private joke between them. She again quashed the notion that maybe the joke was on her.

She walked to Greenwich Street and thrust her arm out for a yellow cab. As the taxi eased its way back past the memorial, she mouthed 'goodbye' to Martin and settled in for the slow crawl to the Upper West Side. Not much had changed: the same *Walk* signs, potholes and steam rising from the sidewalk grates. The same press of people, smart and determined. The same stop-start traffic and constant blare of sirens.

Soon the bustling crowds thinned, office high-rises giving way to apartment buildings. When they pulled in at the corner of 72nd and Riverside, she saw the building had been spruced up: glossy black paint now outlined the windows, and a revolving door had replaced the swing ones. Inside, the doorman's high, heavy oak counter had been taken out, leaving the mail cubbyholes accessible with miniature lockable doors. Even the lifts had been modernised with silent sliding doors instead of concertina gates. Small, disorienting changes that further erased the past, nudging Lucie askew.

A large, liveried black man stood behind the desk, more of a lectern now, that occupied the corner inside the entrance. 'Can I help you, ma'am?' he asked with a bright smile.

Lucie cocked her head. 'Alby?'

'Why, yes.' He looked pleased.

'I lived here. Sort of. Years ago. You wouldn't remember.'

Grey strands now flecked his black hair, and the buttons of his jacket strained a little to hold in his belly. But his eyes still held sympathetic warmth—the eyes of a trustworthy man. He squinted at her. 'I remember you. The Aussie girl.' He pronounced it 'orzi'. Easing his ample frame from behind the desk, he asked, 'You back on holiday?'

'Passing through.' Now that she was standing there, she wasn't sure how to open the conversation. 'Actually, I hoped you'd be here. I wanted to ask you about that day.'

Alby raised his eyebrows. 'You mean 9/11?'

She nodded and bit her bottom lip. 'I'm wondering what you remember from that morning. More specifically, if you remember anything about Martin. Martin Cornish.'

'Let's sit,' Alby said, voice gentle. He took her elbow and steered her through the lobby, and they sat side by side on a hard, stylish bench. 'You're not the first to ask me,' he said. 'His wife stopped by one time . . . Penelope, her name was. Maybe twelve years or so back. She asked questions, too. I didn't tell her nothin'.' He scratched his head. 'Not sure why—didn't take to her, I guess. And I felt sorry for you. Sorrier for you than for her.'

Lucie kept her hands clenched in her lap. She hadn't expected to learn Penelope had come back. 'What questions?'

Alby hesitated. 'About you, I s'pose. She wanted to know if her husband had many visitors. Women visitors. It's not my place to say. So I said nothin'.'

'Thank you, Alby.' Lucie exhaled the breath she'd been holding.

'But Lawson—the other doorman back then—he overheard. "Oh, you must mean the young blonde lady," he said.' Alby tilted his head and spoke to the ceiling. 'That Penelope, she kept her face straight as a poker. "That's right," she said. "I want to find her. I've got something to give her. Do you know where she worked? Or her name?"' Pulling a handkerchief from his pocket, Alby wiped his brow. 'I didn't like her tone. Told her we didn't know nothin'—well, tell truth, I didn't know your name. Lawson, he looked at me and saw I meant business, and he shook his head. "Sorry, can't help," he said.'

Lucie's ears pricked up. Had Penelope really wanted to give her something? Or had it merely been a ruse to get information. 'Is that all?'

'She tried to give us money. I refused, told her she'd be wasting her time. She left then, looking sour as a winter lemon.'

So Penelope had known or had suspicions about the affair, yet it had taken her seven or eight years to start digging. Why? Lucie knew very little about the woman. Would it have crushed her to discover Martin's infidelity, or had she found out and not cared?

Either way, something must have happened to suddenly pique her interest.

A discreet cough from Alby caught Lucie's attention. 'Sorry, I was miles away.'

'There's one more thing,' he said. 'After she'd gone, Lawson told me, "I could've used that money. I could've told her about the other woman."'

'Other woman?' Lucie's voice rose involuntarily.

Alby patted her knee. 'Your Martin wasn't two-timing you. His PA—Lawson didn't know her name—was waiting for him that morning, here in the lobby. She had a whole stack of papers, said Martin had to sign them so she could get 'em to his lawyers, or maybe she said "City Hall"—Lawson couldn't remember.'

'And did he sign them?' Her heart rate picked up at the thought of Martin being delayed, making him late for his meeting, and missing the elevator to the 102nd floor and certain death. *Don't believe it. It's nonsense.*

'Lawson didn't know. Mr Cornish, he just left with the lady in a hurry.'

'Are you in touch with Lawson? Could I talk to him, see what else he can remember?'

Alby's eyes grew damp. 'Sorry, miss, but Lawson passed on three years ago.'

'Oh, sorry to hear that.' Another dead end. 'Did Penelope leave an address or mention where she lived?'

'Nope. She wasn't one to shoot the breeze. Some letters—bills—came for Mr Cornish after he died, but we sent 'em to his office.' Lucie shook Alby's hand and said goodbye. On the sidewalk she scanned the building's facade, and when she spotted the eleventh-floor apartment a swell of memories beset her. Not for the first time, she wondered what Martin had planned to tell her that night over dinner.

Deep in thought, she headed back towards midtown by cutting through Central Park. The chance of locating the PA seemed slim, but as far as Lucie could fathom, she was the only person able to she'd light on Martin's movements that morning, unless she'd shared details of their final meeting with colleagues.

Exiting the park at 59th Street and Fifth Avenue, Lucie walked on until she spied Barnes & Noble, where she took the escalator to the cafe. Once settled with a coffee, she googled Martin's old firm. It had moved premises since 2001; these days it was located in Hearst Tower. She checked out the senior management and saw that most were either too young to have known Martin or had not been with the business long enough. Two names stood out: Lyle Jackson and Teri Radtke. Lyle was described as a founding partner; Teri the whiz-kid who, over twenty years, had climbed the ranks from secretary to director. Could she have been Martin's PA? Lucie's cappuccino went cold as she checked the woman's bio, LinkedIn profile, and many Google mentions—'inspiring speaker', 'dedicated LGBT+ rights advocate', 'occasional New Yorker columnist'.

Before Lucie could tell herself it was a bad idea, she had dialled the firm. Teri was out of the office, so Lucie asked to be put through to Lyle. With scant idea of how she'd explain herself, she plunged in.

'Yes?' he snapped down the phone.

She swallowed, then affected a breezy tone. 'I'm Jane Franklin from *Yesterday's News Today.* I'm researching for a documentary the channel's producing called *The Lost Men!*'

'Yes.' Lyle clearly meant 'get on with it'.

'We're keen to talk to colleagues and friends of up-and-coming business stars whose lives were cruelly cut short by the events of 9/11.'

He grunted. 'Martin Cornish. Don't you people ever give up on new angles that'll dredge it all up again?'

'It's in the public interest, sir. Did you know Mr Cornish? Would you talk to me about him?'

'No.'

'But—'

'Speak to my associate, Teri Radtke. She was his PA. I didn't know the guy well, but I'll tell you this for nothing, and off the record, Martin Cornish would never have made it big. So you're wasting your time.'

For a split second, she hesitated. "That's not what our initial research tells us. How so?'

Lyle paused. 'That's for me to know and you to find out.' He hung up.

Lucie stared at her phone, incredulous. Why badmouth a dead man, even off the record? Perhaps Lyle still felt professional jealousy—or was this a settling of old scores? Her stomach turned. What if something more insidious was going on, something that reflected badly on Martin? Something that could destroy her memory of him, and make a mockery of the years she'd spent idealising and mourning their time together. She put her phone in her bag. *You're being stupid, Lucie, letting your imagination run riot.*

She took the escalator down to Fifth Avenue. As she stepped into light flakes of snow, her phone rang. A number she didn't recognise.

'This is Teri Radtke. You called?'

Lucie hadn't expected her to respond so soon. 'Yes, my name is Jane . . .' Her mind went blank, unable to remember the fabricated name.

'No, you're not,' said Teri matter-of-factly. 'Well, you might be Jane, but you don't work for *Yesterday's News Today.* There's no such program—I checked. Unlike my colleague, I don't speak to media without doing my homework first.'

'Oh.'

'So who are you?' The woman didn't sound unfriendly, just cautious.

'An old friend of Martin Cornish. I'm trying to find out more about the day he died.'

'Almost twenty years later? For Pete's sake, why?' As Lucie struggled to find a reason, Teri broke the silence. 'I get it. You're *her*, aren't you? The girlfriend?'

'Yes,' Lucie admitted, her voice emerging as a squeak. 'Can I talk to you?'

'Well, sister, I know what it's like to have unanswered questions, so sure, I'll meet you tomorrow evening. But prepare yourself, I suspect you won't like what I tell you.'

With twenty-four hours to wait until she met Teri, Lucie played tourist. That evening, she managed to secure a last-minute ticket for an off-Broadway comedy that had garnered rave reviews. It didn't disappoint, but she missed having someone to share the laughs with, and discuss the cleverness of the plot.

In the morning the wind had dropped, so she strolled the length of Manhattan to Greenwich Village, exploring shops that took her fancy and dropping into a cafe for a hot chocolate. She weaved her way towards the Hudson River, ducked into the Whitney Museum for an hour, and walked the High Line, admiring rare-plant gardens, street musicians and eclectic murals.

While she meandered, she chewed on the morsels of information dropped by Teri and Lyle. Lucie couldn't imagine Martin had done anything too terrible. A problem in the office, perhaps. At worst, he'd been sleeping around behind her back, but this wouldn't necessarily mean she'd just been a notch on his bedpost as there was no way he'd had the time to carry on two serious love affairs at once.

By late afternoon, feeling impatient, she arrived early at the Madison Club Lounge in the Roosevelt Hotel. The elegant art

deco design—Tiffany lamps, stained-glass windows—was com-
plemented by stylish period furnishings. She took a table flanked
by deep-cushioned armchairs, with a view of the entrance; she
knew what Teri looked like from the online profiles.

The minutes ticked by, and no one resembling Teri appeared.
Lucie ordered a mineral water. After almost thirty-five minutes,
as she was on the verge of giving up, a short, plump woman in
her fifties, with a flurry of dark curls, burst in and raced over to
her. 'Oh, honey, I am so sorry. Minor work emergency. Another
one of those?' She pointed at Lucie's drink. 'Or a glass of wine?'

The woman's warmth was infectious. 'Why not?' It might help
the conversation flow.

Teri ordered a bottle of chardonnay and filled the moments
between being served with chitchat: the traffic in Manhattan; questions about Lucie's work, where she lived; how Teri would love to
visit 'Down Under' and was still so sad about the Crocodile Hunter.
When the waiter returned, she ordered a cheese plate. 'We need
something to soak up the alcohol.' Her laugh was throaty, perhaps
from years of smoking cigarettes. She passed a large glass of wine to
Lucie. 'Get this into you, and we'll time travel twenty years.'

They chinked glasses, and Lucie sat back. 'First, can I ask how
you found out about me? I thought no one knew.'

'Wasn't too hard to figure out. Men are simple souls. When
their routines change, usually means they're hiding something.'
Teri shrugged. 'Penelope seldom came to town, and Martin was a
good-looking guy. Early that year—2001, I mean—he began to
have mysterious lunches and dinners that he didn't diarise, so I
put two and two together.'

'And do you think I was one of many?'

'Lordy, no. He was too busy making his mark as a finance
hotshot.'

Lucie breathed a sigh of relief. 'Good to know.'

'Gee, you must have been real young back then.'

'Early twenties. I was doing an internship at Lockstein Feltermann, Martin's lawyers.' It was funny thinking back to when she'd struggled to focus on work, consumed by her love and passion for Martin. Whenever he'd left town, she'd counted off the days until his return, crossing her fingers he would tell her he'd left his wife. 'What was Penelope like?'

Teri snorted. 'Beautiful, brainy and highly strung. Reminded me of a racehorse about to bolt at the first sign of trouble. Controlling, too—I think he was a little scared of her. She pressured him to make money so she could give up work. She hated New York, wanted him back in Boston, but the big bucks were here. Commuting between the cities seemed to work fine, except for their issues with the kid.'

Goosebumps crept over Lucie. 'What kid?'

Teri's eyes widened. 'Oh, shit. You didn't know?'

Slowly shaking her head, Lucie stared at Teri.

'Harrison—Harry, they called him. I guess he would have been about ten. I met him once, a nice boy. Quiet. Polite.'

Lucie traced her finger around the rim of her glass. How had she not known? After years of holding Martin's image up to the light, it smashed into shards that crashed down on her head. Why hadn't he told her? Had he been too afraid? There hadn't been any sign of a child in his life—no crayon drawings stuck to the fridge, no phone calls, no photos. She wanted to make excuses and rush back to her hotel, where she could absorb the blow in private, but she couldn't miss this opportunity to question Teri.

Teri smeared camembert on a cracker. 'Well, you know, Martin never talked much about the boy, not like most parents do. I don't have kids, but the other guys in the office, they'd always be bragging about baseball games and SAT scores.'

'Weren't you curious?'

'I asked one time, and Martin said Harry was a bone of contention between him and Penelope. They disagreed about his upbringing.'

'In what way?'

'He said she overindulged Harry, insisted on homeschooling, and the boy was sick a lot. Penelope was an anti-vaxxer, which riled Martin up, but because he lived here he couldn't exert much influence. "Maybe when Harry's a teenager," he said.'

'Still doesn't explain why he never told me about him.'

'Who knows? Perhaps in the beginning he saw you as a fling and thought if you knew he had a kid it'd scare you off. When it got serious, he didn't know how to bring it up.'

Could this be what he'd intended to tell Lucie at dinner? Maybe he'd chosen a smart restaurant to soften the blow and avoid a scene.

'I feel helpless,' Lucie blurted. 'Adrift.' She stared at the stained-glass windows, their colours twinkling in the glow of the chandelier, her stomach in knots. What else might he have hidden from her?

As she dabbed at her eyes with a napkin, Teri stayed silent and topped up their glasses. Lucie appreciated her tact while she took a few moments to gather her wits and remind herself that she needed to make the most of this meeting. 'Can you tell me about that morning? Martin's doorman told me you arrived with some papers to sign.'

Now it was Teri's turn to blink back tears. 'I remember everything about that day. I've gone over it so many times, blaming myself for what happened.'

'Blaming yourself?'

'I met Martin a few minutes before eight. We went round the corner to Rosie's Diner, and I ordered coffee while he called Gus, his broker. We were there fifteen minutes, max. He signed all the papers and left, his coffee half drunk.' Teri closed her eyes, as if shutting out the memory. 'But I'd held him up, and so he changed his plans.'

'How so?'

Teri's voice wobbled. 'His meeting was meant to be at eight-thirty in a Church Street cafe. But when he rang Gus, I heard him say, "Forget about coffee, I'm running a little late. You grab yourself a takeout, and I'll come straight up to your office." So you see, if it hadn't been for me, impatient to get those papers signed off—which goodness knows could have waited—he'd have been a block away. Safe.'

It took a moment for Teri's words to sink in. 'You couldn't have known what would happen,' Lucie said, patting the poor woman's hand while she mulled over the timeline. In peak hour it might have taken half an hour for Martin to arrive at the World Trade Center—and the first plane had slammed into the North Tower at 8.46 A.M. Could he still have been in the lobby, waiting for the elevator? She didn't voice any of this to Teri, not wanting to explain her interest in his last moments. 'How did Penelope take it?'

Teri took a slow sip of wine. 'I don't know, I never saw her again. I had an intern box up the contents of Martin's desk, I couldn't bear to do it, which Penelope collected. She left the States soon after.' Teri paused, frowning. 'She returned, though, a few years later. She came to the office and asked for me, but I'd gone on an extended vacation to India.'

Although Lucie's mind screamed with frustration, she kept her voice level. 'Did she give any indication of why she wanted to talk to you? Or leave an address for you to get in contact?'

'Nope, and that's the last I heard of her.'

'I think she may have wanted to find out if you knew any-thing about me. She went to his apartment block, too, asking questions.'

'Well, she'd have got nothing from me. My loyalty was to Martin, alive or dead.'

The waiter interrupted to see if they wanted anything else; Teri requested the check.

'Can I ask you one last thing?' Lucie said. 'Lyle told me he thought Martin would never have been a big corporate success. Why did he say that?'

Teri slumped back in her chair. 'Wow, what a jerk. The man's been dead twenty years.'

'Please, do you know what he meant? It can't matter now.'

'There was nothing concrete, just some rumours about an off-shore deal. South America, I think. Lyle said maybe Martin had been getting insider-trading tip-offs. But nothing ever came back to roost, so I put it down to idle gossip because Lyle used to be very competitive with Martin—they'd started in the firm at the same time and fought each other for every promotion, bonus and pay rise. Don't worry, sister, Martin wasn't about to be hauled off by the Feds.'

The pendulum in Lucie's head swung back again. Despite Teri's reassurances, could Martin have seen 9/11 as a convenient way to escape discovery of a white-collar crime and evade arrest?

NEW YORK

2001

Martin lay sprawled across the sofa, reading the *Wall Street Journal,* one bare foot caressing Lucie's thigh. He had no interest in *Sex and the City,* but Lucie was glued to the latest episode, unable to believe a woman as savvy as Miranda could get pregnant from a one-night stand.

On the glass-top coffee table, Martin's Blackberry let out its high-pitched, repetitive squeal: Penelope, probably, with one of her ridiculous domestic issues. Whenever she called, he took his phone into the bedroom. When he returned—five, ten, fifteen minutes later—Lucie tried not to ask what they'd talked about. He usually told her, and often it was something inane: the gardener had failed to show up, or Penelope's car needed an oil change. Other times, Lucie wished he hadn't explained. What time did his train get in at the weekend? Which restaurant should Penelope book for Saturday? Friends were visiting, could he stay an extra night? Tart reminders of Lucie's place in his life, the mistress to be fitted in around the wife's agenda.

Martin stretched out an arm and pressed the phone to his ear. 'Yup . . . Hiya, bud.'

So, not Penelope—when for once Lucie wouldn't have minded if he'd slipped off to the bedroom, leaving her to indulge in her favourite program.

'Up a few points.' He scratched his head. 'Good intel. Thanks.'

A business call. She prayed it wouldn't be one of those long conversations filled with jargon about markets, funds, the Dow. She tried to focus on the TV, but Martin's one-sided conversation kept interrupting.

'Whaddaya mean?' His voice had a sharp edge. He swung his legs from the sofa and sat straighter, listening carefully. 'Okay. What's your advice?' Silence. 'Cayman? Uh-huh.' Silence. 'We can't. I can't. You know that, bud.'

Lucie threw him a look, hoping he'd get the hint.

He frowned at her, got up and moved to his desk. 'I can't talk right now. But I can listen. Shoot.' From then on, he spoke only sporadic words: 'trades' . . . 'borrowings' . . . 'too big' . . . 'high risk' . . . 'payback'. Lucie kept following Samantha's quest for a Birkin handbag, until Martin's tone shifted from terse to troubled. 'We'll need a plan B.'

She glanced over, alert to his tension.

He stood facing the window, staring out. 'I'll sort it.' He threw the phone on his desk.

'Everything okay?' she asked.

Swinging around, he gave her a distracted look. 'Sorry, babe, I got work to do. You better leave.'

'No, that's okay, I can read. I won't be in your way.'

'Calls to make. I need peace.' He strode to the bedroom, picked up her overnight bag from where she'd dropped it inside the door, and held it out.

An uneasy sense of being superfluous came over her. Bewildered by his dismissal, she felt tears begin to well. 'Of course.' She made an effort to sound like nothing out of the ordinary had happened. 'Speak soon.'

He didn't answer, tapping away at his Blackberry as if it were a lifeline.

NEW YORK

PRESENT

Chester Lockstein's Greenwich home—a pretentious three-storey, porticoed monstrosity with a stone-and-shingle exterior, unlike its Georgian and colonial-style neighbours—was a fifteen-minute walk from the station. She'd expected her old boss to have aged, but she barely recognised the man who answered the door, shuffling on a walking frame and vastly overweight. The years had not been kind to him, or maybe playing too hard had taken its toll.

'Sorry I couldn't fetch you from the station,' Chester said, waving her in. 'My driver has the weekend off.' "Wheezing from the effort, he led the way across a vast marble entry hall to an airy conservatory with views of a manicured English-style garden. He gestured to a white leather sofa next to a glass-topped table. On a silver tray sat a carafe of water with ice cubes and slices of lime. Lucie took in the elegant pale beige and blue decor, colour-coordinated furnishings and ornaments placed with strategic care. His health might be poor, but Chester had done all right.

And just as she remembered, he was chewing on a fat cigar. 'Well, this is something. Coulda knocked me down with a feather when I got your call.'

'I doubt I'll make it to Sydney for the firm's anniversary, but as I'm in New York for a few days, the least I could do was look you up while I'm here.'

He shook his gold Rolex down his wrist. 'Amy's gone to play bridge, said she'd leave us to talk shop. Truth is, she enjoys a break from me.' He gave his signature booming laugh, which turned into a phlegmy cough; he banged his chest and took a sip of water. 'Living in London, you said?'

'Charnbrook and Henley. I specialise in family law these days.'

'They've a good reputation. We work with them on occasion.'

That caught her interest. 'Do you know Charles Fensham-Smith? One of the senior partners.'

Chester pulled on his earlobe. 'Can't say I do. Fella I deal with is Jack . . . Jacko . . .'

She tensed. 'Jack Hindmarsh?'

'That's him. Heard he broke his neck.'

'He's recovering. Slowly.' She leant forward and tried to sound casual. 'By any chance, did Jack know Martin Cornish?'

Chester squinted at her, eyes alert. 'Mart, eh? Haven't heard that name in a while. Very sad.' He shook his head. 'My first dealing with Jacko was a few years back, long after Mart passed away. Why d'you ask?'

'It's a little delicate. Did you know about our, er, friendship?'

'None of my business. Had my suspicions, of course. A wife in Boston. Him in New York. The way he looked at you.'

Not so secret, after all. 'Could it have come up in conversation with Jack?' A long shot, but worth a try. 'Perhaps in recent times you talked about friends who perished in 9/11?' Jack might have dropped the juicy piece of tittle-tattle to Charles.

'If Mart played away, that was his affair—excuse the pun—not mine. We were old pals but in a business sense. He often came to me for contract advice. He'd stop by, we'd have a drink or two . . .'

'Did he ever consult you over anything else?'

'I managed his estate planning.'

Lucie nodded, glad to have this confirmed. After Teri's bomb-shell about Harry, she'd recalled mailing a copy of Martin's will to him on Chester's behalf. Of course, at the time she hadn't been able to resist reading it, a straightforward document with defi-nitely no mention of a son.

She switched key. 'When was the last time you saw Martin?'

Chester picked up his water glass, his hand quivering. Parkinson's, or something alcohol-related? 'A week or so before that day. Bumped into him on Madison. Didn't stop to chat, wish we had.' He replaced his glass without taking a sip, unable to hold it without sloshing water over the side. 'Funny thing—he called me the day before he died.'

'Really?'

'Wanted to see me asap for a confidential chat. Said something big was going down, and he needed advice. He sounded worried. We made an appointment for the next day.' Chester moistened his lips. 'For eleven o'clock. He had that meeting downtown first.'

Lucie swallowed, unable to speak. Chester's unspoken words, 'At the World Trade Center', hung in the air.

'Ah well,' he finally said, 'So be it.'

Lucie cast around for a change of subject. 'And how well did you know his wife?'

He looked relieved. 'I met her for the first time a week or so later, to go through the terms of his will.'

That would have been the same week Lucie had stumbled from Martin's apartment, alerted to Penelope's imminent arrival. At least Lucie hadn't suffered the painful indignity of coming face to face with her in the corridors of Lockstein Feltermann—or per-haps she had but not known who the woman was, too wrapped in her own agony.

'Did she come with their son?' Lucie asked.

'Son? Oh, I'd forgotten about him. Mart wasn't much of a family man.' Chester coughed again, a deep rattle. 'Let me see . . . I think my secretary took the boy for a milkshake.'

Lucie took a deep breath. 'Did Penelope say anything about their marriage?'

'Like what?' Chester squinted at her, clamping his cigar between his teeth.

'It sounds presumptuous, but did she hint at knowing Martin planned to leave her and marry me?'

Chester's bushy eyebrows shot up. 'He said that, did he? And you believed him?'

'At the time, I had no reason to think otherwise.'

'Well, if Penelope knew about it, she was a terrific actress. She was shocked, in tears.' He sighed. 'Said she couldn't cope with any of it, and just turned everything over to us to deal with— including management of the compensation from the victims' fund. Around three mill.' He chomped down on his cigar. 'We corresponded by mail and email after that. Poor woman couldn't wait to get out of New York, said she'd never set foot in the place again.'

So Chester must have had an address. 'Do you have any idea where she went?'

'Back to Boston, but she sold the house, and once we got the money sorted and invested, I never heard from her.' He cocked his head, gaze sharpening. 'Any reason you're asking me all these questions?'

Lucie shrugged. 'Tying up loose ends, I suppose.'

'Sure.' He was still looking suspicious, but then he glanced to the door and slapped his thighs, brightening. 'That's Amy's car coming up the drive. How about a martini before lunch?'

On the train back to Grand Central, Lucie mulled over Chester's revelation about Martin's sudden need for urgent legal advice. It seemed her lover had been a cheat in every sense. He'd cheated on Penelope. He'd cheated on Lucie by lying about his son. He'd cheated on Harry by not acknowledging his existence. It was also possible he'd cheated at work to make an easy dollar. And maybe he'd cheated death.

Anger knotted in her chest. Only a despicable man would fake his death to save his own skin. If he'd abandoned her and his family without a backwards glance, he'd never loved any of them; never cared about their grief, the wasted years spent mourning him.

Could he have plotted how to slip from sight? Had he intended to tell Lucie, take her with him, or just walk out? Or did he seize the opportunity to disappear on 9/11, while everyone was looking in the other direction?

If he'd fled the country, there would be flight records. What if he'd somehow obtained a fake passport? Then again, he might have taken on a new identity in America and laid low. Or moved around, never staying long enough to raise suspicion.

As she gazed out the window, suburbia giving way to industrial granite, an idea formed. On her phone she searched for *Penelope Cornish*. Why hadn't she googled the name before? Probably because back in 2001, no one had searched for everyone and everything online.

There were over nine hundred results. When Lucie narrowed the criteria to Boston, there were almost three hundred. Martin had once told her Penelope worked as an academic, wedded to some ongoing research project. *Penelope Cornish, Boston University* yielded nothing relevant. Lucie racked her memory for the correct university but wasn't sure she'd ever known. Certainly, she didn't know the specialisation or faculty, and it wouldn't have occurred to her to ask Martin; she'd had no interest in Penelope other than seeing her and Martin get divorced. Another search told Lucie there were fifty-two higher education institutions in the Boston region—and for all she knew, Penelope no longer lived or worked there.

She checked LinkedIn and only got one result, in the UK, with no profile attached. She tried *Penny Cornish* and found eight women, none in academia. If Penelope worked under her maiden name, the haystack became truly impenetrable. Or she might have remarried, taken her new husband's name.

Lucie put away her phone, but she was undeterred: there were other avenues she could pursue. Tomorrow, she'd go back to the past.

That night she applied online for a New York Public Library card and emailed the DeWitt Wallace Periodical Room with her request. Hours of library research had been the norm for her twenty-five years ago at university, but now she had no idea how to interrogate the vast databases on offer. She'd have to interface with a human to have any hope of finding what was out there in the public domain.

The library opened at ten. Buoyed by a double-shot espresso, she walked at a brisk pace down Fifth Avenue to 42nd Street. She passed between Patience and Fortitude, the stone lions at the library's imposing-entrance, and made her way up to the Rose Room on the third floor. The librarian sported spiky black hair streaked with purple and pink, and an earring through her left nostril. She located Lucie's email and took pity when Lucie fibbed that today was her last day in New York. 'I'll do a search now,' she said, and email you the links.'

Lucie surveyed the majestic room lined with thousands of reference books and lit by massive chandeliers. At the long wooden tables a few students were buried in study, backpacks at their feet, brass reading lamps turned on. She set up her laptop in the middle of an empty table, where she wouldn't be distracted by visitors browsing the shelves.

Emails from the librarian trickled in over the next hour. In the uninterrupted hush of the library, she examined each one. Some articles she discarded as mistaken identity; others caught her attention. She printed out the few that referred to Martin Cornish: his death and memorial notices, a brief profile, and a *Women Today* interview with Penelope.

Boston Globe. September 17, 2001.
Martin Franklin Cornish, aged 39
January 2, 1962—September 11, 2001

Most adored husband
Lost too soon.
In anguish and heartache
Always in my thoughts.

Your loving wife, Penelope

Odd, thought Lucie: no mention of Harry. Even after such a passage of time, she found the language galling, given the marriage had been an empty shell. On first reading, she assumed Penelope had written what everyone would expect the grieving widow to say. But when Lucie re-read the notice, both the written and unwritten words were revealing. Had Martin lied about Penelope's feelings for him? *Most adored—In anguish and heartache—Your loving wife,* with no mention of 'husband and father' or 'wife and son'. Did the omission mean Penelope had been so broken, her mind was solely on Martin?

Boston Globe, November 21, 2001
In Memoriam

To grieve and celebrate the Life and Loss of Martin

Franklin Cornish, beloved husband of Penelope Cornish. Cruelly taken, September 11, 2001.

St Cecilia Roman Catholic Church, Belvidere St, Boston. November 29, 2001. The service will begin at 12 P.M..

There will be no wake.

Lucie read the notice twice, struck again by no reference to Harry—surely Martin's role in his son's life, even if it had been as his stepfather or adopted father, deserved recognition.

Strangely, the librarian's search didn't throw up an obituary. *The New York Times* had run the short profile piece in April 2002, but it read like a professional biography, detailing his schooling, academic, sporting and career achievements. It did, however, end with: *He leaves behind his wife, Penelope, and son, Harrison, 12.*

The *Women Today* article, dated June 2002, was the one that most intrigued Lucie. She stared at the photos, unable to tear her eyes from the hero shot of Penelope and Martin in an embrace, beaming into the camera. She'd never seen Penelope before, and for the first time since 2001, Lucie looked into the face of the man she had loved: soft brown eyes, immaculate dark hair, and a crinkly grin on his clean-shaven face— the smile Lucie had believed he reserved for her. Penelope was raven-haired with high cheekbones and startling blue eyes, her bright-red lips pouted; by any reckoning, she was beautiful. Martin's hand rested on his wife's shoulder, and she reached up to entwine their fingers.

Alongside it were two smaller photos, the first from their wedding day: Penelope in white, Martin in a tuxedo, both looking high-school young, standing stiffly under an archway of pink and white blooms. Lucie barely recognised this baby-faced man who wore horn-rimmed glasses, but there was something familiar about the way he stood, tense and focused. Underneath was a snap of Penelope, gaunt in a black dress, which hung from her emaciated frame like a rag, and incongruous sheepskin boots. She also wore a fur-trimmed black hat, and held black gloves and a Bible. Other mourners mingled in the background—the photo must have been taken either on the day of Martin's memorial or a service at Ground Zero.

There was no image of Harry.

Lucie read the article. Sandwiched between knitting patterns, recipes and celebrity nonsense, she expected it to be lavish with sentiment, and she was right. The sympathetic reporter gushed about the agony of Penelope's loss, while references to terrorism were artfully avoided.

> Penelope's hands tense into tight balls as she remembers the tragic day when she lost her soulmate. "What kind of people, what kind of evil people fly planes into buildings? Destroy lives? Destroy hopes and smash dreams to smithereens?"
>
> Her tears are never far from the surface. "How can he be gone? Someone so vibrant, so full of energy, so full of plans for our future. All he wanted was to make enough money to maintain our lifestyle. 'I'll work my butt off for the next twenty years,' he said, 'and then we'll retire to Florida.'"
>
> But Florida is now a tarnished dream. Penelope describes how, on September 11, she and Martin were due to fly to Miami for a holiday at their condo. "But our son contracted whooping cough, so I stayed in Boston while Martin decided to remain in New York until the incubation period passed."

So that was the 'change of plan' Martin had referred to.

Lucie frowned, something niggling at her. Penelope might have been an anti-vaxxer, but wouldn't Martin have been immunised as a child? A Google search confirmed that the likelihood of infection increased with the time since vaccination; it made sense he hadn't wanted to put himself at risk.

Sitting back in her chair, Lucie gazed up at the intricately carved ceiling, realising she would never know if Penelope's take on the marriage was a lie, a delusion or the truth.

Penelope is loath to talk about their son, Harrison, except to say she intends to move with him from Boston to settle in the UK. "I can't live with the memories. The house we chose together, the restaurants we ate in, the hospital where our baby was born."

But Martin Cornish will never be forgotten. Penelope plans to remember him every year, on the anniversary of his death, in her own special way. I ask her how she will honor him, and she replies: "Wherever I live, he will have a presence, and with each passing year, it will become greater, not lesser."

Lucie rubbed her forehead. There was something forced about Penelope's words, or was she reading too much into them?

At least she was closer to locating Penelope and Harry. If they had gone to the UK as planned, it pointed to Penelope holding British citizenship, something else Martin had never mentioned. It also fitted with what Teri told her, that Penelope had taken Harry overseas. But how could she discover where exactly they had moved, short of hiring a costly private investigator?

Of course she could use Charnbrook and Henley's legal channels but she baulked at using the firm's resources for her personal business. She looked at her laptop. Somewhere there would be records in the public domain, and a good starting point would be births, marriages and deaths. Maybe Harry had married, possibly fathered a child, or Penelope had re-married.

She registered on the official UK government website and quickly discovered she'd need the date and place of marriage in order to obtain a copy of the certificate. Birth records were only available to 2004, when Harry would have been an extremely young dad. On the off-chance, she did a pre-2004 search but there were no relevant results, so if he'd had children, it had been more recently.

Finally, she searched under 'Deaths' for *Penelope Cornish*. But the search came back blank, so she tried again, this time for all women with that surname. About twenty entries appeared, the fourth for *Beatrice Penelope Cornish* who had died late 2018, in Oxfordshire. To obtain further information, Lucie had to apply for the death certificate. She paid the express delivery fee and received notification a copy would be mailed to her London address within twenty-four hours.

Then she searched on *Harrison Cornish,* and also men named *Cornish,* but when no possible matches came up, she assumed he must still be alive.

LONDON

PRESENT

When Lucie arrived home, she picked up her mail from the hall mat, tossed aside a few circulars and kept one letter to read. Still in her overcoat, she went through to the living room and placed the official-looking brown envelope on the side table next to the fire. An unfriendly winter nip penetrated the night air. She flicked on the gas jets, and went in search of Trim.

He sat on the kitchen counter, glaring at her. When she approached, he flicked his ears back in disgust.

'Pleased to see you, too.' She ruffled his coat, and he arched his back, jumped down and stalked off, leaving her in little doubt of his feelings about being left for a few days with only Mabel for company.

She hung up her coat and poured a glass of wine, then undertook the evening ritual of drawing curtains, lighting lamps and selecting music. Dame Kiri hit the high notes of 'O mio babbino caro'. Settled in the armchair, Lucie tapped the envelope on her palm, turned it over and slid her finger under the flap.

The single sheet of paper was headed *Certified Copy of an Entry*. Beneath that: *DEATH*. Lucie took a deep breath and scanned the details.

Beatrice Penelope Cornish, aged fifty-three, had died at Forget-me-not Cottage, Link Lane, Shipton-under-Wychwood, Oxfordshire, on 18 October 2018. Cause of Death: *Aspiration pneumonia.* Her death had been registered by Harrison Franklin Cornish, Son.

Lucie blew a long breath from pursed lips and leant back against the chair. 'Wow,' she murmured. It was a lot to take in. She re-read the certificate, trying to get her head around the small details that revealed so much.

It struck her that Penelope had chosen to live near Oxford, the place of Martin's dreams, and call her home Forget-me-not. A coincidence—or at Martin's bidding? And she'd said, *Wherever I live, he will have a presence, and with each passing year, his presence will become greater, not lesser.* Taken literally, could that mean he'd escaped death and fled to England with his family?

Lucie shook herself, picked up her drink, and put it back, untouched. She needed to stay focused, not be sidetracked by wild theories. If Martin had lived with Penelope and Harry in the Cotswolds, he would have been discovered in a nanosecond. In order to stay undercover, the whole family would have had to assume new identities.

Lucie took her laptop from her briefcase and googled *Forget-me-not Cottage, Link Lane, Shipton-under-Wychwood, Oxfordshire.* The first listing showed it last sold a few months after Penelope's death. Lucie flicked through photos of the picture-perfect stone cottage. Ivy framed the windows, while established trees shielded the home from nosy neighbours. A large vegetable patch dominated the side garden, and at the back a small circular stone table and two chairs nestled beside a well-kept lawn surrounded by flowerbeds. The interior was stripped of furniture, with low beams and whitewashed walls giving the rooms character. Hooks dotted one wall where a collection of photos or artworks must have hung. A mud room and laundry flowed into the eat-in kitchen.

The tiny living area was dominated by a narrow, open staircase, which led to two bedrooms.

It would have been cramped accommodation for Penelope and her growing son, let alone a man in hiding as well.

Lucie's living room was toasty now. She kicked off her shoes, sat on the fireside rug with her laptop on her knees, and reclined against the sofa. Trim slunk in and allowed her to stroke him; he even purred. She pulled him closer, glad to be forgiven, giving him a cuddle as she watched the gas flames flicker.

With no news on Jack Hindmarsh's prognosis or a date for his return to the office, Lucie grappled to meet competing deadlines, swamped by a workload that kept mushrooming. Every time Charles F-S dropped another file on her desk, she grimaced. She couldn't complain about Jack's ongoing absence, but she wasn't a machine: it became impossible to keep up.

A couple of cases strayed beyond her area of family law into more complicated property matters. When she pointed out to Charles that she didn't think she had the necessary qualifications or understanding of the UK tax system, he was unsympathetic. 'Do what that lot do.' He tipped his head towards the hot desks staffed by millennials. 'Google it!' He guffawed at his own joke.

The time spent in the office stretched into an ever-thinner elastic band of hours. In by seven, home by midnight—eleven, if she was lucky. By the time she had a few drinks to unwind, she had to survive on four or five hours' sleep. It took at least two strong coffees to kickstart her day. Saturdays, and often her sacrosanct Sundays, were spent in the office, further draining her tank. She had to cancel a trip to the Vienna State Opera, and another to visit an Australian friend in Ireland.

When Alan was in town for a few days, she used work as an excuse not to see him. At Claridge's she'd realised how boring he was: nice eye-candy, without much else to offer. He kept texting her with bawdy, adolescent messages, which he must have presumed would turn her on but had the opposite effect.

A couple of emails from Everett went unanswered. When she received a third—*Did I offend you?*—she rattled off a quick response: *Under pump at work. Not ignoring you.* He wrote back: *Got it!* But as the days passed, she heard nothing further from him and felt snubbed by his sudden withdrawal.

Despite the pressure, she loved the buzz of working in London, the complexity of the cases and the demands on her expertise. That was, until the morning when she arrived at work just before 7 A.M. to be greeted with three emails from Charles. Each one contained a time-consuming, menial task that should have gone to the lazy graduates in the back office who drank cappuccinos and swapped Tinder stories.

Her anger brewed, and as soon as Charles strutted into his office well after midday, haughty and important, she followed him and slammed the door. He turned to her, his eyebrows arched in lazy curiosity.

Hands on hips, she confronted him. 'This has to stop. I'm not your bloody work mule.'

His expression hardened. 'Your billable hours are behind those of the other team leaders. How will you cope when you are at maximum capacity, Lucinda?'

'You know damned well I work longer hours than most people in the firm,' She found it inconceivable he'd question her output.

He flicked through a pile of papers on his desk. 'The proof is in the numbers.' He tapped a page in front of him. 'We've had to adjust several of your invoices. We can't charge clients for work that has mistakes.'

Lucie bit her lip. Yes, there had been some confusion on a property settlement—she'd mixed up English law with Australian tax rulings on capital gains. But that was nothing major, was it?

It had soon been sorted. She swallowed hard, determined not to give way. 'Don't play me for a fool, Charles.'

'No, Lucinda. Don't assume we don't see what's under our noses. Now if you'll excuse me, I have work to do.'

Lucie returned to her desk, chafing under the injustice, and tried to focus on *Wetherby v Armstrong*.

'Ahem.' Kristy stood by her workstation, holding a hamper. 'This came for you.'

Lucie didn't look up. 'I'm drowning here.'

Kristy, sharp as a steel knife, spoke her mind. 'You stabbed his pride, not his foot, with that stiletto. This is payback.'

'Would Charles be so unprofessional?'

'Trust me, he's a vindictive little shit.' Kristy paused. 'By the way, you got your billings entries all mangled up last week. I've sorted it, but be careful.'

Another slip-up, so soon after Charles's reprimand, took Lucie off guard. 'Did you ask again about getting a contractor for me?'

Kristy snorted. 'Charles referred me to his memo of September decreeing a hold on additional staff due to Brexit uncertainty, although why that affects how many people divorce is a mystery. I argued that this is a special case—an unforeseen hiccough. Charles said I exaggerated and dismissed me. Fluttered his regal hand at me and said, "Get out, get out. I'm busy." You know how he does.' She tapped the hamper. 'Eat.'

The smart woven basket had a Fortnum's label. It was probably from Jonathan. He'd been so sweet lately, calling her a couple of times a week but never pushing her to find time for him. 'I'm sure you'd rather recharge your batteries when you have a few hours to yourself, not be bothered by me,' he'd said. Down the track, she'd make it up to him.

Kristy eyed the hamper. 'Nice one. Someone knows you're not eating properly.' She leant over the desk. 'There's a cooler bag. Check it out.'

Lucie found a pair of scissors and snipped open the bag. A tray of oysters on ice. 'What the—?' She hated oysters: slippery, nasty things you had to swallow whole. She couldn't see the point of them. Still, Jonathan wasn't to know that. She opened the typed card: *I thought this would make you laugh.*

'What is it? You've gone white.'

Lucie rifled through the rest of the hamper: a block of tofu, a tub of rice pudding. 'I don't understand . . .'

Kristy jumped off the desk. 'Gotta go. Can hear my phone. Enjoy lunch—and get more sleep. You look like you might faint.'

Hands over her mouth, Lucie closed her eyes and sat for several moments, horrified. *He's dead, he's dead.* She grabbed her coat from the back of her chair and headed to reception, where she thrust the hamper at Kristy. 'Take this. I'm not hungry.'

Kristy raised an eyebrow. 'You okay, girl?'

'Got a meeting,' Lucie mumbled. Rather than wait for the lift and be forced to make idle chat, she ran down the fire stairs.

Out on the street, she took several gulps of air and looked from left to right. She needed space to think, somewhere she wouldn't be disturbed. She walked to the next cross-street and pushed through the door of the Olde Cheshire Cheese.

One table of late lunchers lingered: a few businessmen finishing up a bottle of red, and a couple with coffees—no one she recognised. She ordered a brandy and took it to a corner table. Even in her distressed state, as soon as she sat down she realised being seen mid-afternoon on her own in a pub next to her workplace wasn't a good idea. She just had to pull herself together. Her hand shook when she lifted the brandy balloon, then the fiery jolt soothed her. She took another sip. And another. When the barman approached—a weasel of a man with a droopy moustache—and asked if she'd like a refill, she nodded.

Her brain darted erratically. *You're being a fool. He's dead, and this is David's work. Only David would know the foods you hate.*

Or could it be Alan, Jonathan, Charles, Mr X? Everyone talked about food. Maybe she'd said something at dinner, over a drink, a jokey chat at the water cooler. Even Kristy, who often picked up lunch for her, might have worked out what she didn't eat. Tofu. Oysters. Rice pudding. She rootled around her memory bank, retrieving conversations, snippets of things discussed, likes, dislikes . . . Once, with Alan, perhaps, when he ordered at Claridge's. Or had they? She couldn't recall . . . Jonathan? Wine, yes, but food, he never showed much interest . . . Images of Charles, whisky in hand, boardroom lunches . . . Would Martin have known? Too far in the past . . . *Think, Lucie, think.*

David, it must have been David. Ten years of marriage. He knew it all—from her favourite toothpaste to the brand of washing powder she favoured.

'Another one for you, ma'am?' the barman called over to her.

She looked up. The pub had emptied, now in its afternoon lull before the evening crowd descended. 'Thanks,' she said. 'A double. And the bill, please.'

She nursed the drink and focused on getting her mind into neutral. Having finished the brandy, she left a fifty-pound note tucked under a beer mat. Her head swam, and she went to the ladies, where she splashed cold water on her face and pinched her cheeks. On the way back to the office, she stopped by the corner newsstand and bought a tube of peppermints.

LONDON

PRESENT

Later that night at home, when she'd sobered up, her confusion turned to anger. If David thought it funny to send her a basket of foods she disliked, he had serious issues to address, and she didn't intend to waste energy on him. Right now, she needed to vent her frustrations about Charles. She'd write to Everett—a fellow lawyer would understand—although she'd heard nothing from him in weeks, and hoped she hadn't destroyed their friendship. Had he misunderstood when, time poor, she'd stopped corresponding?

> I don't understand the Brits. They won't come out and say what's on their minds. You have to read between the lines, try to work out the innuendo, the body language. I ask a question and get an answer that bears little relevance to the issue at hand. It's all smoke and whispers. I feel like I'm constantly ten steps behind.

She paused. She really wanted to cry on someone's shoulder; unload about how the whole Martin thing had upended her, scared her to the point she'd now messed up at work. If only she could call Em, but she'd gone skiing to Japan, and it wouldn't be fair to burden her in the midst of a snow fling. And it wasn't Everett's problem, either. If Lucie blurted her fears, he'd think her a neurotic fantasist.

> Sorry, feeling bit raw and overworked. Hope all well with you? Lucie.

Everett pinged back instantly, and her tummy took a small leap. So he wasn't cross with her. He'd obviously taken her at her word that she had no time to write, and hadn't wanted to crowd her inbox.

> Glad to hear from you. Discuss it with that English boyfriend of yours? Maybe he can decipher the code for you! Seriously, I think you're being oversensitive. Your Australian down-to-earthiness, coupled with all that straight-shooting you would have learnt from your years in New York, doubtless intimidates your UK colleagues. Ignore them. Breathe. Go smell some roses.

She slumped back in her chair, disappointed by his flippant response. It was no use asking Jonathan's advice—she tended not to involve him in work stuff, as he'd never had a corporate job. Despite his thoughtfulness, she doubted he'd get the politics, the jostling for advancement, the constant focus on bottom-line profit.

Alan might have more insight, as he also worked in a pressure cooker, but Lucie had a horrid sense he'd try to rescue her with a stream of 'good' advice on how to handle Charles F-S. And there was something off about Alan. That expensive watch had spooked her, with its eerie echo of Martin's. Those juvenile text messages annoyed her, too—sent as roundabout way of alerting her to their next shag.

She took a large mouthful of wine and pulled out her phone, before she could change her mind. Never mind the great sex—her safety was more important.

He picked up on the fourth ring. 'Hey. What's up?'

She took a deep breath. No point procrastinating. 'There's no easy way to say this—'

'But you don't want to see me anymore.'

'That's about the gist of it.'

Silence fell for one second, two. 'Not even once more, for old times' sake?'

'No.' The idea now revolted her, rather than filling her with excited anticipation.

'That's a shame. Sure I can't change your mind?'

Definitely not. 'I want to return the watch. Could you give me your address?'

'You don't have to. Actually, I'd like you to keep it—my thankyou gift.'

'I want to.'

'O-kaaay.' He sounded reluctant. 'I'll text it.'

She hung up, relieved at taking back control. No one could sort her problems for her; she'd have to battle through on her own. *As* far as Charles's insufferable behaviour went, she'd stand up for her rights and not be bullied. First priority: no more weekends spent in the office.

With Alan out of the way and more free time, she'd up the ante with Jonathan. Add some sizzle and spice. True, they shared a love of opera and enjoyed exploring London together, and he made intelligent conversation. But physically, he held back. When she tried to initiate sex in the shower or on the rug in front of the fire, he always led her to the bedroom. He never kissed her, except on her cheek in greeting or farewell. On the few occasions she tried to tease his mouth with her lips and tongue, he kept it shut firm—like in a 1940s movie. When they had sex, he rejected her attempts to stimulate him, more interested in her orgasm than his. It was so one-sided, she felt selfish.

There had to be some of way of unleashing his inner fetish. She just needed to find the right buttons to press.

By close to midnight, Alan still hadn't texted his address, although she'd sent him a couple of reminders. Perhaps he had the serious shits with her for pulling the pin. Guys like Alan— good-looking, wealthy, masters of the universe—didn't appreciate not having their own way. No matter: she'd send the watch to him at Moore's Bank.

She went to the hall table, certain she'd put it in the top drawer, and rifled through the contents: envelopes, flyers, pens, spare keys. A blank envelope caught her attention, and she pulled out a sheet of paper: that note, the one that had started everything. *At last, I've found you. A shock, I'm sure. But in time, I'll explain. Martin.* A lump rose in her throat and she forced herself to examine the handwriting—it appeared the same but memory played tricks, and writing changed over time. With unsteady fingers she replaced the note, and peered to the back of the drawer, but found only the cheap Parker pen from Alan.

With methodical care, she checked through the antique mahogany desk in the living room, and the shelves of the dining room dresser. Then she searched the kitchen, though why would she have stored a Longines watch with cutlery or tins of food? Perhaps she'd taken it upstairs, thinking it safer among her jewellery. But the leather pouch yielded nothing, and neither did the bedside drawers, linen closet or the bathroom cabinet.

She ran downstairs, replaying Christmas Day. She'd drunk a lot, so she could have stuffed it somewhere peculiar. Or—God forbid—could she have scrunched it up with all the wrapping paper and thrown it in the bin, as she'd done with Martin's card in the shoebox? With frantic zeal she pulled off cushions and seat covers, got on her hands and knees and peered underneath every piece of furniture. She re-checked all the drawers, looked in every saucepan, and even ransacked the downstairs bathroom cupboard where she stored rolls of toilet paper.

A sick sensation took hold. When she'd been in New York, could someone have stolen it? The letting agent had a key. So did Mabel. And Lucie had told Kristy where her spare keys lived in her desk—which meant anyone at the office could, in theory, have broken in. Even Charles. But why would anyone want to burgle her home and only take a watch? Unless Kristy, who'd dated Alan and been spurned, had sought payback?

No, Lucie refused to believe she'd been robbed, or that she'd been stupid enough to discard the watch. It had to be here somewhere. Going upstairs again, she went through all the clothes racks and drawers. Checked coat pockets. Peered into boots. Emptied handbags. Yanked out shoeboxes.

The Manolos from Martin showed no sign of interference. But the new pair, in their soft drawstring bag, felt lumpy. She tipped them out.

As she reached into the toe of the right red stiletto, her fingers brushed cold metal. A link chain. In disbelief, she withdrew the Longines watch.

For several long minutes she sat on the floor, the watch in her hand, desperate to recall the moment she'd hidden it there. She focused again on remembering Christmas. The call from Martin. Her decision to go to New York. Organising flights. Packing. It was possible, she had to admit, she'd shovelled the watch into the shoe to keep it secure. If only she could remember doing it.

LONDON

The kitchen needed more romance than the aroma of slow-cooked lamb shanks, which had been stewing for a few hours. She lit a trio of candles, set them on the table and switched off the harsh downlights, except those over the hob. In the living room, she drew the curtains, lit more candles, and chose a jazz play-list. Strains of Dave Brubeck filtered through to the hallway and followed her up the stairs. In the bedroom she lit clusters of tea lights, placing them on the bedside tables and around the bathroom. From the top drawer of the dressing table she selected a few silk scarves—Hermès, Versace, Gucci—and laid them on the bed.

After undressing, giggling to herself, she popped a frilly red polka-dot French apron over her head and tied it around her waist. Jonathan was in for a treat. To complete her ensemble, she put on a pair of skin-tight, black leather, over-the-knee boots and stood back to admire her reflection. *If this doesn't do the trick, maybe next time I'll try a nurse's uniform—or go all out with dominatrix gear.*

The doorbell tinkled, and Lucie ran down the stairs. She stopped by the kitchen, picked up a small tray with a tumbler of whisky, and answered the door. 'Good evening, sir.' She curtseyed before Jonathan's astounded face, holding the tray at shoulder height. 'Come this way.' She swung around, giving him the full benefit of her naked backside, and sashayed along the hallway.

Behind her, he said nothing. The silent plod of his footsteps made her feel silly and self-conscious.

She led the way through the flickering candlelight and stood next to the armchair. 'Make yourself at home.' She waited for him to sit down, handed him the tumbler, and perched on his knee.

He squirmed beneath her, and sniffed the air. 'What's cooking?'

'Me.' She rubbed her boot along his calf. 'Hot and saucy.'

'Jump up,' he said, patting her bottom. 'You're making my leg go to sleep. And I expect you want to finish getting dressed.'

She gaped at him. 'Are you kidding me?'

He blinked. 'Hadn't you noticed? You're still in your apron. Lovely smell from the kitchen, by the way.'

'Oh gosh, so I am.' Lucie undid the apron's tie, whipped it over her head, and placed one booted foot on his knee. Maybe leather was more his thing, particularly when made into shoes. 'Unzip me.'

'You're not wearing anything.'

'Oh, for Christ's sake, are you being deliberately obtuse? Doesn't seeing me naked, behaving like a French parlourmaid, turn you on?'

'Not really. I prefer you in proper clothes, not dress-ups.' He stood and put his glass on the mantelpiece. 'Let me come upstairs with you. Show you how much you mean to me. My way.'

He took her hand, and Lucie, bemused, allowed herself to be led up the stairs. Did she make a lousy femme fatale, or was he just completely oblivious? Maybe she was being unreasonable: growing up a loner, he'd have had no friends with whom to swap stories of sexual conquests or explore pornography. And he hadn't been forthcoming about past girlfriends—perhaps there'd been none. Of course, he'd never tell her.

He grunted in appreciation at the sight of the candles dotted around the room, then walked around the bed and picked up one of the scarves. 'Nice,' he said.

'To tie you to the bedhead. For fun. While I have my evil way.' Lucie grinned at him, hopeful he still might be persuaded to play a game.

'I don't think I'd like that.'

'Why don't I blindfold you?'

He frowned. 'If it's what you want.' He unbuttoned his shirt, slipped off his trousers and underpants, and lay on his back on the bed.

Lucie tugged off her boots, knelt beside him and picked up a blood-red paisley scarf. Careful to ensure his eyes were covered, she tied it around his head. She took him in her mouth, and he rubbed her back while she sucked and caressed him. Eventually, his body showed a semblance of interest, and she sat astride him.

He quickly came—and, without a word, pushed the scarf onto his forehead, blinking in the light. His eyes focused on Lucie. 'Move off me.'

She rolled to one side, and he went into the bathroom. She listened to the sound of running water. When he reappeared, he reached for his trousers and phone.

'Aren't you going to join me?' she asked. 'Finish what we started?'

He glanced at her, sprawled on the bed, waiting for him. 'I need to send a couple of messages, and then I want to taste whatever you've cooked up for me.'

She stifled a sigh and swung her body off the bed. Another fail. He hadn't even tried to give her pleasure, which wasn't like him; he was too preoccupied with his phone. Maybe she should confiscate it. But was he worth the effort, or had their friendship run its race?

* * *

Lucie woke the next morning to a note propped against the bedside lamp. *I had to leave early so left you sleeping. Jonathan.* She looked at the clock: 10 a.m., and her bones ached. She must have been desperate for sleep to still feel tired. It was a bitterly cold day, so she turned up the heating before she put out food for Trim and tidied away the remains of dinner. By midday, chills began, and she took paracetamol. Her throat burned, and her eyes stung.

She hauled herself upstairs, snuggled into bed and fell into a deep, restless slumber. Her temperature rose, and she flailed around under the covers, dipping in and out of consciousness. Peculiar dreams accosted her: a giant rabbit chasing her through a shopping centre; flying a plane, empty of passengers, to Antarctica.

Loud knocking and the tinkle of the doorbell roused her. Disoriented and drenched in sweat, she heard another bell chiming closer by: her phone. She tried to sit up, but her stomach roiled, and she swallowed down a churning wave of nausea. Hand over mouth, she pushed back the bedclothes and lurched to the bathroom. Leaning over the toilet, she threw up until she was exhausted, but kept dry-retching. Heat flushed her face, and her head thundered in pain.

More knocking rumbled from downstairs. The phone rang again. She crawled back to the bedroom and fumbled for it. 'Hello?' Her dry throat made her voice rasp.

'It's me. Jonathan. I left my gloves behind. You sound terrible.'

'I think I've come down with a gastro bug that's whipping round the office.'

'I'm outside. So's your boss, Charles—he's got an urgent file for you.'

Lucie pulled on her dressing-gown. Clutching the bannister, she made her shaky way downstairs and wobbled along the hall-way. She opened the front door and almost collapsed into Jonathan. 'I feel sick.'

He put his arm around her and led her to the guest bathroom, where she heaved up again in gut-wrenching, noisy anguish.

Charles's muffled voice penetrated through the door. 'I tried to telephone, Lucinda. Urgent court hearing tomorrow afternoon. Con with client in the morning at ten. I'll leave the paperwork on your kitchen table. Mind if I borrow your loo?' And she heard his footsteps on the stairs.

'I don't want him to see me like this,' she mumbled. 'Get rid of him.'

'Stay there.' Jonathan slipped out.

Lucie splashed her face with cold water and leant her head against the cool wall tiles. Her mouth tasted of stale vomit, and she yearned to put her head on her pillow and fade into nothingness. She listened as Jonathan farewelled Charles, waited to hear the front door close, then staggered into the hallway. With Jonathan's help, she made her way upstairs, changed into a clean nightdress and clambered into bed.

Hours later, the click of the bedroom door woke her, and she sensed Jonathan hovering in the doorway. She lifted her heavy head from the pillow and squinted at the clock, but the numbers blurred.

'Would you like a cup of tea?' Jonathan tiptoed to the bedside and laid a cool hand on her forehead. 'And some aspirin? You're very hot.'

She raised herself on one elbow. The room was dark. 'Why are you still here? It's late. You should go home.'

He drew open the curtains, and a dull grey light penetrated the air. 'It's morning. You slept right through.'

'Oh, no.' She had that ten o'clock conference, and she hadn't yet read the file Charles had dropped off. 'I must get in to work.'

'Don't worry, I called your office. Charles seemed unfazed.'

Her relief was mixed with resentment at Jonathan taking liberties. She lay back on the pillow. 'Right, thanks.'

He sat on the side of the bed. 'You should stay home for a few days. You're running a temperature. I can look after you.' He smoothed the covers. 'I'll change your sheets. You'll have drenched them in sweat.'

It was too much: he was her lover, not her nursemaid. She didn't want him clucking around her, seeing her immobilised. 'No, please, really, I'd much rather be on my own.' Her stomach lurched, heralding another bout of retching.

'Shall I take a key, so I can look in on you every day?'

'No need,' she mumbled, mortified. She closed her eyes, shutting him out, needing to get to the bathroom. 'I'm very tired.'

He took the hint and left.

That night, her fevered brain whirled with nightmares. Martin, maimed and hideous, unrecognisable. His eyes gouged out. Buried alive.

Burning up, she threw off the sheets. Then, chills coursing and wet with perspiration, she burrowed under blankets. She told herself Martin was dead, gone, his ashes mingled with those of hundreds of strangers, but a spike of uncertainty persisted . . . What if? Like a mantra, she kept repeating to herself, *There's an explanation, there's an explanation*, until sleep overtook her.

In daylight her fears shrank, and she relished time on her own with only Trim for company.

After three days she stopped throwing up, but her body was sapped of energy, and she stayed away from the office for the rest of the week. However, she couldn't escape the mounting pile of work; each day, Kristy couriered over files with instructions from Charles. His little yellow sticky notes demanded attention: *Hearing set for next Monday. Client anxious. Prioritise this one!* Lucie lit the gas fire, turned on all the radiators, and enjoyed the rebellious act of attending to client issues in pyjamas and a dressing-gown.

Jonathan rang every evening at six o'clock, concerned and solicitous. He carried on as if she'd survived a life-threatening disease. She stifled her irritation, thanked him for his kindness, refused his offers to shop for her, and hung up with promises that yes, she'd keep warm, drink lots of fluids and have plenty of rest. As each day passed, it became clearer Jonathan had reached his use-by date. Things that had once appealed to her about him she now found hard work. She didn't want an old woman fussing around, mothering her. Or his presumption that they were a couple, and he had a right to intrude into her home, make decisions for her.

By Friday, her depressed mood had lifted, and she felt much perkier until her phone rang on the dot of six. If she didn't pick up, Jonathan would come over and start banging on the door, and although she had little desire to see him, she owed him the courtesy of winding back their relationship face to face. When he offered to bring dinner, she asked for Thai cuisine.

For the first time all week, she got dressed and smoothed on a light layer of make-up. Humming a Mozart clarinet concerto, she cleared the dining table of paperwork, then stacked the dishwasher with the plates and glasses that had congregated on the drainer.

He arrived with a large white plastic bag and unwrapped two containers sheathed in butcher's paper. 'I realised spicy food might not be a good idea, so I got grilled fish and mash instead.'

Invalid food. 'Shame. After nothing more than soup all week, I was looking forward to something with flavour.'

'Chilli might upset your tummy.' He kissed her cheek. 'You look better, but thin. Have you thrown up again?'

She bit back an angry retort. 'I lost my appetite.'

Bustling around in the kitchen, he found plates and cutlery. 'That's good, I suppose.' His voice carried an edge of disappointment.

'Good that I couldn't eat? Are you saying I need to lose weight?'

He frowned, then quickly smiled. 'You're perfect. But you should be resting. Go sit down, put your feet up. I'll serve the food on trays.'

She grabbed the cutlery and a bottle of Coonawarra shiraz. 'Let's sit at the table. You can tell me what you've been up to all week while I've been malingering in bed.'

'Not malingering, Lucie—taking care of yourself. After all, you never know, you may be—'

'May be . . . what?'

As she brushed past, he swiped the bottle from her grasp. 'Should you be drinking?'

'Why on earth not?' She grabbed it back and unscrewed the top. 'Stop suffocating me,' she snapped.

'But what if . . . what if. . . ?'

'Oh for God's sake, Jonathan, what is it? You're clucking around me like a mother hen.' She poured herself a defiant, extra-large glass of wine and a smaller one for him. 'You're driving,' she said pointedly.

'Oh, am I? I rather hoped, now you're feeling better . . .'

Lucie took a slug of wine and firmly set her glass down on the table. 'It's lovely to see you. Thank you for the food and your solicitations. However, I have been feeling rotten all week while simultaneously keeping up with my not-inconsiderable workload. So I'm a bit tired and irritable. Plus, I don't need to be lectured by you on whether or not I can have a drink.' She took another mouthful of wine and sat down.

Without a word, Jonathan placed her fish in front of her. He handed her a serviette and sat down opposite, shoulders tensed, lips pursed. They ate in silence.

In one gulp, Lucie emptied her glass and started to pour another. 'There's something I need to talk—'

Before she could say anything more, he took the bottle from her and screwed on the top. 'What if you're pregnant?'

His absurd question hovered between them. She shook her head. 'You're not serious. How on earth could I be pregnant? Whatever makes you think such a thing?'

'You were sick. And that night you spent at my flat, you didn't have your pills with you.'

She did a quick mental backflip, remembering how the sterile atmosphere had doused any desire. 'Sorry, Jonathan, but what century are you from? A, we have protected sex, and B, I threw up. I was running a fever. I had a stomach bug, or I ate something that disagreed with me. End of story.' She caught the sound of herself, harsh and mean, and saw dismay on his face. 'Don't worry, you're not about to be a father.'

'I was only afraid for you. Still, it wouldn't be so terrible, would it?' He tipped his head to one side. 'Children?'

'For me, yes. And at my age, it's almost impossible to have a spontaneous pregnancy.' She had to put an end to this. 'I think it's time we had a chat. About us.'

When he splayed his hands on the table, she noticed his fingernails were chewed raw. 'I've been selfish,' he said. 'Upsetting you when you're tired.'

'Listen, Jonathan, I need to straighten out a few things between us. You're very kind, and I appreciate everything you do for me, but I'm not looking for anything serious.'

'Aren't you? The other night, before you got ill, you dressed up for me.'

'That was sex. A game. Don't you get it?'

'It was much more than sex. It meant something to you because you put my enjoyment first. Do you realise how happy that makes me?'

Was she hearing him right? 'No, no—you've misunderstood. We're on completely different wavelengths.'

'Were not.' His voice went up an octave, and he clenched his hand around his phone. 'We're good together. Can't you see? I'm here to look after you, make your life easier so you can concentrate on your work. It's perfect, isn't it?'

'You've got it so wrong. I'm not looking for a partner, or to be taken care of. I'm sorry if somehow I've misled you—it was never my intention.'

'Then why lead me on? Was it all a pretence?'

'You misread the whole situation. I've enjoyed our friendship, but it's time to call it a day, before you get hurt.'

'It's because I asked if you were having a baby, isn't it? I thought you must want a child, before it's too late for you.'

Anger bubbled. 'Drop it, Jonathan, I don't want a fight. Let's part on good terms.'

'Can I still see you? Take you to the opera?' A childish note of hope in his voice.

'We'll see.' She wouldn't, of course.

After he'd gone, she finished the bottle of wine and poured herself a brandy. She stared into the fire, mesmerised by the fake flames, glad she'd put a lid on the relationship. He was a nice guy but plainly had issues—that whole pregnancy thing was, well, nuts. And she was better off without him and Alan. Right now, she was too on edge to be with any man. Waiting, waiting. Wondering what would happen next.

LONDON

A good night's sleep, and a brisk walk around Hyde Park in the winter sunshine, lifted Lucie's spirits. Returning home and not being bothered by a call from Jonathan made her wonder why she'd tolerated him so long. Perhaps because work hadn't allowed her the luxury of making new friends—aside from her correspondence with Everett. She vowed to change all that. Next week, once back into her routine with Sonya, she'd invite her to go for dinner one evening. And she'd organise a drinks party for her neighbours, whom she ought to get to know better. She'd also make a bigger effort at work, and ask Kristy to organise a get-together for the department—with their partners. It would be good to mingle with people who did something other than legal work for a living.

This past week, without frequent interruptions from staff, clients and meetings, she'd managed to get on top of most of her files. When she returned to work on Monday, she'd have a clean slate. No more stuff-ups. There was something to be said for working from home: maybe she'd suggest to Charles F-S the firm consider offering staff more flexible hours. With luck, he'd see the advantages—improved productivity and better health—rather than dismissing the idea as impractical and an excuse to skive off.

She made a pot of coffee, pulled out her laptop and began framing her argument. The decision wouldn't be Charles's alone, as the other partners would have a say, too. She listed those who'd be onside, the ones she'd need to lobby, and those who no matter how hard she campaigned would flatly denounce any change to working conditions. By late evening, she'd also come up with a shopping list of other innovations for the firm to consider: implementing a four-day week once a month, reconsidering annual leave, partnering with other firms to provide childcare facilities.

The ringing of her phone broke her concentration. No Caller ID. Her newfound optimism faltered, replaced by an odd sense of relief. If this was 'Martin,' she'd give him what he wanted: an assurance of her belief in him. In that way, she might get the answers she needed.

'Hey, Lucie, are you quite recovered?' That soft, gravelly voice: Martin. His words at once put her on guard, but she ignored the implication that he had her under surveillance.

'I'm glad to hear from you.' She kept her voice steady, while her heart thumped against her ribcage.

'You don't know how much that means to me. I guess you're now satisfied it's really me, and you're ready to hear the truth.'

'I keep going over in my mind that last morning. But a lot is a blur. So much time has passed.'

'I'm gonna explain. Fill in the gaps for you.'

He hadn't taken the chance to show he knew she'd been to New York, and to probe why she'd gone there and what she'd found out. She'd told no one where she was going, merely that she'd had a few days' break—which surely meant no one in New York was part of this charade, capable of alerting him she'd been sniffing around.

'All I want is the truth,' she said.

'You got it.' He coughed, cleared his throat. 'I never made it to the World Trade Center. I watched those planes hit, then I ran like everyone else. I panicked. Bodies dropped from the sky, and thick smoke made it impossible to see. I remember the screaming, and the sirens. All those tall buildings, Lucie, and no one knew when the next one would be hit. I prayed you'd be safe in midtown and figured my best bet was to get as far away as I could. I walked across Brooklyn Bridge with hundreds of others. Everyone held a mask or a scarf to their face, and that's when I had the idea to disappear.'

She remembered seeing those pictures in the paper: disoriented strangers fleeing in a cloud of dust. Despite his credible story, it made no sense that Martin would have walked off without a backwards look, when he could have returned to her, in one piece, and they might have had their happy ever after. But she had to play along with the pretence. 'I still don't understand why.'

'I'd gotten deep in debt. Been trying to dig myself out with huge trades, big overnight positions. It might have paid off, but once those planes hit I figured the markets would go haywire, and I'd be sunk. Worse, I'd gotten loans from people who'd demand payment. Let me tell you, dying in that inferno would have been a better way to go. So I thought, *That's what I'll do. I'll lay low, let things settle down, let them think I'm dead.*'

'And me?' She couldn't help asking.

'I couldn't risk telling you. Better you believed me dead. One day, I told myself, I'd be back for you. I didn't think it would be almost twenty years.'

'Where did you go?'

'I waited a couple of days, holed up in a motel, and caught a bus to Boston. Even if I wasn't alive to pay up, it wouldn't stop those goons going after Penelope. I had to warn her to get out of America as soon as she could. I gotta hand it to her, she kept her cool. She said she'd keep me hidden, play the grieving widow and claim my life insurance. As it turned out, she also got almost three mill in victims' compensation. But the twister was, we could never reveal I was alive. I just wanna say, Lucie, I always loved you, I never stopped. I sometimes wonder if a part of me wanted Penelope to find out about you, bring things to a head.'

Lucie's chest tightened, constricting her lungs. Words roared in her head, but she held back. 'Go on.'

'I slipped up. Big time. There was a box of my stuff in the attic. Penelope collected it from my office after 9/11 and stored it away. A few years back, she went through it, looking for another photograph of me. You see, every anniversary of 9/11 she added another picture of me to her shrine: her wall of remembrance, she called it. That year she wanted the one of my graduation from Columbia Business School, remembered I'd kept it at work and figured it'd be in that box. She found it, all right—on top of your love letters. Things turned nasty then. She didn't know who you were, just that you'd signed with the letter L.'

She'd forgotten about her quirk of signature. Intended to cover her tracks, it had also sounded sexy: Elle.

He went on. 'When I refused to tell her your identity, she made my life miserable and said if I ever tried to find you or get in touch with you, she'd turn me in.'

Lucie's temples throbbed. 'I've some questions—'

'Let me finish. Please. Penelope's dead now. That's why I'm back at last. If you'll have me. Think about everything we shared, everything we meant to each other. Give it another chance. Give me another chance. You won't regret it.'

She paused. If this man wasn't Martin, and she asked him more about the logistics—*Where did you live? How did you explain away your presence? What about your son? Weren't people suspicious?*—she might lose the advantage. She needed him to believe she trusted him, so he'd come out of hiding. All she needed was concrete evidence to take to the police. Even if her stalker turned out to be Martin, he had no right to pursue her and frighten her. 'Can we meet?'

He exhaled. 'Thank you, Lucie. I'll call you with a time and place.' He hung up.

A half-drunk bottle of brandy stood on the side table, and she poured a slug into her cold cup of coffee and leant back against the cushions, deep in thought. His story sounded plausible, if fantastical. Was there anything he'd said that he couldn't have discovered through research? That cottage wall dotted with picture hooks, for example, was in the real estate photos. And it turned out he hadn't destroyed her letters, but stashed them in his office. The intern who had packed up his belongings might have read them, so perhaps there had been gossip. His rival, Lyle—and Teri—would have been familiar with the photos on his desk, and may have seen the letters. And, of course, Penelope, who might have told their son—or anyone she knew.

Dead men didn't make phone calls. To unlock this puzzle, Lucie had to remain sensible. *Stay logical. You're a lawyer. You don't deal in emotions, you deal in facts. Tick them off. Fact: Martin Cornish died on 11 September 2001. Fact: Martin Cornish lied to you about having a son. Fact: No Caller ID means the caller is at pains to remain untraceable. Fact: The shoes could have been sent by anyone—Charles F-S, David, Jonathan, Alan, Mr X. Fact: David knows more than anyone about your time with Martin. Facts, Lucie, facts.*

She turned to Google and searched for 9/11 victims. Martin's name had been etched into the memorial, so didn't that mean his remains had been identified and catalogued? Apparently not. She learnt that more than a thousand people believed dead were yet to be positively identified. But every year, armed with breakthroughs in DNA technology, scientists gave one or more positive IDs. Just the year before, bone fragments already tested six times had finally yielded their owner's name. All unidentified remains were stored in a sacred repository located at bedrock between the footprints of the twin towers. The Reflection Room offered a place to go, in lieu of a grave, for consolation or prayer. If she'd known, she could have visited and tried to discover if Martin remained on an unknown victims' list—except it was only open to family.

Newspaper archives turned up stories of missing men found a year later, suffering amnesia and schizophrenia. A woman who'd gone missing the day before 9/11—allegedly troubled and in trouble—was believed by some to have used the attack as cover to disappear. Or perhaps her murderer had used it to cover their tracks.

The slim worm of possibility that Martin might have staged a similar Houdini act wouldn't wriggle away, and Lucie opened a bottle of wine.

Fact: Penelope was dead. But Harrison might have some answers: if his father was somehow alive, they might be in touch. All Lucie had to do was find Harrison and work out a feasible reason for contacting him. As it remained most likely that Martin had perished, the last thing she wanted was to upset his son with spurious suggestions of reincarnation.

Her earlier search had been fruitless, only proving Harrison was alive if he still resided in England. She scoured social media sites and dating apps but found no matches. He'd be what, thirty? Perhaps one of those young people who valued anonymity over having their personal data available for commercial enterprise to interpret and target.

Taking a punt he'd have gone to a fee-paying school in Oxfordshire, she found a list and began searching. It soon became evident the schools valued their alumni's privacy: the few websites she scanned offered no listings or yearbooks of former students. To get a result, she'd have to phone each one with some bullshit about trying to locate a long-lost relative. Maybe he fulfilled Martin's dream of studying at University of Oxford, although she doubted it. Unlike Australia, it was a rite of passage for tertiary students in England to move away from their home town.

As a last-ditch effort, she turned to the online phone book, although few people his age had a landline. Several listings came up for Cornish in Oxfordshire, but none with a first initial H. She tried London, and her eyes widened when one H Cornish appeared. In NW3—the North Western postcode area. She noted the address.

The facts became blurrier as Sunday afternoon faded into evening. She poured a large brandy, hoping it would help her sleep. Half an hour later, still feeling wide awake, she poured another and sat in the dark, unable to erase the growing conviction that David must be at the heart of this. Surely he had the strongest motive to punish her, scare her. How sad if his suppressed anger had turned into sadistic revenge. If only she'd understood him better, seen behind his veneer of geniality, she could have handled their separation with more sensitivity.

She woke at six, curled up with her head resting on the sofa arm. Temples pounding, mouth dry, neck stiff from being propped at an unnatural angle, she staggered into the kitchen and switched on the coffee machine. A shot of caffeine, and she'd be right. The stale taste of alcohol lingered, so she went upstairs to brush her teeth and raid the medicine cabinet for paracetamol and vitamin C.

In the bathroom mirror, her pallid complexion gazed back at her. Mascara-stained bags had formed under her bloodshot eyes, and her tousled hair was matted to her head. She grimaced and gingerly returned downstairs.

Lucie's head was still throbbing as she walked to the Tube, and her legs shook with the effort of placing one foot in front of the other. Her enfeebled state compounded when work on the Central Line meant fewer trains. Commuters squashed together in damp torture, with bodies, briefcases and umbrellas jamming the carriages. She hid behind incongruous sunglasses, clutching a hand pole, trying to ignore the woman next to her who yelled instructions down her phone to her nanny. At last, Lucie disembarked at Temple station, found her way into grey drizzle and attempted to switch into work mode. She took several deep breaths and forced her body towards the inevitable mountain of work waiting on her desk.

Arriving at the office, she pushed her sunglasses onto the top of her head. The glare from the overhead lights penetrated to the back of her eyeballs.

Kristy raised her head above her computer screen. 'Christ, you look terrible. You sure you're over that flu?'

Lucie squinted at her. 'I could use a coffee. Strong and black.'

'A party weekend, I take it?' Kristy smirked. 'Lover boy pulled all the stops out, eh?' She laughed. 'Half your luck.'

Lucie gave a weak smile, the best she could muster, and walked carefully to her desk, feeling sick. A folder greeted her, with a yellow sticky note attached: *Urgent. Opinion needed by 9 A.M. con. CF-S.* Jesus, that was all she needed, a client meeting and an assumption that she held the answers to whatever problem they expected her to solve.

She opened the folder and began to read. The words swam in a haze. Kristy banged down a mug of coffee, further jangling her nerves. She re-read the last three paragraphs, trying to formulate an understanding of the issue. A residential apartment block with no electricity in a third-floor flat. The recent buyers wanted to run a cable through the building, but the other tenant owners objected: they didn't want their walls and cornicing altered to accommodate the new boxing. It was a simple enough problem—one that could have been sorted by a junior associate. Mediation should do the trick, but Lucie grappled to balance the arguments that would be put up by the other side.

At nine o'clock, Charles clicked his fingers. 'Lucinda, my office.' He stood over her desk, nostrils flaring. 'And take those sunglasses off your head.'

She closed the folder and stood up too fast, needing to grasp the back of her chair. Her stomach rolled, and she choked back rising nausea. It took a couple of seconds for her head to clear. Then she walked with slow precision into Charles's office.

An elderly man and a small, grey-haired woman sat at the meeting table. Charles frowned at Lucie, flicking his eyes upwards. Oh shit, she still had her sunnies on her head. She whipped them off and stretched out her hand. 'Good morning,' she struggled to say, 'I'm Lucie Wilkinson.'

Charles carried most of the meeting, while Lucie took notes and tried to ignore the waves of hot flushes that kept surging through her body. She eyed the water carafe but wasn't sure she'd be able to keep fluid down. Perspiration seeped through her clothes, and her face was clammy. The couple ignored her, and for once she was thankful for the slight. They preferred to deal with a man? So be it—today, they could.

At last, everyone stood and shook hands. 'Excuse me,' Lucie said, edging to the door. 'Another meeting.' She pushed past the couple, out into reception. Ignoring Kristy's raised eyebrows, she almost ran to the ladies where she threw up, noisily, in the nearest toilet. She knelt on the floor, head spinning, waiting for the next stomach churn.

When it was finally over, she washed her face and tried to gargle away the taste of vomit. She looked in the mirror. Her complexion was grey, her eyes were red and puffy. The door swung open, and she bent her head, not wanting to engage with anyone.

'Here.' Kristy rubbed her back. 'I've got your coat and bag. Go home. Sleep it off.'

'I can't,' mumbled Lucie. 'I've got to log notes from this morning's meeting.'

'Directive from F-S, I'm afraid. And he wants to see you first thing tomorrow.'

Lucie groaned. Oh well, she'd claim she still hadn't got over the gastric bug—Charles couldn't give her a hard time for being genuinely sick.

After ten hours' sleep, she awoke the next day feeling rested but foolish. She stood in the shower, water spilling down her body, and remonstrated with herself Yesterday had been no way for a lawyer to behave. Clients paid good money for her counsel, not to have someone in a substandard, hungover state deal with their business. When she reached the office, she'd apologise to Charles, explain she was unwell, and assure him that it wouldn't happen again.

She dressed in a sharp navy-blue suit over a white fitted top, clipped on gold earrings and a cuff bracelet, and stood back to look in the mirror. Her hair, loose and flowing, was too informal; she knotted it into a loose bun.

On the way to Bouverie Street, she stopped at Two Hens for toast, coffee and orange juice, and steadied her nerves by reading *The Times*. At the till, she paid and dropped a pound coin into the tip jar. 'Wish me luck,' she said to the waitress, who grinned and gave a thumb's up.

Head up, ready to do battle, Lucie strode through Charnbrook and Henley's lift doors. Kristy flicked her eyes towards the boardroom. 'His lordship awaits you.'

Lucie frowned. Charles always held meetings in his office, on comfy leather armchairs around a low coffee table. He made a point of describing himself as 'a man of the people' who 'never stood on ceremony. She asked, 'Is someone using his office?'

Kristy raised one eyebrow. 'Search me.'

Lucie squared her shoulders. This face-off was going to be harder than she'd anticipated. 'Be ready to pick up the pieces.'

The heavy arched door closed behind her with a deep thump, blocking all sound from prying ears. Charles stood under the portrait of founding partner Ellsworth Henley, a po-faced man with hollow cheekbones and a thin moustache. Neither of them looked welcoming. Charles gestured Lucie to the far end of the oak inlaid table that seated twenty-four at full stretch.

She walked the length of the room, conscious of his eyes on her, and tried to appear unperturbed. 'Morning, Charles. Lovely day.' She kept her voice professional.

He sat next to her at the head of the table, coughed, and placed a folder in front of him. 'Before you say anything, Lucinda, and dig yourself into a deeper hole, I want a few words.' He tapped the folder. 'You came to us from a well-respected firm—and prior to that, from Lockstein Feltermann in New York—with excellent credentials and a flawless record. No one gave any indication that you had personal problems. And yet it has not gone unnoticed here that you appear to have a relationship with alcohol that at times impairs your work.'

Lucie opened her mouth to protest, to defend herself. A glance at Charles's stern face stopped her. Her cheeks grew warm, and she looked down at her hands.

His tone softened. 'I like you, Lucinda. You are a good law-yer. But this cannot go on. It's bad enough that we can smell the alcohol on your breath. But when there are repeated mistakes, errors our clients find inexplicable, which make them question their judgement in using our firm . . . well, then it is my duty to take action.' He straightened his tie, waggling it from side to side under his collar.

He's going to ask for my resignation, she thought, *and I can't blame him.* She'd never get another job in London—word got around the legal community like greased lightning. She'd have to leave her beautiful mews house and return to Sydney, tail between her legs, partnership aspirations thwarted.

Charles leant across the table and placed a hand over hers. 'I told you I could help your career.'

She tried not to recoil from his touch. Right now, she needed his mercy. She'd sit tight and listen to what he had to say, and then decide whether to kick him in the balls or eat the crumbs of humble pie he offered.

'Take some time off. Clean up your act, and solve whatever it is that's troubling you. I'll tell the staff you're on secondment to Australia, recalled by its government for a previous case of yours. They may not believe it, but that's immaterial. When you can prove to me that you've—ah—turned over a new leaf, so to speak, then we'll take you back.' He patted her hand and sat back. 'Your call.'

She had little choice. "Thank you for your understanding, Charles. I won't forget it.'

He smiled. 'Be sure of it.'

When Lucie parroted Charles's trumped-up story about her sudden 'relocation', Kristy was upbeat. 'You lucky diva. What I wouldn't give for sunshine and bronzed lifesavers.'

Lucie assumed the receptionist's cheery words meant she was unaware of the circumstances, and decided it prudent to keep her in the dark. 'I'll try to get a flight tomorrow or the next day.' The sooner she went, the better, Charles had said. He'd asked—no, *insisted*—she clear her desk, write up progress notes on all her clients and be gone by midday.

What if Kristy was pleased to have her out of the way, so she could make another play for Alan? Good luck to her.

'Would you like me to check on things for you while you're gone?' Kristy asked.

'Not necessary. My neighbour will look after Trim.' Lucie hated being suspicious of Kristy and Charles, or anyone at work; nevertheless, she retrieved her spare keys from her desk.

She left the office with mixed feelings. Shame, for her behaviour. Relief, that she still held her job. Excitement, at the prospect of going to Sydney—because in that regard, the cover story would hold true. Rather than cool her heels in London waiting to be released from gardening leave, she'd take this opportunity to go home.

Although she'd never wanted to set eyes on David again, seeing him had now become her main priority. She'd email that she was flying over, and would like to see him. If he held the clues to solving the riddle of 'Martin', she'd know as soon as she asked. David could never lie to her face—he always looked away.

SYDNEY

PRESENT

Ensconced in her sister's weatherboard house in Crows Nest on the lower north shore, Lucie retreated to a bedroom that Zoe had reconfigured from its use as a study, and hinted at the need for total peace and quiet. Not an easy goal to achieve with two noisy boys hooning around, but Lucie didn't want to be quizzed about her sudden reappearance, knowing she couldn't brush Zoe off with a glib story.

'I'm on stress leave,' she told her and Jake. 'I'm here to recuperate.'

Zoe, older and wiser than her younger sibling, asked ho questions, busying herself with the daily pandemonium of juggling a job, a home, a husband and the twins. Jake accepted his sister-in-law's presence with his usual equanimity.

Relieved at their apparent lack of curiosity, Lucie spent the first few days running, surfing, and drinking in moderation. Before she met with David she wanted a clear head, no jet lag fogging her brain. After London's inclement winter, Sydney's hot, humid summer was a balm to her frazzled nerves. Her jitters eased every time she pulled on shorts and a singlet—rather than trackpants, several layers of tops, gloves and a beanie—before jogging out onto the street and shielding her eyes from the onslaught of bright sunshine. She followed the running tracks around the parks and harbour foreshore, stopped at local cafes, and swam at her favourite beaches: Balmoral, Edwards, Chinamans. "When smoke from out-of-control bushfires engulfed the city, forcing her indoors, she treated herself to an avant-garde musical at the Opera House, boutique shopping in Woollahra, and lunch with former colleagues.

The only blight to her carefree days came in the form of texts from Alan. *How's your pussy? TRIM and taut?* She ignored his childish humour, but another quickly followed. *Playing HARD to get, huh?* Then a third: *I don't go easy, but I do COME in a FLASH.* The rest—pinging like rapid gunfire—she didn't open. The next day he sent an insincere apology, saying he'd been drunk. She didn't believe him and sent no reply.

By the weekend she felt almost ready to confront David, but first she wanted Em's advice. They met near The Rocks, at the top of the Hotel Palisade. Em snaffled a table on the deck with a smoke-hazed view across the harbour.

'You look fabulous.' Lucie wasn't joking: Em's chestnut hair gleamed, cascading onto her shoulders; her skin had a light golden tan, and her eyes sparkled. 'Who is he?'

'A surgeon at Vinnies. Tall, dark and handsome. I'm smitten.' She handed Lucie her drink. 'What's with the mineral water?'

'I'm doing dry February.'

'Yeah, right.' Em sat back and crossed her arms. 'Tell me everything.'

Lucie was sparing with details; she didn't need a whole lot of psychobabble from her best friend, so she sketched only the bare bones of her concerns. 'Remember I thought David could be stalking me? I'm pretty sure he is, and I think the best thing for me to do is see him, have it out with him. He hates confrontation, though, and wants me to go to his apartment.'

Em's eyes widened. 'You've already spoken to him?'

'Not exactly. I emailed—said I'd be in Sydney and that I'd like to clear the air.'

'There is no way on this planet you are going to his place. Are you mad? After what Zoe told you about his angry accusations? He sounds like he's got into a real state. He could be dangerous.'

'Don't be ridiculous. We're talking about *David*.' However anguished, David would never lay a finger on her. He wasn't the type—or was she being naive?

'I mean it, Lucie. Don't be alone with him. Meet him on neutral ground, preferably outdoors, so if he does cause a scene it won't be quite so hard to handle, or you can just walk away.'

'You're worrying me.'

'Good, you should be worried. If he's pretending to be Martin— God, I can't believe I just said that—then he's got serious issues.'

Lucie wrestled to take Em's advice seriously, but had to concede that as her friend counselled damaged souls every day, she knew the signs. 'I'll suggest Centennial Park, by the cafe. What if he refuses to come?'

'Then you'll know you made the right move. But I think he'll meet you. It's not over for him. He's obviously still got questions, things he never thought to ask at the time you separated. However . . .' Em hesitated.

'Yes?'

'Have you considered he might not be the one doing this?'

Lucie ran her fingers through her hair, and stared at the Harbour Bridge in the distance. 'One thing at a time, Em.' She snapped on a smile, keen to block any further supposition. 'Enough about that—I'm dying to hear more about your new man. "When can I check him out?'

Lucie borrowed Jake's car and parked near Federation Pavilion. She stood in the shade of a sprawling Moreton Bay fig tree, overlooking the park below. Joggers, parents pushing strollers, and those out for a morning walk navigated the wide tree-lined path. In the central fields, a group of police exercised their horses, and schoolboys kicked a football as their coach yelled to them. Cyclists whizzed by, ignoring the speed limit. Lucie squinted into the glare, put on her sunglasses and squared her shoulders.

She wasn't sure she'd spotted him at first. The man on the bench at the top of the steps to the cafe entrance looked too dishevelled to be her ex-husband. As she came closer, she saw he'd angled his body away from the approach. A pot belly now protruded over his drawstring pants, and his hair—unkempt and in need of a cut—had turned steel-grey.

No mistake, however . . . 'David?'

He turned, and jumped up. 'Lucie. Hello.' He'd put on his 'client' voice: stern, distanced.

They stood a few feet apart, not kissing or shaking hands.

'I got you a coffee,' he said. 'Skinny cap.'

He'd got that right. 'Thanks.'

They sat, and while he fiddled to take the cups from the cardboard tray, she examined him. He hadn't shaved, and his skin appeared blotchy; he didn't look healthy. Nor had he made the slightest effort, his t-shirt looking as if he'd slept in it, with a stain on the chest—ketchup? In fact, his unkempt appearance struck her as deliberate, crafted as if he wanted her to feel sorry for him.

'How's business?' she asked. Safe territory.

He rubbed his hands together. 'Going well. Markets are at an all-time high. May not last, though.' David, always the doom merchant. 'How's London?'

'Good.' She took the opening. 'Zoe said you'd been travelling. Did you go anywhere nice?'

'Here and there.'

'Oh?' Zoe had also said she'd heard rumours he'd taken off to a clinic in the country, where they offered healing programs for people suffering relationship trauma, though he'd never admit to that. 'In Australia or overseas?' Lucie pressed.

He took a large slurp of his coffee. 'What do you want, Lucie?'

That surprised her. 'I thought, from your behaviour . . . that you needed closure.'

He hung his head, avoiding her gaze. 'I shouldn't have done any of it, I realise that now.'

Her anxiety levels heightened. 'Any of what?'

'Sending those emails to our friends. Your family. Your boss.'

Her boss? 'Who do you mean?' Her senior partner in Sydney hadn't mentioned receiving any venom from David. They were good mates—she would have told Lucie.

'Charles . . . Charles somebody or other . . .'

The Christmas party. She tried to keep her tone steady. 'What precisely did you say to him?'

David scratched the side of his nose, and lifted his eyes to the sky. 'Was I the last to know that you were leaving me for someone else? You never did me the courtesy of telling me, just let me think you were bored, you'd had enough. After all I'd done for you.'

'There was never anyone else. You can believe it or not, your choice. My conscience is clear. Where I went wrong was thinking you felt the same way about the parlous state of our marriage.'

His head jerked up, a perplexed crease across his forehead.

She softened her tone. 'That we'd run our race, that it was the right time to part ways, while we could remain friends. I had no idea it would be such a shock for you.'

'I loved you. Lucie, for better or worse. But you—you never got over that American bloke, did you? Oh, I never mentioned it after you told me all about him, but he was always there between us. I knew you measured me against him. Do you know how hard that was, being second best?'

So she'd been right—David had come back to haunt her, masquerading as Martin. 'Why pretend to be him? What did you hope to achieve?'

David shook his head. 'I could never be that man.'

'So why make me think he's still alive?'

'What are you talking about?'

'The phone calls, the shoes . . .' Her voice rose an octave.

'What calls?'

'I know it's you. It has to be.' She knew she sounded a little hysterical, but she couldn't tone it down. 'Don't keep lying to me. *Look at me.*'

A few cyclists at the base of the steps turned their way. David placed a hand on her arm. 'Ssh. Calm down.'

'Don't touch me.'

He backed off. 'Lucie, listen. I got drunk, worked myself into a jealous fit, I suppose. I wrote to Charles, I admit it. Said some bad things about you . . . I called you a slut, told him you'd had an affair with a married man in New York who was a friend of your boss. I said I thought he'd want to know what sort of person he'd hired.' David put his hands over his face, and his shoulders heaved in silent sobs.

'And did you give him Martin's name?'

'Yeah. I'm sorry. I'm so, so sorry.' He dabbed the bottom of his t-shirt over his eyes. 'I'll hate myself for the rest of my life. I know you can't forgive me. I could write to Charles, say I made it up, anything you want.'

Sicker and sadder than she'd believed possible, Lucie took in the broken man next to her—hard to remember happy days with him, their joy at being husband and wife. 'Just answer one question truthfully.'

'Of course. Please. Whatever you need to know.'

'Are you responsible for phoning me and claiming to be Martin?'

'No. No.' He clutched her arm and looked straight into her eyes. 'Absolutely not.'

'Then there's no more to say.' She picked up her bag. 'I hope you find your way back to a good place. Don't let our divorce define you and leave you bitter. If you want my forgiveness, then make a fresh start. Let go.'

She didn't wait to hear his response; David had to sort his own demons.

Lucie and Everett had exchanged a few emails after she wrote to say she was in Sydney and would be able to attend the firm's one-hundreth anniversary celebration after all, but he hadn't suggested they get together. Given they'd become such regular correspondents, she was puzzled by his lack of initiative; she'd imagined he'd be eager to meet her. Perhaps disturbing his Sydney routine, taking time from his day to catch up face to face, held little appeal to him. Then, two weeks into her visit she received an unexpected apology from him and an invitation to have coffee.

They met at Tre Pani, in Dover Heights. Lucie recognised him straightaway from his image on LinkedIn: dark, slightly swarthy, with neatly cropped hair. He stood at the back of the café, waving to her—lanky and well over six foot tall—and she became conscious of his gaze as she wove through tables packed with Saturday brunchers.

A lopsided smile broke over his boyish face. *He's a very young-looking forty-something,* she thought. His engaging grin brought back no flickers of recognition, but as a fresh-faced intern he would have looked very different. If anything, his tidy appearance—button-down shirt, trim haircut—reminded her of Martin, who back in 2001 would have been close to Everett's age now.

'Should we shake or kiss?' Everett asked.

She laughed. 'Kiss, I think. I feel I've got to know you too well to shake hands.'

The light peck on the cheek was friendly, and she sensed no reserve. She shouldn't have assumed she'd be a priority; he must have been busy, maybe his sons were in town for a visit.

'I've snared a spot outside,' he said and led her to a table on the street, shaded by a large umbrella, with views over terracotta rooftops to the harbour.

They ordered coffee and chatted about the bushfires roaring through the country, the destruction of the land, the devastated lives.

'Bloody awful start to the year,' said Everett. 'Hope things improve.'

Lucie nodded. For her, his words conjured not bushfires, but Martin and another inferno. Since discovering David wasn't her tormentor, her anxiety had reignited. She'd become convinced the answer lay with him, so the let-down was double-edged: she was relieved his hurt hadn't extended to such cruelty, but also sickened at the prospect of more hounding by an unknown person.

The waiter served their coffees, and Lucie focused on Everett. 'It's good to meet at last,' she said.

'I only got back yesterday, otherwise I'd've caught up sooner.'

She couldn't recall any mention in his recent emails of a trip. 'Business?'

His forehead crinkled. 'Didn't I tell you? I've been in Europe for the past four weeks.'

Odd, he definitely hadn't alluded to being overseas—in fact, she'd had the distinct impression he'd been in Sydney the whole time.

'What took you to Europe, and where did you go?'

'Scandinavia—had a conference in Copenhagen followed by a university lecture tour through Gothenburg, Stockholm, Oslo . . .'

She stirred the milky froth. 'You should have popped over to London.' A mere hop, skip and jump, and yet he had never mentioned he was a couple of hours' flight away. It was unreasonable to be miffed, yet she couldn't help feeling slighted.

He shrugged. 'No time for a holiday, I'm afraid. I had to get home.'

'Ah, of course, your boys. They'd miss you.' An explanation of sorts, albeit a weak one.

'I flew back via Brisbane to see them, then I had to return to work. Quite a backlog had built up. You must know how that feels, Lucie.'

The sound of him saying her name struck her as intimate, crossing a boundary. Her cheeks flushed. 'You never considered moving to Brisbane, to be closer to your sons?'

'I played with the idea, but I couldn't trust Wendy not to flit off somewhere else if the mood took her. Work-wise I'd have ended up on a constant commuter flight as all the big cases I handle tend to be here. And the boys love coming to visit me, and seeing their gran and cousins.'

'Is your family from Sydney?' It struck Lucie that throughout their correspondence, she'd never asked about his parents, and he'd never offered any information.

'Yes and no. Mum's side is from the States, though she lived here for, oh, best part of thirty years. Until Dad . . . well, until he left us.'

Ugh, messy, she thought. 'What happened?'

'Do you mind if we don't? I'd hate to spoil our first meeting.' He coughed. 'Anyway, I'm thrilled you'll be here for the celebration next weekend. It's incredible how many people are showing up. I wonder . . . would you like to come with me? So you're not faced with walking into a roomful of lawyers, most of whom you don't know.' He made it sound like what it was—a kind offer—not a way of hitting on her.

'That's thoughtful. Thank you.'

'Don't thank me. Remember, I'm the guy who harboured secret longings that one day you'd agree to come on a date. Imagine, two decades later, I'm getting my opportunity. See where patience got me?'

She couldn't stop the giggle that escaped and self-consciously tucked an imaginary strand of hair behind her ear. 'I'll have to make a special effort, then.'

'Okay, that's enough small talk.' Everett focused his gaze on her; his eyes, gentle and direct, unnerved her. 'I've like to hear more about how the years have treated you. I keep thinking about that guy who died in 9/11, trying to imagine how I would have coped with something similar—the enormity of it, and the random nature of chance.' He narrowed his eyes. 'I can't get my head around it.' Then he paused. 'Sorry, am I being inappropriate?'

'No, I've just never talked about Martin much, except with close friends. When we were together, I got used to keeping our relationship a secret because he wanted it that way, afraid of his wife finding out. Even all these years later, it's something I tend to avoid mentioning, as it raises too many intrusive questions. People have this ghoulish interest in 9/11. But recently—' she took a deep breath—'I've had some weird stuff happen.'

'Oh?'

'If I told you, you'd classify me as a certifiable lunatic. Which I may well be . . .' She hesitated, anxious for his interest, afraid of his rebuff.

'I'm a good listener. Try me.'

This was just what she wanted: not only his opinion, but also another opportunity to describe the troubling series of events. Everett's dispassionate demeanour—honed from years of taking legal statements—helped relax her while she told the story, his face giving little away as she went back over every confounding detail. He listened without comment until she said, 'Well, there you have it.'

'Wow.' He ran both hands through his hair. 'I can't blame you for being freaked out.'

She grimaced. 'Does that mean you don't think I'm some madwoman, making up fairy stories or attention seeking?'

Although he pulled a poker face, his eyes twinkled with mischief. 'Well, I don't know you very well yet. I'm giving you the benefit of the doubt.'

'For which I am truly grateful. Amen.'

He bowed his head in acknowledgement. 'You told me about some guy in London. Has he helped?'

Jonathan. Lucie had barely given him a thought since her return to Sydney. He'd texted a couple of times, trying to persuade her to see him again, but he'd stopped after learning she'd returned to Australia. Admittedly, she'd made it sound as if she had permanently relocated. 'That's over,' she said.

Everett grinned. 'Good. I'm in with a chance.'

Coffee morphed into lunch. Lunch lingered until late afternoon, when the cafe owner slipped them the bill. 'Sorry, we're closing soon,' he said.

'This is mine.' Without checking the amount, Everett dropped his credit card on the table. 'On one condition.'

Lucie rested her chin on her hand. 'Which is?'

'Have dinner with me tonight? I can't bear to stop this conversation yet. How does kicking off at a great martini bar in Darlinghurst sound?'

It sounded like the precursor to spending the whole night together. 'I'd like that. Very much.' She saw little point in being coy when it was pretty obvious the attraction was mutual.

He tucked her arm through his and they strolled towards Old South Head Road. 'Let's fill in the time 'til cocktail hour with a walk,' he said.

'On one condition.'

He laughed. 'I can see I'll have my work cut out trying to one-up you. Go ahead.'

'Why didn't you let me know you were in Europe? I mean, it wasn't a secret.'

He closed his hand over hers, and she relished the heat and strength of him—but sensed a reluctance to answer her question. When at last he spoke, he stumbled over the words. 'I reasoned if I told you I was in the region, you might suggest we meet, and I'd be so tempted I wouldn't be able to say no.'

'But—' Lucie looked up at him, trying to read his face but he avoided her eyes. 'I don't understand.'

'I was afraid to meet you—scared, I suppose, I'd fall for you. I might come across as a hardened lawyer, but I have a rather fragile heart.'

'Oh.' She didn't know what else to say.

They walked on in silence until they reached a pocket park. He led her to a wooden bench shaded by a flowering crepe myrtle. With the back of his hand, he swept away clusters of blush-pink blossoms, and they sat in the late afternoon sunshine, surrounded by lengthening shadows that played across the small lawn and flowerbeds.

'I knew from our emails I'd like you,' he said. 'You'd become a real person, no longer simply a girl I'd once had a big crush on, who'd rejected me—worse, not even noticed me. I began to think of you as my friend: someone I'd probably never meet, but someone I enjoyed chatting with, who cheered up my otherwise dry bachelor evenings.'

'I felt the same,' Lucie ventured.

His explanation gathered pace. 'When I accepted the Denmark gig, my first thought was, *Great, I'll go via London, drop in on Lucie.* My second thought was, *Lucie has a boyfriend, my presence could be difficult for her, and what if I really, really like her? I live in Australia, and she's spoken for and living in England.* Do you see my point?'

'I suppose . . .'

'So I decided it'd be better not to mention the trip. And then you dropped on me you were coming back to Sydney.'

'But you still didn't let on you were overseas. Why?'

He pulled a face. 'I'm a dickhead bloke. And you still had a boyfriend.'

'But you changed your mind?'

'I had an awakening.' He gave her a sheepish smile. 'When I went to Brisbane, my ex, Wendy, galvanised me.'

Lucie squirmed at the idea of being discussed by Everett and his former wife, but her desire to learn more won out. 'How so?'

'She's a blunt women who tells it how she sees it. We were having an argument about the boys, old ground—me complaining about not seeing them enough since she moved up north. Wendy looked at me square on and said, "You have to grab life's chances when they present themselves." I thought about that a lot on the plane home. And here we are. I'm bloody glad, whatever does or doesn't come of it.'

Lucie stood up and adjusted her handbag over her shoulder.

His face fell. 'Oh shit, I've blown it, haven't I?'

Oh no you haven't, she thought, *quite the opposite.* 'There's a couple of hours or more until cocktail time,' she said. 'Shall we go to your place?'

SYDNEY

PRESENT

Lucie examined her reflection in the mirror, and with care applied face base, blusher and mascara. Zoe sat cross-legged on Lucie's bed, watching her sister get ready. Jake had taken the twins to the aquatic centre, and without their constant noise a rare peace had descended on the Crows Nest home.

'So much for my sister living with me for a few weeks,' Zoe grumbled affectionately. 'I've hardly seen you. Ah well, at least you're a cheap guest.'

'Stop complaining. You're thrilled to bits by anything that means I might be tempted to stay in Oz. But you forget, I have a job back in London.' Lucie slithered into the navy silk shift she'd bought for the now-postponed anniversary dinner. Fears of a global pandemic had restricted travel in parts of Asia, and with more hotspots daily added to the list of no-go zones, the firm had put caution ahead of mass celebrations in key hubs. Instead, Everett had secured a table for two at Quay restaurant, posh enough to call for the new dress. 'And if I'm a good girl, I'll make equity partner. At long last I'll have a piece of the action and the salary package to go with it.'

'Bullshit to that.' Zoe had never put career before love. When she'd married Jake, she'd asked her boss for a lower-grade, nine-to-five job so she could give him more attention. In her book, sane people put life before work. 'Anyway, I want the dirt on this guy. What's so special about him? Or are you just in a frenzy over the legal wig and gown?'

Lucie spun around, checking the drape of her dress in the mirror, then lifted her hair on top of her head. 'Shall I put it up?'

'Yes,' said Zoe. 'And spill.'

'He's funny. Interesting. Intelligent. Fabulous in bed.' That was an understatement: the sex was a revelation, a mutual exploration of pleasure, a fascinating journey of discovery. He could be gentle or rough, serious or joking, a man in a hurry or a man with all the time in the world. When he buried his head in her neck and whispered, 'You drive me crazy,' she never wanted him to let go. When he kissed her with soft lips, she never wanted him to stop. When he smiled at her, her insides melted, and she wanted to touch him, stroke him, make love to him again.

'That much is clear—your bed hasn't been slept in all week.'

'What are you, my mother?' Lucie took her Manolos from their soft drawstring bag.

'Oh my God, where did you get those?' Zoe snatched up the shoes. 'Seriously, can you walk on those heels?'

'They were that anonymous gift.' Lucie clicked her fingers. 'Shoes, please.'

'You never said they were *Manolos*.'

'Probably from Alan.'

'The stitched-up Englishman?'

Lucie slipped her feet into the luscious confines of the variegated red satin. 'No, Alan's the full-of-himself Californian. Jonathan's the serious one, too keen and not my type.'

'Oh, Miss Popular.'

The deep crimson in the shoes popped, enhancing the navy

dress to give her outfit an understated elegance. 'I had an email from Jonathan today. Foolishly, I opened it.'

'And?'

'It was a sort of stilted outpouring. He begged me to return to London. Said he missed me. What a great couple we make. Blah, blah. To be frank, it left me numb.' She remained quiet about the persistent voice in her head that queried why she'd kept seeing him when her feelings, in a romantic sense, had never run hotter than lukewarm.

Her sister propped herself up against the pillows. 'Have you told him?'

'I made it clear the last time I saw him . . . or thought I did.'

Zoe rolled her eyes. The peal of the doorbell rang throughout the house, and she leapt off the bed. 'That'll be the horny legal eagle. I'll get it—I want to check him out.'

Lucie appraised herself in the mirror. Her uncharacteristic behaviour over the past week had unsettled her. She wasn't used to waiting for her phone to ring, becoming fretful if a few hours passed with no call. Not since Martin had she so wanted to please a man, win his approval. When she had introduced him to Em, Lucie felt like a thrilled teenager when they hit it off. She laughed at her reflection. Her feminist side should have been appalled, but she didn't care; she felt energised and was tingling with excitement.

She flipped her delicate lace wrap around her shoulders, picked up her evening purse and went to rescue Everett from her sister's inquisition. The two of them were standing at the bottom of the stairs, and they watched her descend.

'Stunning,' said Everett, smart in an Italian-tailored suit. 'And those are the infamous red stilettos, I take it?'

Lucie frowned as an odd sense of deja vu caught her: dancing for Martin, naked except for the red shoes. Distracted, she tilted her cheek for him to kiss—and, over his shoulder, saw Zoe give her a broad grin and the thumbs up.

'You may not know this about me yet,' he said, 'but shoes are my thing. Shoes are the sexiest thing ever invented.' He gave her his arm. 'Shall we go?'

After an eight-course degustation dinner, marred only by a cruise liner blocking the harbour view, they strolled around Circular Quay to the Opera Bar. Ahead, the sails of Sydney Opera House soared, and over the water intrepid tourists climbed the Harbour Bridge. A jazz band played, tourists and revellers packed the tables, and passers-by jockeyed to get through the crowd. Everett elbowed his way to the bar, then in standing room only they listened to a set of music. A roar of applause went up when the announcer gave thanks to firefighters and rural fire brigades, everyone cheering and raising their glasses. Young and old stuffed coins and notes into collection tins, proceeds for bushfire victims.

'It's refreshing to see how tragedy can bring out the best in people,' Lucie yelled above the raucous crowd, which swirled around them. She shifted her weight onto one foot to ease her aching heels and toes.

Everett tossed a few twenty-dollar bills into the hands of a charity worker. 'Time to go home,' he shouted in her ear. 'I've walked you too far. Let's see if we can find a taxi.'

At his apartment, he made her sit on the sofa, legs up, then removed her shoes and rubbed her feet. She sighed in pleasure as his gentle hands massaged the sore spots.

'I'll get you a sparkling mineral,' he said, bustling off to the kitchen.

She relaxed into the soft folds of the sofa, glad to be away from the noise and press of the crowds, happy to submit to Everett's ministrations. Being together, ordinary and untroubled, was restful.

He turned on the television to a golf tournament in America. She didn't understand the rules but was lulled by the soothing tones of the commentator. A great waft of weariness hit her. 'Do you mind if I go to bed?' She hoped he wouldn't be miffed, after only a week together.

He smiled. 'No problem. I'll be there as soon as Jason Day wins this.'

Jason Day? She picked up her shoes and kissed the top of his head. 'Thanks, and sorry to be—'

'No worries, it's been a big week. Go and sleep it off.' He brushed his hand against the side of her face. 'Don't forget your phone.' He passed it over to her.

A deep swell of happiness enveloped her as she cleaned her teeth, undressed and slipped into Everett's bed, where they had shared such connection, such desire. Within moments, she drifted into welcome sleep.

A dull, insistent buzzing penetrated the night. Disorientated, she fought against waking up, but the buzzing didn't stop.

She rolled over and felt across the bed for Everett's warmth. A murmur of voices came from the TV in the living room. The buzzing continued. Her head throbbed as she became aware of her surroundings. Her phone, *buzz-buzz*, was a flickering light source in the shadowy room. She groaned, positive she'd put it on silent.

Groggy, without lifting her head, she pressed the phone to her ear. 'Hello.'

His voice. 'It's me, Lucie.'

She shut her eyes tight, her heart hammering. *How dare he intrude here, in Australia, with Everett?*

'Are you there, Lucie? Are you listening to me?'

She glanced towards the closed door. 'I don't know who you are or why you're playing this game, but I'm sick of it.'

'It's me. Martin. You know that.'

'You could be anyone. If you're Martin Cornish, prove it to me.'

'Come back to London. We'll meet.'

So he knew she'd left London—well, it wasn't a secret the way her New York trip had been. A chill ran through her all the same. What if he'd followed her across the globe? 'After all the lies you've told, I don't want to see you. Leave me alone.'

'Lucie, Lucie, I explained. Now Penelope's dead, it's all different.'

'If you really are Martin, then you're a criminal on the run. You stole millions of dollars, then pretended to be dead rather than face the music.'

'I know, it's bad. But I swear—'

'And what about your son? When were you going to tell me about Harrison?'

A heartbeat. 'Harry is no son of mine. Harry is his mother's son.' Silence.

The line dropped out.

Fully awake now, Lucie slumped into the pillows. The TV still droned in the living room, and she was reassured by knowing Everett was a few metres away. Moonlight seeped through the shutters, splaying its beams across the bed. With hands pressed together, fingertips against her nose, she stared straight ahead into the silent shadows. This had to stop. Martin the cat, Lucie the mouse. Whichever way she turned, he came too, taunting her, reaching out and pulling back. What the hell was his game?

Some time after midnight, when Everett slipped into bed and stroked her leg with his foot, her mind relaxed. She lay quite still, feigning sleep, enjoying the feel of his body, his toes soft against her skin, his breath fluttering against her back. After a few minutes his breathing steadied into a deep rhythm, but he kept a protective hand on her buttock.

She fought the pillow for a comfortable position, while her body remained restless and her brain kept spinning. Everett didn't deserve to be messed about, and Martin wasn't his problem. Martin was most definitely her problem—one she must solve to save her sanity. With David eliminated, the answer wouldn't be found in Australia. Yes, she'd only been away from London for three weeks, but if she convinced Charles F-S she was sober, fit and bouncing with intellectual energy, he'd probably be happy to see her return. The firm couldn't afford to be down a senior staffer for long, and she'd taken her punishment like a good girl.

Plotting her next steps seemed easy in the darkness of night. But in the light of day, her resolve teetered when Everett rolled over, cradled her to him and murmured in her ear, 'Are you feeling rested?'

Nestled against his warmth, she faltered. 'Let's go for breakfast.' Easier than a difficult conversation in bed.

'Right now?' He raised himself on one elbow.

'I had another call. Last night.' Best to be blunt. 'I need to talk to you.'

He hesitated. 'Okay.' He peered at her. 'You don't look like you had much sleep.'

An understatement. To avoid his touch undermining her fragile determination, she pushed aside the bedclothes, then pulled on jeans and a crumpled t-shirt. 'Let's go.'

Soon they sat across a rickety table on the pavement outside Cafe CC. Everett ordered them orange juice, coffee and croissants. The flaky pastry stuck to the roof of Lucie's mouth; she had little appetite.

He squeezed her hand. 'You've got to sort this out, haven't you? It's eating you up. You're being haunted by these calls, and to you they are real.'

'What do you mean?'

'I mean, they are real. Of course.'

She took a deep breath. 'I'm going back.'

'Yeah, I know. And I hate it. But I get it.' He stroked her fingers, but she resisted responding. 'If I could come with you, I would, but I've just had four weeks away.'

'I don't expect you to. Your work is here. Your sons.' In truth, she didn't want him with her, complicating things further.

'It's bigger than that, Lucie. I'm falling for you.' He laughed, self-deprecating. 'Well, I guess I did that when I first met you, and it's never left me. Perhaps it's like you and Martin—you have to go back to find out what's what. Where your heart is.'

She swallowed hard and blinked away unexpected tears. 'I'll stay in touch. If you want me to.' She couldn't—wouldn't—promise more. Easier to walk away now, after a week together, than make unrealistic plans.

After all, her future lay in London, not Sydney. Whatever happened with the Martin mystery, it would be foolish for her to embark on a relationship that could go nowhere. Given Everett's evident keenness on her, he'd end up hurt, and she couldn't bear more emotional blood on her hands.

He leant across the table and placed a gentle kiss on her lips. 'Hey, it's all right,' he said. 'If we can't be lovers, I want us to be friends, good friends. Let me know what's happening. Use me as a sounding board. I'm here if you need me.'

Lucie nodded, glad to have his support but doubtful she'd share too much, at least when it came to Martin.

She began a mental to-do list. Now she'd made the decision, she wanted to leave as soon as possible, before anything could change her mind. First, she'd email Charles to reassure him she was rested, healthy and keen to return. Next, a heads up to Kristy. And she'd book in more self-defence sessions with Sonya.

LONDON

Five days later, almost recovered from jet lag, Lucie stepped out of the lift and through the portals of Charnbrook and Henley. Nothing much had changed. The scent of hothouse roses wafted around reception. Stressed executives hurried to their desks. The office's manicured, olde-worlde charm and genteel public face belied the pressure and long hours behind the scenes. A typical Monday morning.

Kristy flung her arms around Lucie, hugging her tight. 'I've missed you, girl,' she said. Without being asked, she filled Lucie in on the office gossip: Jack Hindmarsh, in rehab and unable to come to terms with his broken body, had lost all motivation to return to work; rumours circulated Charles F-S's wife had kicked him out; and his PA had resigned, fuelling more scuttlebutt and surmise. 'He wants to see you as soon as you get in.' The receptionist winked. 'Don't take no shit from him.'

Lucie grinned and headed towards the work hub. 'I'm on it.'

Charles's email in response to hers had been professional: *I'm glad to hear matters which took you to Australia have been successfully resolved. There is no need for a debrief. Onwards and upwards!* In Charles-speak, it meant he didn't want to rehash old ground or discuss her personal issues. The proof would be in the quality of her work.

She dumped her bag on her desk, acknowledged the warm greetings of her colleagues, and sought out Charles in his office.

He gave her an effusive welcome. 'Lucinda, my dear girl, how we've missed you. Wonderful to have you back, wonderful.' He got up from his desk and clasped her by the shoulders. 'My, you look well. The break has done you good.'

His bonhomie made her suspicious. 'Nice to be back, Charles. Yes, I'm quite, er, better, and ready to hit the files. What have you got for me?'

'There's a celebrity divorce in the wings.' He tapped his nose. 'Highly confidential, and it involves royalty—well, minor royalty.' His glee was obvious. 'It's a coup for the firm. A feather in our cap.'

Lucie immediately envisaged doorstop interviews and an unwelcome spotlight. 'Have you done any sort of risk management plan?'

He leant against his desk. 'Don't be ridiculous, we are perfectly capable of handling any public curiosity. However He examined his hand and flicked an invisible speck of dirt from under his thumbnail. 'There are a few considerations and vested interests.' He checked his watch. 'I've a busy schedule today. Dinner tonight? Full briefing?'

She sighed—nothing had changed. 'I don't think so. Let's keep work in the office.'

His face hardened, but his voice was light. 'We mustn't get off on the wrong foot, Lucinda.'

'We're not going to "get off" at all, Charles. I hope I'm making myself plain.'

He cleared his throat and handed her a folder. 'Read this. I'm sure you'll have questions. I'll be available at, say, 6 p.m. My office.'

Lucie took the brief. 'Not a problem.'

'I'll have champagne on ice ready as a welcome back gift.'

'No thanks, I'd like water and tea. Any hint that you're stepping beyond the bounds of a professional relationship, and I'll make good on reporting you to the Law Society.'

He opened and closed his mouth, a fish gulping for air. Then he laughed. 'Very droll.' He didn't look amused, though. Clenching his fists, he turned his back on her.

As she strode from his office, she was shaking a little at her audacity but grinning like the Cheshire cat.

Her evening meeting with Charles was tense. He exuded hurt indifference and responded to her questions with a pedantry she found puerile. 'As an Australian,' he said, you cannot possibly appreciate British sensitivities around the Royal Family.'

She kept her temper by telling herself a man scorned was a man who needed to grow up. 'I understand the public's insatiable appetite for gossip, Charles. In this instance, we need to keep our client out of the media—or, at the very least, ensure careful management of messaging. Not a time to be blowing our own trumpet, eh?' His jubilant attitude could come back to bite him where it hurt if he didn't settle down.

'Quite, quite,' he said, straightening his tie.

She registered his discomfort with a kick of satisfaction. He deserved a put-down—and not just for his outrageous conceit. As an experienced lawyer, he should know better than to take scurrilous, unsubstantiated accusations at face value. 'There is one other matter I'd like to discuss.'

'Oh?' He peered at her from under hooded eyelids. 'Not another request for extra staff, I hope? Budgets are still very tight, and with business set for tough times—'

'It's about my former husband, David.'

Charles flinched and tugged at his shirt cuffs. 'How so?'

'Why on earth did you take heed of anything—*anything*—my ex-husband, a man you've never met, wrote in an email to you? You're perfect strangers, and yet you took his snide insinuations about me as evidence of my character. After years in family law, surely you can spot an angry divorcee?'

'A terrible misunderstanding, my dear, as I said at the time.' He looked at his feet. 'I don't know what came over me.'

She stood. 'That's not the point, though, is it? You didn't do me the courtesy of telling me you'd had a nasty note from David. Rather, you used his words to sexually harass me.'

'No, no, not at all,' Charles blustered, 'you've got me all wrong.'

'The world has changed, and luckily for you I'm not going to take this further. Let's just say I'm aware you're having some private difficulties of your own, and that no doubt your advances to me were a misguided attempt to find some solace.'

'Yes, that's it. Spot on.' His relief was palpable. 'I'm terribly sorry, you're quite right. Appalling of me. Thank you for showing such sympathy to my situation. Never easy, is it?'

How true: she'd never imagined that climbing to the top of a British legal firm would involve fighting dirty. But keeping a little something up her sleeve for insurance purposes could well come in handy. She had Charles where she wanted him now; he wouldn't risk getting her offside again.

'I think we understand each other?' she said, stretching out her hand.

He shook it. 'Perfectly, my dear.'

LONDON

Lucie regarded the imposing residence from her vantage point on the opposite side of the street. Edwardian, she guessed, judging from the bay windows and distinctive brickwork. The two-storey semidetached house was set back from the street, and a tall privet hedge shielded it from its neighbour. Harrison hadn't stinted himself; a short walk from Hampstead Heath, it would have cost a pretty penny. His inheritance plus the proceeds from the Cotswolds cottage and the 9/11 victims' compensation fund had set him up well. Still, if 'Martin' was only spouting inventive lies, the poor guy had lost both parents, and nothing could compensate for that.

As she scanned the neat proportions of the building, a curtain twitched in an upper room. It occurred to her the house might be divided into apartments. Perhaps she should do a little more homework before banging on front doors, uninvited.

She strolled along Downshire Hill and found a coffee shop on the corner of Keats Grove, run by a pair of Aussies, Dougie and Max. She ordered a three-quarter latte and took a table by the window. When Dougie—wrinkled and tattooed, wearing a red bandana—delivered her coffee, it was a taste of home: strong and creamy. He lingered by her table, on for a chat with a fellow Antipodean. 'What brings you over here?'

She grinned. 'The usual. Work. But I'm here in Hampstead to track down an old family friend.'

'Everyone local comes in here.' He flung his tea towel over his shoulder. 'Well, they do if they appreciate coffee.'

As she'd hoped. 'His name's Harrison—Harry, maybe. Thirties. He's English, but he might have an American accent. Ring any bells?'

Dougie cocked his head. 'Caucasian? Handsome? Short? I might need a few more details. We get a lotta blokes in here.'

Lucie realised she couldn't answer any of those questions. 'Er, white. I think.'

'Max might know.' He nodded at the plump, middle-aged barista with a bulbous nose. 'Know a Harry, Max? From round here?'

Max spoke without looking up from the milk frother. 'Soy flat white. Initials HC. Always takes two packets of sugar. Comes in every morning for a takeaway at nine, and again for a cuppa in the arvo—well, some days he misses.' Max winked. 'Probably when he's being a dirty stopout.'

Sounded like it could be a match. 'How old is he?' she asked.

Max wiped clean the steam wand with a dishcloth. 'Late twenties, early thirties at a guess. We got talking one day, and he told me he'd moved from Oxford way. Said work brought him here.'

Lucie pushed her luck a little further. 'Did he ever mention where he lives now?'

'Yeah, back up this street and round the corner, a few doors up. I know 'cos he once asked if I could recommend a chimney sweep. He's got four fireplaces.'

That clinched it: Harrison owned the whole house. She downed the dregs of her latte. 'Thanks, guys. Appreciate it.'

After strolling back to Downshire Hill, she stopped for a moment at the bottom of Harrison's driveway. Nothing ventured, nothing gained; she walked to the front door and banged the brass knocker. She heard a rustling inside and waited, expecting the approach of footsteps. After a minute, she rapped her fist on the shiny black woodwork and pressed her ear against the panelling. She could have sworn she heard distant music and a door being shut, but still no one came, so she took a pen and small notebook from her handbag.

Attn: Harrison Cornish. Please contact me, she wrote. *I think your father may be an old friend of mine, in which case I have something of his which is rightfully yours.* She jotted down her name and mobile number, folded the note in half, and pushed it beneath the front door, praying there wasn't a mat under which it might slip.

One last time, she listened at the door. Silence greeted her. She raised her fist to knock again, and hesitated. Whoever was inside clearly didn't want to be disturbed. With luck, her note would pique Harrison's curiosity. If he called and confirmed that he was Martin's son, she'd explain that Martin had lent her his Parker pen to sign some papers, and she'd forgotten to return it. Then she'd buy a replica pen, invite Harrison to meet, and trust he'd be fooled. What clues he might hold about his father, she couldn't fathom, but felt good to take active steps rather than waiting like a jilted bride for 'Martin' to show himself.

It was dark by the time she returned to the mews where the streetlights illuminated her way. A cyclist went past and rang his bell, causing her to jump aside. Up ahead, Mabel put out milk bottles and called out a cheery good evening. 'I wouldn't be surprised if we saw snow,' she said.

Lucie waved to her. 'You must be the last person I know who still has their milk delivered.'

'Can't be losing the old ways.' Mabel tugged her cardigan around her frail frame.

'I've a small gift for you, for looking after Trim. I'll drop it over tomorrow?'

'I love that boy. He puts a smile on my face. You've no need to thank me.' But she looked pleased. 'I'll catch my death out here.' She shuffled back behind her magenta front door with its gleaming brass knob.

Lucie scrabbled in her bag for her keys and, not looking where she was going, tripped against a lumpy mound close by her front door.

Her ankle turned on a cobblestone, and a sharp pain shot up her leg. 'Ouch.'

Looking down to see what had blocked her path, she spotted a familiar swirl of grey fur. She dropped to her knees, the contents of her handbag scattering to the ground. *'Oh no, no.'* Bile rose in her throat, and she clamped her hand across her mouth.

She knew straightaway Trim was dead. His eyes stared, sightless, skywards, and his neck twisted at an unnatural angle. His body appeared shrunken, his red collar loose and floppy, name tag dangling. She swallowed, took a deep breath and forced herself to look closely, desperate for signs of an accident—broken bones, blood. She pressed her hands to his coat and, choking back horror, examined his fur and limbs. Even her untrained eye could see he hadn't fallen from the balcony—he'd been strangled.

She scooped him into her arms and scoured up and down the mews for movement in the shadows. All quiet. The cyclist had long gone in the direction of Fulham: a neighbour, a delivery boy, or a killer? She pressed her face to Trim's coat. No heartbeat, but some warmth still emanated from him—this was a recent act of malice.

Stroking his soft fur, she held him tight, sickened by such cruelty to a defenceless animal. Her beautiful Trim.

As she knelt in the doorway, light flakes of snow swirled, and her queasiness gave way to tears of anger. She gathered her belongings and, still clutching Trim, opened the door, half-expecting to see a note, a warning, an explanation, but nothing greeted her except the low whirr of the heating system. In the kitchen, she laid Trim on sheets of newspaper, found a towel to cover him, and phoned the vet, who offered to collect and dispose of his body that night, after his surgery ended.

Under the harsh downlights, Trim's corpse lay stiff and sad. Without warning, Lucie began to shake in uncontrollable judders, and she yearned for a glass of brandy. But she wouldn't favour who-ever had done this with the enjoyment of driving her to the bottle. She rocked back and forth, determined to keep a sane head. Trim's death couldn't be connected to the Martin business. She mustn't try to join dots where none existed. It must have been a random act, perhaps a gang of kids looking for a thrill. And yet . . .

It was too early for a phone call to Sydney, so she emailed Everett. He'd offered his friendship, and she badly needed some perspective. As she typed the details, the ugly reality of losing Trim took shape.

Moments after she pressed *send,* her phone lit up. 'Everett,' she said. 'You're up early.'

'Couldn't sleep. I was reading the news on my phone when your email popped up. What a horrible thing to come home to.'

'I'm waiting for the vet.' She choked on the words. 'What do you think? Do you agree it's a coincidence?'

'I'd like to say yes, but be extra vigilant, eh?' He was clearly picking his words with care. 'To be honest, I wish you weren't on your own.'

While his concern touched her, she bristled a little at the implication. 'I'm fine. I can take care of myself.'

'I think you should report it to the police.'

'Hardly practical. What would they do?'

'I agree, nothing, but if anything else were to happen . . . it would paint a picture, don't you see?'

She stiffened . . . *anything else* . . . 'Let's change the subject. How have you been?'

'Same old. Missing you. Can I say that?'

She missed him, too: his body wrapped around hers, and his sharp intellect, tart sense of humour and balanced attitude to life. A genuine nice guy, the one who got away, timing all wrong. 'Of course,' she said lightly, and changed gear. 'I went to Harrison's house today and left him a note.'

'Was that wise?'

'It can't do any harm. For all I know, it'll turn out to be a case of mistaken identity.'

'If he gets in touch, don't see him by yourself.'

The doorbell prevented her making a defensive response. 'The vet's arrived. Go get some sleep.'

'I'll call in a few days.'

'Thanks. I'd like that.'

Much as she hated Everett treating her like a maiden in distress, his protective advice wrapped her in a blanket of reassurance.

She patted Trim one last time, then went to answer the door. A moment's hesitation before she called out, 'Who is it?'

'Jamie. You phoned about your cat?' Freckle-faced with unruly red hair, he didn't look old enough to be a vet, but he had genuine compassion in his eyes when he saw Trim laid out on the table. 'Do you know anyone who might have done this? Someone in your street who might've taken a dislike to him? Does he stray into a neighbour's property, perhaps?'

'Not that I'm aware. The only neighbour he has anything to do with is an elderly lady who feeds him when I'm away.'

As Lucie watched Jamie parcel Trim up in the towel, she chewed over his question.

Charles had a reason to hurt her: she'd punctured his ego, shown him up as a sleaze. Hard to picture him cycling down the mews, though, with menace in mind—especially disguised in lycra and a helmet. Did he even know she had a cat?

Alan had a reason, too, and he loathed cats. Fuelled with resentment at being ditched, he might have visited on impulse and taken out his animosity on Trim.

What about Jonathan? Perhaps he'd wanted to punish her for their break-up. Except he'd shown no sign of being heartbroken; after a couple of texts and an email, he'd stopped contacting her, and he believed her to be in Australia.

Further afield . . . the Saudi father who didn't want to return his children? Someone at work she'd slighted? Mr X?

After saying her goodbyes to Trim and Jamie, she sat for a long time at the kitchen bench. A note. Shoes. Pens and watches. A food hamper. A man's voice in the night. Martin. 9/11. Was it all connected?

LONDON

By the end of the week, twelve-hour days had again become the norm. Jack's remaining files all landed on Lucie's desk, together with a couple of urgent child custody cases.

Charles F-S's manner towards her remained cordial but distant. Her threat to report him to the Law Society had evidently hit home, but nevertheless, twitchy and self-important, he kept passing by her desk to remind her his celebrity divorce case should be her priority. While she couldn't believe he had strangled Trim—Charles fought with wits, not fists—she sensed his lingering rancour. He engineered small slights: not inviting her to the firm's Future Directions brainstorm; not introducing her in a client briefing; insincerely apologising when he scheduled a teleconference at 3 A.M., accompanied by a smirk and, 'Sorry, Californians, you know.'

At 7 P.M. on Friday, he insisted she provide an update on the royal divorce. 'Can't risk the juniors eavesdropping.' More likely, he didn't relish returning to an empty house, with no wife and no dinner on the table. He kept yarning on about protocols, and it was well after 8 p.m. when Lucie left the office and stepped out into the black night, amid evening diners and other workers straggling home.

She'd never get used to arriving at work in the dark and leaving in the dark: she felt like a mole digging away underground. Pulling up the collar of her new Burberry coat, she hunched against the wind and headed to the station. Sporadic train service due to repairs on the District line meant it was almost nine when, cold and hungry, she at last made her way along the cobblestones to her cottage. In her hurry to leave the office, she'd forgotten to change from her heels into boots; head down, she picked her way along the uneven surface.

A shadow fell across her path. Startled, she gasped, looked up and almost lost her footing. In front of her door, a man loomed in a black fleecy jacket, with a beanie pulled down his forehead and over his ears. Her heart rate jackknifed, and she raised her arm, ready to shout for help.

Alan smiled, handsome and sure of himself.

Her already damp mood plummeted, and she clutched her briefcase tighter. 'What the—?'

After pulling off his beanie, he shook out his blond mane and kissed her cheek. 'You're looking good. Radiant.'

She flinched in dismay. His behaviour was unacceptable, inexcusable. 'How long have you been here?' Surely not long—the neighbours would have noticed and been suspicious.

'I got back Wednesday.'

That obviously wasn't what she'd meant, and she didn't appreciate his cockiness. 'You seriously don't get it, do you?'

His mouth turned down in a babyish pout. 'I've missed you. Big time.' His eyes travelled in a lazy movement over her body. 'C'mon. Admit it. You feel the same way, huh?'

'As I told you weeks ago, it's over.' She realised a white-ish lie might be her easiest get-out clause. 'There's someone else now.'

He narrowed his eyes, reminding her of a boxer waiting to take a punch.

'He's called Everett. I met him in Australia.'

Alan's entire body stiffened. He reached forward and, for an instant, she feared he might grab or hit her. Under the dim street-light, his face appeared grey and threatening. 'What do you know about this man in Australia?'

'It's none of your business,' she said, taking a small step backwards.

'Oh, but it is.' He lunged, seizing her shoulder, and she froze. 'Let's go inside. We can't talk out here.'

She glanced around the mews. Aside from a light in a lower-floor window a few doors down, every house remained cloaked in darkness. The traffic thrummed in the distance. She tried to tug her shoulder from his grip, but he held fast. 'No,' she said. 'I've no time. Work to do.' Her breath, high in her chest, came in sharp gasps. 'Please go.'

'Oh my, you're fickle, Lucie. First you had that guy Jonathan, the world's lousiest fuck. Then me, who you couldn't keep your hands off. And now some outback dude. You need to get real. If this *Everett*—' he spat the name '—was serious about you, he'd be here.' Alan's eyes darted from side to side. 'I know how to treat you. Give you what you want.'

His mood swing frightened her, but she needed to stay calm and do what she could to get rid of him. 'Let me think about it. I'll call you.'

He eased his hold on her. 'That's more like it. You upset me, returning that watch.'

'I couldn't keep it.' She pictured Trim, rigid on the table, eyes bulging—Alan's work?

The sound of heavy footsteps filtered down the mews, and Lucie exhaled. A man she recognised, portly, wearing a dark over-coat over a city suit, walked at a brisk pace, swinging his umbrella. 'Good evening,' he called out.

'How are you?' Lucie prayed he'd stop to chat, but he just waved his umbrella and kept on going.

'Who's that?' Alan snapped. 'How do you know him?'

'Alan, you must go. I'm tired and I have work to do.' She watched the businessman's back disappear into a house at the end of the mews. Too late now to shout out to him.

Alan pulled her into an embrace. 'Of course. I'm being selfish.'

When he thrust his body against her, she pushed him away in revulsion. If only she could get into the house. 'We can talk another time.' She held her breath. *Please go.*

Her phone trilled from the depths of her briefcase, and she flipped open the bag's clasp and scrabbled inside. As she answered, the call cut out. 'Oh, Charles, good evening,' she blustered, then mouthed 'sorry' to Alan. 'The Hardings case? Yes, of course I can discuss. One moment . . .' She clutched her phone against her shoulder and thanked God for whoever had tried to call. 'Bye, Alan. Chat soon.' She turned her back, fumbled for her keys, quickly let herself in and—relief flooding her body that he'd made no move to follow—pressed her ear to the door until she heard him retreat down the mews.

Legs shaking, she double-locked the door and, overwhelmed by the urge to wash away all traces of Alan, secured the top and bottom bolts before going upstairs to run a bath. She drew the curtains, then stripped off her clothes and threw them in the laundry basket.

As she lay back in steaming water, she replayed the run-in. His overbearing jealousy bordered on obsession. But given he hadn't tried to come into the house, she reasoned he didn't mean her any real harm; after all, he could have easily overpowered her.

She soaped her legs, unable to shift her apprehension that his erratic moods might manifest in any number of ways. She shouldn't be laissez-faire about his threatening behaviour, as it could suddenly escalate—and there were plenty of women who rued the day they hadn't taken better notice of early warning signs.

In fact, now she considered it, there had been an indication right at the beginning. He'd asked Kristy for an introduction, and Lucie, rather than finding such a request odd, had been flattered. Kristy had tried to warn her, told her he was 'awful', but Lucie had put that down to Alan dumping her via text. Maybe there'd been more to it. She'd talk to Kristy, take her for a drink, see what else she could find out about him.

And she'd text Sonya, ask her to include martial arts training in their self-defence sessions.

Lucie snaffled a table at the back of the wine bar, next to the fireplace. Seated on a taupe leather bench seat, leaning against the button-studded backrest, she surveyed the press of office workers, noisy and earnest, out for an early snifter. It was good being surrounded by a gaggle of people. *Safety in numbers.*

Kristy waved at her from the bar, jabbed a finger at the menu and gave a thumbs up. Lucie responded in kind—having a bite out meant longer before she returned to Bellings Mews. Once her haven, home now spooked her, as she was fearful of who or what she might find on her doorstep.

Kristy edged her way through the crowd, holding a bottle of wine and two glasses. In a flurry of dumping her bag, taking off her coat and unwinding her scarf, she settled opposite Lucie. 'I ordered tapas.' She poured the wine. 'Cheers.'

They chinked glasses.

'I like your hair,' said Lucie. 'Suits you.'

The braids had gone, replaced with riotous curls.

'Charles hates it. He didn't dare comment, but his expression said it all—you know, that frown where his nose turns up like he's stepped in dogshit.' She roared with laughter. 'So, what's going on?'

Lucie took a deep breath. 'It's a bit tricky . . . There's something I need to ask you about . . .'

'Don't tell me. Alan.'

'How did you know?'

'He's a grade A asshole.'

'So I've discovered. When you dated him, was he ever . . . weird? Almost a split personality?'

'Hell, what are you saying? Do you mean, like, violent?'

A waiter approached, a tray above his shoulder, preventing Lucie from answering. He placed four dishes on the table. 'Sardines. Chorizo. Meatballs. Haloumi.'

Over his shoulder, Lucie noticed a man at the bar on his own, head down, hunched over his phone. Had she imagined it, or had he been staring at her and glanced away as soon as she looked across? He wore a peaked cap that shaded his face. She shifted sideways to look between two men, heads together, blocking her view. But the man had swivelled on his seat and now had his back to her.

'Lucie?' Kristy asked.

'Sorry . . . what were we saying? Oh yes, Alan. A bit overbearing, not violent as such.' Possibly violent to Trim. 'More stalkerish. Possessive.' She took a piece of spicy chorizo but had lost her appetite.

'Interesting.' Kristy strummed her fingers on the tabletop. 'He wants everything his own way. And he's all talk. Where's this leading?'

'I've ended it with him, not that he was ever more than a fling. But he won't give up, he seems to think I don't mean it, and—am I exaggerating all this?' She ran her fingers through her hair, suddenly unsure what she'd hoped to gain from Kristy. 'Oh, forget it. I'm being stupid.'

'You're not.' Kristy speared a meatball with her fork. 'He called me today.'

'Alan?'

'Wanted to take me for dinner. Said he'd made a mistake. I told him to piss off and never call again.'

'But last night he bailed me up on my doorstep.'

'Told you. He's an asshole, a player, and I reckon he wants to play you against me.'

That had a ring of truth. Lucie's mind flashed back to the night they'd met, when as a joke—or had he been serious?—he'd suggested a threesome. She let her gaze stray around the packed room, still harbouring discomfiture about the man at the bar, although now she couldn't see him. 'What do you know about Alan, aside from where he works? Have you been to his place, met any of his friends?'

'He's got a flashy bachelor pad in Shoreditch with a large-screen TV, vodka in the freezer and a king-size bed. I suppose he might have a wife and four kids stashed away somewhere. As for his friends, I only met guys from the bank, the kind who like cocktails and cocaine. Fast-talking dickheads.'

'Did he ever talk about what he does in America?'

'Nah. To be fair, I never asked. I think he stays in five-star hotels, does deals and flies back. Maybe that's where he keeps the wife and kids.' She gave a hearty laugh. 'Eat up and let's change the subject.'

Kristy's vivacious company cheered her. By the time they parted, the receptionist's down-to-earth pragmatism had brushed off, and Lucie walked to Temple station in a more optimistic mood. The after-work crowds had thinned, and the city streets were quiet. Ahead, a man talked into his phone with little regard for keeping the conversation private. Behind her, footsteps rapped in time with hers. A Swedish couple, tourists, asked her the way to Fleet Street, but no one overtook her. When she kept walking, the footsteps started up again. She glanced back and saw the shadowy figure of a man. Her heart picked up pace, and so did her feet. Behind her, the steps seemed to mimic hers.

At the newsstand, she lingered over a rack of magazines. A

man in a hoodie passed by, and she stared at his back. Alan had a similar hoodie—but so did lots of people. The man loitered at the station entrance, hoodie shielding his face, and she swung in the opposite direction, desperate to get away. Along Embankment, she couldn't see any taxis for hire. A bus pulled up a few yards ahead and she jumped on, heart pumping, willing the driver to pull away before the man in the hoodie followed.

Her heart rate slowed to normal, and she slumped in her seat, appalled she'd let her imagination overtake her good sense. Of course the man hadn't been Alan, or anyone else she knew.

The bus indicator board signalled they were headed to Lark-field and West Mailing—places she'd never heard of. At Tower Hill, she got off and hailed the first black cab she saw. Twenty minutes later, it drew up outside her house, headlights illuminating the front door. No one in sight, no packages. She asked the driver not to turn the cab around until she was safe inside, then paid him and hurried to the door. She pushed her key in the lock and waved to him before entering.

Brightness streamed down the hallway where she'd expected blackness. She frowned, trying to recall if she'd left the lights on. After putting her bag and keys on the hall table, she went to the kitchen; in there, too, lights shone bright on every surface. In a panic, she dashed to the sitting room, where darkness greeted her. Shaky, she ran upstairs and flung open the bedroom door, letting free a blast of freezing air. The room remained as she'd left it that morning: bed made, lights off. But light glimmered under the bathroom door.

With trepidation, she tiptoed forward. 'Is anyone there?'
Silence.
She turned the handle, stepped back and kicked open the door.

Light streamed out. A whistling sound, a whooshing behind her. She swung around and ducked her head as something flapped at her face, wings battering the air around her. She screamed, covering her head with her arms. The bird, not large, brown and ordinary, a sparrow, flew across the room and landed on the chest of drawers.

Terrified, Lucie backed into the bathroom, keeping her eyes on it, and grabbed a towel. She edged her way to the balcony door and noticed it was ajar. Had she left it open? Was that how the sparrow got in? Keeping one eye on her quarry, she pulled the door wide open and crept across the room. As she neared, the bird took off. She flipped the towel in its direction, but it needed no help to find its way out into the evening air.

She shut and bolted the door, drew the curtains, then sat on the bed, trembling and angry at her stupidity. Still out of kilter after Alan had bailed her up, she must have gone through the motions that morning in a dream, leaving lights on and forgetting to close the balcony door after watering the plants.

Jittery, she went downstairs, double-checked all the doors and windows, and turned off the kitchen lights. Maybe she'd left them on for Trim by mistake, a reflex action. The hall light could stay on.

Before she went to bed, a little against her better judgement she wrote to Everett. She knew she shouldn't lean on him, playing with his emotions, but she felt vulnerable and needed to share the burden.

I'm getting jumpy over silly little things. I thought someone was following me tonight. Possibly a guy I saw a few times casually who turned up at home uninvited last night. He won't accept it's over between us. I think he's the one stalking me, maybe who killed Trim. To be honest, he scares me a little. I'm going to get in touch with Women's Aid, see if his actions warrant reporting him to the police. Lxxx

Knowing she'd have difficulty turning off her anxious mind, she took half a sleeping pill and fell into a fitful slumber.

In the night a distant bell dragged her into consciousness. Her head was heavy with drugged sleep. The ringing persisted. Her befuddled brain concluded it must be Everett, worried by her email. Disoriented, she reached for her phone. 'Hello,' she murmured.

The sound of breathing. Soft and rhythmic. In, out. In, out. 'Who is this?'

In, out. In, out. Steady, repetitive. In, out.

'Who are you?' she screamed. '*Stop.*'

A light chuckle. The call clicked off.

Lucie shivered under the duvet and lay on her back, preparing for a long night.

LONDON

Everett's response to Lucie's late-night email was swift. She read it, strap-hanging on the Tube, on her way to work the next morning.

> Good idea to see if the police can step in. This guy sounds like a looney-tune. I'm worried, you sounded so distraught, I'm flying out on Qantas this afternoon, getting in 5.25 A.M. Saturday. If the police can't help, I'll meet him; make it clear he has to stop bugging you. We'll get to the bottom of this. Everett. PS. I'd be lying if I didn't admit I can't wait to see you.

The train jolted to a halt, and Lucie glanced up from her phone. Engrossed in Everett's note, she'd missed Temple station and gone on to Blackfriars. She pushed her way to the platform and followed the pack of commuters up the escalator, mentally mapping how she'd backtrack to the office.

An icy wind whipped off the Thames, and she buttoned her coat, tugged on gloves and pulled her beret over her ears. She wouldn't get lost if she walked alongside the river, and it would be good thinking time. Everett's visit thrilled and unsettled her—she needed to unpack her emotions. The idea that she needed rescuing was a bit offensive. She was quite capable of handling Alan. She'd even arrange a restraining order if she had to, although on what grounds? He hadn't forced his way in, and she had no proof he'd strangled Trim.

A man hurrying past bumped her shoulder, and she recoiled. 'Sorry,' he said.

Everett surely knew she could deal with Alan, so his sudden decision to fly Sydney-London on the pretext of confronting an ex-boyfriend sang of an excuse to see her. Which meant he was very serious about her, didn't it? *I'd be lying if I didn't admit I can't wait to see you.*

She turned right into Bouverie Street, glad to be out of the eye of the cold breeze. Since she'd come back from Australia, Everett had never strayed far from her thoughts. But did she want a long distance romance? How would that work? Besides, she needed to clear a few things up—it was all very well for her heart to yearn to be with him, but her head had a say too.

Much as she hated to admit it, a few things about Everett bothered her. His reticence to talk about his father, for one. Whenever she asked, he shut her out, yet he was fulsome about his sisters, his kids, and their extended family. He didn't talk much about his mother either, other than to say he wished he saw her more often. The fact Lucie didn't remember him from New York niggled, too. Sure, it had been twenty years ago, and she'd been young, busy, and in love with Martin. But those eyes and smile would surely be impossible to forget, and she only had Everett's word he'd interned at the same office. Then there was that month he'd spent in Europe with no mention of it in his emails. Did his reasoning ring true— that he'd been too afraid of meeting and falling for her?

Taken individually, nothing he'd said or done ought to ring alarm bells. While in his company, she'd always felt relaxed and safe. But what if he wasn't who he said he was? Could he have made the calls, sent the gifts? Had he already followed her back to London?

She quickened her step and thrust her hands in her pockets, her brain darting in and out of dark corners. She'd reached a point where she trusted no one, not even her own judgement. *Get a grip, Lucie. Em met Everett. Zoe met him. He's a lovely guy.*

But although Lucie hated doubting him, she needed to be sure. As soon as she reached the office, she'd email Chester in New York and ask him for a favour—to see if the firm still held records of interns from 2000.

The cottage held no surprises when Lucie returned that night. The same lights blazed that she'd left switched on. All the windows were closed and shuttered. No packages or letters awaited her. Wanting to ease the eerie silence, she found a YouTube production of *Last Night of the Proms.* To a hearty singalong of 'Land of Hope and Glory', she checked her email, on tenterhooks to hear from Chester, although the mere act of reaching out to verify Everett's credentials had already calmed her anxiety about him. Once again she'd allowed her imagination to run away from her.

Chester's response was brief and incurious: he'd passed her query to HR and asked they contact her direct. In a PS, he commiserated about the postponement of the firm's celebrations, adding: *You'll be on the invite list when there's a new date.* She scrolled through the remaining emails; nothing yet from Lockstein Felterman's HR department, but a few hours remained of the New York workday.

After a light supper, she tidied the kitchen and went upstairs to give the bathroom a quick once-over. She opened the door slowly, listening for flapping wings. All remained as she'd left it that morning.

While she washed down the basin, her phone rang. She didn't recognise the number.

The man's voice carried a transatlantic twang, British with a soft edge of American. 'Is this Lucie Wilkinson?'

She tucked the phone under her ear while she wiped her hands on a towel. 'Harrison?'

'Yes. I got your note. I must say, I'm most intrigued. Something to do with my late father?'

'Was your father Martin Cornish?'

'The same. He died in the World Trade Center attacks.'

She briefly closed her eyes, trying to keep her voice steady, I'm sorry'.

Harrison sighed. 'It was a long time ago. One moves on. I'm amazed you found me.'

'It wasn't hard.' She forced a light tone. 'Your father's old workplace told me the family had moved to England, and the phone directory did the rest. I took a chance.'

'You can run but you can't hide, eh?' Harrison gave a fake-sounding laugh. 'And what is it that you have of my father's?'

Lucie hesitated. He might not be concerned about an old pen. Suppose he told her to keep it, or even chuck it out? She needed to talk it up. 'His fountain pen. An antique, I believe. I'm certain it's very valuable.'

'And how did you come to have it, may I ask?' His accent bewitched her: an odd mix of American vowels combined with English parlance.

'I worked for the legal firm he used and was called in to witness some papers. He handed me his pen and—I'm not sure how it happened, but I forgot to return it. I found it a couple of days later and phoned his office.' Her story sounded convoluted, unrealistic, but she kept going. 'His secretary told me to hold on to it, he'd collect it next time he came in. I remember her saying it held special sentimental value, that it had been a gift from his wife on the birth of his son. You, I guess.' Did that sound over the top? But she had to make sure he wanted it. 'And then 9/11 happened. I forgot all about it and later moved back to Australia. I found the pen when I cleared out my flat in Sydney before moving over here, and vowed I must return it either to you or his wife, if I could locate you. To be honest, I felt guilty I hadn't done so at the time. My poor excuse is being young—I didn't give it enough importance. I would imagine anything of your father's would be extremely special for you.' She stopped, hoping she'd laid the groundwork well enough and hadn't stretched the truth too far.

If she had, it appeared Harrison didn't notice. 'Yes, indeed. How marvellous. I have so little of my father's. My mother has passed, but I will most happily take it in her memory.' He sounded formal; if she didn't know better, she'd say rehearsed. 'May I ask . . . you said in your note my father was a friend of yours?'

Lucie froze. How stupid of her. 'A . . . a small exaggeration on my part. I should have said "acquaintance".'

'Oh, that's a shame. I'd hoped . . .' His voice trailed off, leaving his hopes unexplained. Did he know about the affair? Could he have suspicions of Lucie? Or was he just naturally curious about the father he'd lost? On the other hand, he might know everything and be taking part in this charade.

Although a meeting with Harrison seemed unlikely to yield answers, she needed to pursue this opportunity. 'Well, then, let's arrange a time to meet.' Somewhere public but discreet, where their conversation wouldn't be overheard.

'What are your whereabouts in London?' Again, that strange old-fashioned phrasing.

'Fulham.'

'Ha! I'm in Paddington as we speak. Why don't I pop over to your place? I can be there in half an hour.'

Her shoulders tensed. Much as she wanted—*needed*—to solve the conundrum around Martin, she didn't want a strange man coming to her house. With Everett due to arrive in the morning,

she would wait until he was with her, just in case. 'It's not convenient right now. How about tomorrow, midday? I can text you
the address.'

A long pause. 'Fine, fine.'

She rang off, a plan forming. *Safety in numbers.* Not just with
Harrison, Everett too—at least until she absolutely confirmed he
held no secrets. She sat on the edge of the bath, drumming the
phone on the palm of her hand. *Safety in numbers.*

Everett's flight got in at 5.25 A.M. If he wasn't held up in
passport control and customs, Lucie estimated he'd be with her
somewhere between 7 and 8 A.M. By then, she should have heard
back from Lockstein Feltermann.

She tapped out a text to Sonya: *Can we schedule a workout at
8.30 tomorrow? Meet at mine?* A back-up plan: if the news from
HR wasn't what she wanted to learn, she'd have an excuse to be
out of the house, with time and space to decide how to proceed.

The phone beeped with Sonya's response: a thumbs up and a
smiley emoji.

On being awoken by a persistent ringing, Lucie opened one eye.
In disbelief, she saw the clock next to the bed read 8 a.m., and her
phone showed *Everett Black.* What the hell?

'Shit.' She picked up the phone, heart pumping, for once
relieved she'd forgotten to put it on silent. 'I overslept. Are you
here?' Everett laughed. 'Almost. About ten minutes away, the
driver says.'

She leapt out of bed and into a fury of activity: showering,
pulling her hair into a ponytail, slapping on foundation, and
dressing in stretch pants, a fleecy top and thick socks. As she put
on her running shoes, she heard the diesel chug of a London
black cab coming along the mews, and dashed down the stairs.

Flinging open the front door, she was greeted by Everett's
curled fist, poised to knock. He tossed his bag down the hallway,

kicked shut the door and enveloped her in a huge bear hug within his Driza-Bone jacket. She breathed in his familiar smell.

'Oh, Christ, I've missed you.' He tilted up her chin, his soft brown eyes sparkling. 'Beautiful woman.'

She wriggled from his grasp. 'The alarm didn't go off, or maybe I didn't set it, sorry. It's all a mess, and my personal trainer's due in fifteen minutes.'

Everett's face fell. 'Your—?'

'Yes, I know. Inconvenient, but it's a regular thing. I couldn't alter it, and I figured you'd want a shower, breakfast.' She backed down the corridor to the kitchen. 'Follow me, I'll show you where everything is.' Speaking in a nonstop gabble, she opened and closed kitchen cabinets, pointing out tea, coffee, bread, eggs. 'Bathroom's upstairs. Apologies for the unmade bed. Hot water takes a few minutes to come through. Towels on the rack. If you want to sit outside, the balcony door opens inwards. Cushion covers are under the bed, next to the barbells.'

'Wow,' said Everett, 'is it nerves or have you plain gone off me?'

Lucie gaped. She noticed he sprouted stubble and needed a shave, or maybe he'd decided on a new look. It suited him. 'I haven't, but . . .'

'But. . . ?'

Typical Everett, unable to let an elephant sit in the room. 'Let's sit for a minute.'

She perched on a stool, while he took one at the end of the counter, probably realising it was best not to crowd her.

'There's a couple of things I need to clear up,' she said. 'Things that, right or wrong, I find worrying.' Should she be saying this before checking her email? Too late now. 'First, why do you avoid talking about your father?'

His body tensed, and a light flush reddened his cheeks. 'Why do you ask?'

Good question. 'I don't like secrets, I suppose, or evasive

behaviour.' She frowned—he deserved better than that. 'I've had some shocks, you know that. Someone's trying to spook me, and I don't know who.'

His eyes widened. 'Are you saying you think I might be involved?'

She crumpled. 'I don't know. I can't see straight anymore. Things I took as given, that I'd believed in for years, have turned out to be fake. Martin never told me he had a son and probably a happy marriage. David harboured deep resentment of Martin, saw him as the enemy. Of late I've dated two hopelessly unsuitable guys, God knows why. Loneliness? Or maybe a desire to prove I can be a serial dater and not get emotionally tied.' She looked him in the eyes. 'I guess what I'm trying to say is, from now on, if all the cards aren't on the table I don't want to play.'

'I get that. And hearing you say it pleases me. It means you care.'

She let his comment pass. 'So don't hold back on me. Please, tell me about your father.'

'I'm ashamed of him.' He swallowed. 'Because I'm terrified I might be like him—a weak man, when push comes to shove.'

'Weak? How?' It wasn't a word she would ever have used to describe Everett.

He rubbed his hands over his head. 'This is hard for me to talk about. In fact, I never speak of it. I've buried it in a place marked The Past. So forgive me if I get emotional. My father is someone I deeply despise.'

He sounded so distressed, she was apprehensive about pushing him further, but until she had answers she'd be plagued with uncertainty. She pressed her hand against his chest. 'It's between us. I promise.'

Everett looked up at the ceiling. 'Twelve or so years ago, Mum was diagnosed with a rare blood cancer, and the prognosis was pretty bleak. The doctors warned us there would be a long, painful period of treatment, and even then they only gave her about two years. I was in law school at the time, over in Perth. I offered to defer, but Mum wouldn't hear of it. Dad took early retirement so he'd be able to take care of her.' He shut his eyes. 'For a few weeks, that's what the bastard did. And then, right in midst of her first bout of chemo, he failed to wake her up one morning with her usual cup of tea.'

Oh my God, thought Lucie, *he ran away.* 'Go on,' she murmured.

'Poor woman found him dangling from a rope in the guest bedroom. It's amazing the shock of the sight of it didn't kill her, but turns out she's a lot stronger than him. She's still with us— been in remission more than ten years.'

'But . . . why? Why did he do it?'

'Because he was a selfish old man.'

'You don't know that, Everett.'

'Oh yes I do. He knew it, too. He left a note to justify his actions. Said he couldn't cope with watching her die. And thanked her for all the good years she'd given him.'

'Jesus.' No wonder Everett was still angry. But she couldn't help thinking there must be some compassion for his father's actions, surely? 'He must have been suffering from depression.'

'That's what Mum said, too. I've always had trouble buying it. Feels like a poor excuse.' Everett pressed his thumb and forefinger across the bridge of his nose. 'I know I sound like an unsympathetic prick, but you've got to understand how many times I've rolled this around in my head. Of course he was depressed, to some extent, that much is obvious. But he had a duty to her, and he failed in it.' Lucie waited, sensing him do battle with his memories. After a few moments he turned to her, his eyes dark with sadness. 'Drop it, Lucie.'

She stood, intending to put her arms around him, when the doorbell rang out, so she squeezed his shoulder instead. 'That'll be Sonya.'

'Wait.' He took her hand. 'What else has been gnawing at you?'

She hesitated. 'Later.' He'd already explained about his time in Europe, and she saw no point going over old ground. 'After my run.' She grabbed her zipper jacket from the back of the chair and picked up her phone. 'See you in an hour or so. Help yourself to whatever you want.'

With mixed emotions—shame at doubting him, fear he was lying, sadness about going out and leaving him—she opened the front door. At least a run might clear her head.

Outside, Sonya ran on the spot, wearing shorts and a lycra top. Her muscles rippled and gleamed with sweat. 'Boxing lesson?'

'A run and a few stretches.' Her concentration couldn't manage anything more strenuous.

'Ready to go?'

'In a tick.' Lucie turned and called down the corridor, '*Everett.*'

He appeared in the kitchen doorway, hope on his face, and walked towards her.

'If you need to go out, there's a spare set of keys in the hall table drawer.'

'Right. Thanks.' He peered over Lucie's shoulder and waved at Sonya. 'Hi there. Enjoy the workout.'

Sonya's right eyebrow raised a fraction, but she waited until Everett closed the door, and they were jogging up the mews. 'My, my. A new man in your life?'

'A friend from Australia. We met when I was back home.'

'Pretty fit friend. Staying with you, is he?'

Good question, and it reminded Lucie—she stopped at the next lamppost and pulled out her phone. 'Something I have to do. Give me a minute.'

'Sure. I'll see you at the park gates.' Sonya took off at speed, dodging into the gutter to avoid a man walking his dog, and narrowly missed colliding with a cyclist.

Lucie scanned through her inbox until she found an email from a woman she didn't know, Hermione Fletcher, with the subject header: *Everett Black*. Lucie stared at the screen. What if he turned out to be a fraud? She'd have to get rid of him somehow. Ahead, Sonya disappeared round a corner; Lucie would ask her for help, if it came to that.

The email was comprehensive. Everett Black had interned at Lockstein Feltermann during the summer of 2001, following his graduation from the University of Western Australia. His ID photograph was attached. Holding her breath, Lucie clicked on it.

She examined the youthful face that stared back at her. This version of Everett had a mass of black curly hair and a terrible moustache, which drooped a little at the edges. The eyes were unmistakeable, but as for the smile—he had bad teeth, stained and crooked. Since those days, he'd spent a small fortune at the dentist. She laughed out loud—no wonder she didn't remember him.

With a bounce in her step she jogged towards the park, figuring out how to curtail the run without appearing rude so she could get back to Everett.

Sonya was on the phone, leaning against the wall, and hung up as Lucie approached. 'You look like the cat with the cream.'

'Good news,' said Lucie.

'Care to share?'

'A work thing. But I have to run a couple of errands before I get home, so okay with you if we only do one lap?'

'Sure. Are you cooking a gourmet meal?'

She hadn't planned that far, but Sonya had a point: a cosy evening at home would be far preferable to going out. When Everett's jet lag kicked in, he'd be able to crash on the spot. 'Yes, I need to pick up groceries and wine from the specialty deli.' And stop by one of the antique shops on King's Road for a vintage fountain pen, a Parker if she could find one, Harrison might know his father had favoured them. In all the morning's drama, she'd forgotten to tell Everett that Harrison would be visiting later. But she'd be home long before he was due, leaving her plenty of time to explain how she'd located him.

Sonya clapped her hands. 'Let's get that body in action. One circuit of the park, and then some drills: press-ups, stretches, side-steps, lunges. First, some sprints. Ready? Go.'

Lucie groaned at Sonya's idea of a shortened session, but dutifully took off from a standing start. The quicker the workout, the sooner she'd be home.

LONDON

PRESENT

It was nearly 11 A.M. when Lucie returned, arms heavy with shopping. She hastened to the kitchen, calling down the hall, 'I'm home. Where are you?' She cocked her head but could hear nothing. She smiled: Everett had probably taken a shower and fallen asleep.

Humming under her breath she put the kettle on and unpacked the groceries. After discarding the receipt and wrapping from Antiques & Everything, she placed the oblong box in the drawer of the hall table, alongside the unaddressed envelope containing the note from 'Martin' that had started all this. She'd show it to Everett later, but first a cup of tea was in order. With Harrison due in less than an hour, she needed to freshen up and brief Everett. If he had taken a nap, he'd be groggy when he woke, needing a few minutes to orientate.

Realising she had no idea how he preferred his brew, she put the two mugs on a tray with sugar and milk. The bedroom door was closed, and she had to put the tray on the floor before turning the handle and peeking inside. The bed remained as she'd left it—unmade, the duvet thrown back.

'Everett?' She peered into the bathroom. Empty. Then, even though the doors were shut, she scanned the Juliet balcony. Just the chair and flowerpots.

He must have popped out for something. She put the tray on the bedside table, pulled off her jacket and decided to have a quick shower. Her back pocket vibrated, and she pulled out her phone, expecting Everett. *No Caller ID*. She grimaced. *Oh no, not today.*

'I'm here.' Martin's voice, clear and close. 'Waiting for you. It's time to celebrate.'

She froze. *I'm, here?*

Blood pounded in her head. She raced down the stairs. Grabbed her keys from the hall table and flung open the front door. Stopped. Could he be here in the house? What if he'd broken in, hidden somewhere downstairs? She swung around and kicked open the guest bathroom door. No one.

Her mouth dry, she ran to the kitchen. The laundry door stood ajar. No shadow. Heart racing, she ventured closer and pushed it further back. Machines, a basket of washing, Wellington boots.

The living room . . . She darted along the hallway. Hung back for an instant. Took a breath. Grabbed the doorhandle. Turned it. Screamed.

Everett lay on the floor, badly beaten, blood gushing from his face. Immobile. Dead? She rushed to his side and put her ear to his chest, listening for a heartbeat. 'Everett . . .'

He stirred a little. Tried to speak, but no words came.

'Oh my God, what happened? What has he done to you?' Lucie looked wildly around the room. It was swathed in half-light, curtains drawn.

In the corner, a man with his back to her, face half-turned. She recognised the tilt of those shoulders. The sleek cut of fresh-trimmed hair. The outline of his jaw. These past months he'd invaded her dreams, challenged her deepest-held beliefs. Made her question her sanity. A man who would put himself above others. A man not to be trusted. She clamped a hand across her mouth. *It couldn't be.*

And then he spun around. Lucie jumped up and took an involuntary step backwards. Not a ghost from her past but an unwelcome incarnation from her present. 'You.' A sick thump roiled her stomach. 'What are you doing here?'

Jonathan grasped her arm and tugged her from Everett. 'I'm Harrison.' He spoke with an American twang, mimicking Martin's voice. 'The man you invited here.' He giggled. 'You only had to ask, you know. Harry was right under your nose, after all.'

She stared at him, unable to fathom his words. 'What are you saying?' She tried to pull away, but he held fast. Gripped her so tight, she winced. 'What have you done to Everett?' Her voice rose, panicked. Everett lay quite still. 'We need a doctor.' She tried to shake him off, but he held firm. 'Jonathan, let go. We have to get help.'

'I don't believe a doctor is necessary. And it's Harry. Call me Harry.'

Her chest tightened. 'Where's Martin?' She scanned the room, still confused by that call—*I'm here*—and half expecting him to emerge from behind the drapes.

'You mean Daddy?' Jonathan spat. His face contorted.

She went limp in his grasp. 'Daddy?'

'Let's leave this wanker—' he kicked Everett in the guts '—and have a quiet little discussion. The two of us.'

'*No*,' she yelled. 'He'll bleed to death.'

'Oh dear.' He dragged her across the room, grabbed his backpack from the armchair, and yanked her towards the open door. 'What a price to pay.'

He kicked out a kitchen chair. Pushed her onto the seat. His strong hands pressed her shoulders hard against the bentwood frame, while his breath came in heaving gasps. Sour. Nauseating. Sweat peppered his forehead. He thrust his face near hers. 'You didn't guess, did you? I knew you wouldn't.'

Clamping his forearm around her neck, he grabbed her right arm and yanked it behind the chair. She tried to struggle, but he kept her motionless. Quivers of fear bubbled. 'Let go of me, Jonathan.' Her voice cracked. 'This is crazy.'

With his free hand, he flung the backpack on the table and spilled the contents. Coils of rope. Masking tape. Knives. He slipped rope around her wrist and pulled it tight. The rough edge dug into her skin. He forced her left arm around the back of the chair. Bound her hands together. 'Be quiet, Lucie. Do as I say and maybe you won't get hurt.'

Her guts clenched. *What the hell does he intend to do?* She held back from kicking out at him—that would make him angrier, and she couldn't counter his strength. She needed to calm him down. 'I just want to understand what's going on.' Her voice escaped in breathy staccato.

Jonathan knelt before her and twisted masking tape around her feet—five, six times. His fingers were red raw where he'd bitten his nails to the quick. Without taking his eyes off her, he reached over to the tabletop and fumbled until he found a slim-bladed paring knife. She stared back at him, refusing to be intimidated. He cut a length of the tape. Tossed the knife back on the table. 'Daddy. Harry. Jonathan. All me.' He smiled and went back to imprisoning her.

She squirmed, helpless, as she finally understood. All along, it had been Jonathan playing a sick game. No, not Jonathan: Martin's son, Harry. But she couldn't think of him by that name—to her he was Jonathan.

'Why the pretence?' she asked.

A glint of victory lit his face. 'It was a bit of a gamble. Mommy always said I was quite like Daddy in many ways, but I figured if I grew my hair long, played up my British accent and changed my speech patterns, you wouldn't notice. And you didn't, did you? Pretending to be Jonathan meant I could have you where I wanted you.'

'But Harrison lives in Hampstead.' She floundered, trying to join the dots. 'You took me to your flat in Pimlico—'

'I set it all up in advance,' he crowed. An Airbnb. I chose somewhere I knew you'd hate, where you'd never want to return.'

Remembering the times they'd had sex, she tasted bile and swallowed hard. Pushed away the image of Jonathan thrusting on top of her. 'How could you, you bastard?'

He took another coil of rope from the table. 'Oh, Lucie, Lucie. Your sins will always find you out. You should know that.'

'My sins?'

After winding the rope around her waist, he knotted it behind the chair. Took two steps back and leant against the counter. Contempt sputtered from his lips. 'You think—you really think I did all those things to you because I wanted to, you whore?' She blanched. 'Yes, you're a despicable whore. You were my father's whore and you are still a whore—with me, Everett, Alan, Charles, anyone who takes your fancy. Fucking you made my flesh creep, but it had to be done. You had to learn what suffering means.' He jumped up; paced back and forth, tapping his fingers along the counter. 'My mother thought my father was a saint. She trusted him. She loved him. And when he died, she blamed me. *Me.*' He thumped his chest. 'She made my life hell. Do you know what that's like—to bear the brunt of someone else's grief?'

Keep calm, Lucie. 'Your father *was* a saint. He would never have left your mother.' Not a saint but a spineless two-timer who'd abandoned Penelope, leaving her to look after their damaged son, while he made hollow promises to Lucie.

He spun around. Struck her hard across the cheek with the back of his hand.

She gasped, tears springing to her eyes.

'You stupid bitch. I found your letters after Mommy died. She'd kept them hidden in the attic.' From the front pocket of the backpack, he pulled out a wad of paper and envelopes. 'Would you like to be reminded?' He unfolded a document. '*M—The weekend was endless. I hate weekends. Well, unless you're here with me, not home with her. Sorry, that sounds so selfish, doesn't it? But I dream of the day when we won't need to hide anymore. I know you've promised me it won't be long now, but I get so scared that she'll cling on to you and not let you go. I wouldn't let you go. I won't let you go, not ever, not once you're finally in my arms every night and every weekend.*' He waved the paper in her face. 'It drivels on like this. They all do. You aren't much of a writer, are you, Lucie? Or should I call you "L"—that's how you signed them all.' He chucked the letter aside. 'Daddy was no saint, but Mommy was. She knew about you, and she never said a word, not to anyone. She kept his memory unsullied and kept her hurt, her terrible hurt, hidden.'

So, Penelope must have spent years brooding about her husband's girlfriend, poring over Lucie's letters, her bitterness brewing until she finally revisited New York in an attempt to seek Lucie out.

He clenched and unclenched his hands. 'I had to take Daddy's place. Care for her, be there for her, help her through her dreadful pain. She couldn't be left alone. I had to be there, every evening, every night, every hour. At night, I shared her bed to share her pain.'

Oh my God. 'What did she make you do?'

'Never you mind, you floozy. Mommy was pure, not like you with your dirty ways, wanting to do it in daylight or on the floor or as a sex doll. I helped Mommy keep Daddy memory's alive.'

Lucie's stomach lurched. Jonathan was painting a vile picture—if everything he said was true, not an evil phantasmagoria.

He pinched her chin. Forced her to look into his eyes, pinpricks of hate. 'She taught me how no one ever loved Daddy more than her. How being in England meant we were safe from nosey parkers. How the attic was her precious space to be with Daddy. She forbade me to go up there, the place where she kept his dirty secret. I expect it drove her a little mad, never knowing who you were. She tried to find out, though—when I was eighteen, she went to New York for a few days while I was in hospital having my appendix out. She said she had to tie up some loose ends of Daddy's business. But of course she went looking for you, his whore. I think she didn't go sooner because she disliked leaving me at home alone, fearful I'd break into the attic.' He paused. Took a deep breath. 'And she couldn't bring me with her because I wouldn't fly. After Daddy's death, planes gave me nightmares. When Mommy made me go with her to England, I screamed for the whole flight.'

Pieces of the puzzle dropped into place: Penelope had taken so long to hunt for Lucie because she wouldn't leave Jonathan on his own. But who revealed her identity to Penelope?

He released his grasp on Lucie's face and resumed pacing. 'When Mommy came home, I asked her if she'd found what she was looking for. She said, "No, but they're all liars in that city." I worked it out, though, later.' Triumph crept into his voice. 'Before she died, when she was too ill to leave her bed, I found those letters. There were no words for my anger. You stole my father and destroyed my mother. You ruined our lives. So I vowed to Mommy I'd get even. In the end, it wasn't hard to unmask you when I found what Mommy had missed. Her biggest mistake was never checking my father's will.'

Lucie frowned. What on earth could he mean? Martin had left her nothing; she knew that she wasn't mentioned in his will because she'd read it before mailing Martin's copy.

Jonathan scrabbled through the pile of letters and pulled one out. 'This one has the clue. *17 July, 2001: I hate it when you go* to Florida. *Two weeks! With her! How can you bear it? How can I bear it? I keep myself together imagining how it will be when finally we're together ALL THE TIME. I'm staying super busy banking lots of billable hours so I can take some time off when you're back. I know you won't read this until you're home but it helps me not miss you so much to write anyway. Love you to bits and back, Lxxxxxx.'* He dropped the letter on the floor. *'Banking lots of billable hours,* eh? That told me you were some sort of consultant—public relations, or a lawyer, maybe.'

He was pacing again. Circles of six steps, looping around Lucie's chair. She braced for a blow. *Don't hit me.*

'That's when I went through all of Daddy's personal files. They were in the same box as your filthy letters. Bank statements. Tax returns. Medical. Car. Personal. Will. I checked every line of every bank statement. I read his personal address book and all of his diaries and found nothing. His will was still in its envelope. I doubt Mommy read it other than to make sure that you—his *bitch whore*—weren't mentioned. She would have left all the details to the lawyers. It was a simple document leaving everything holus-bolus to her.' His eyes hardened. 'Even *I* wasn't mentioned, not by name. Just some legal words about if Mommy predeceased Daddy, his fortune would be divided among any progeny.'

She hadn't found that clause strange, assuming Martin had written it that way because he'd expected to have children with Lucie. He must have wanted to ensure they'd be recognised as beneficiaries alongside Harry.

Jonathan snapped his fingers under her nose. 'Are you listening to me? Aren't you interested to know how I found you out, you slut?'

'Yes, of course I am. Tell me everything.' *Keep him talking. Let him show off.*

He obviously wanted to boast about his cleverness, and she still had her phone in her pocket. If she could find a way to get him to leave the house, then she'd escape from the handcuffs, call an ambulance . . . Even as she thought it, the idea appeared impossible. 'Go on. Please.' She dragged her mind from the image of Everett bleeding into the carpet.

'The will was only a few sheets of paper. Teri Radtke and Aaron Flood, presumably members of his staff, witnessed Daddy's signature.' Jonathan turned back to the table and picked up a sheet of paper. Held it close to Lucie's eyes. The letters blurred, but she recognised *Lockstein Feltermann* at the top. 'The best bit is this covering letter that acknowledges the contents and promises an account to follow. Do you recall what else is in this letter, Lucie?'

Her mind jumped erratically. 'No, I'm afraid I don't.'

Jonathan flipped it over. 'Blah, blah, blah, etcetera, etcetera. *Yours faithfully, Chester Lockstein Jr, Attorney At Law.* But look at the signature, Lucie.' He held the piece of paper in her field of vision this time.

Across the signature box, in neat, familiar script, was *p.p. Lucie Wilkinson (paralegal).* 'Oh,' she whispered, remembering now. She'd often signed on Chester's behalf; it was commonplace for simple correspondence.

'Lucie. L. Who banks billable hours. Once I knew your name, it was a simple Google search to find you in Australia. And once I tracked you down, I checked your social media every day. I got to know you. Your sister. Your husband. Your friends.'

'What if you'd been wrong?'

'But I wasn't, was I? I proved that the first time we had dinner and I tried to get you to talk about New York. Most people who've lived overseas can't wait to show off. You clammed up and changed the subject.'

She wished she'd known it was a test. 'So it wasn't an accident, meeting me in Two Hens? It was all a plan?'

Jonathan tipped his head on one side. 'Well, if I'm honest, I didn't have a plan then. I hated you, of course, and you had to be punished. I mean, you couldn't get away with it—that would be wrong.' He stood behind her. Pressed his hands flat against her cheeks. Squeezed her face until her teeth bit into her gums. Laughed. 'And then you announced to the online world you were moving to London. Oh my, that was a grand day. Then I began planning in earnest. You've no idea.' He slapped her cheeks and stepped back. She gasped, the rope digging into her wrists. 'I worked out what needed to be done.'

'What do you mean?' Her face smarted.

'I would become my father. Mommy always wanted me to be just like him—worship her, study finance. She wouldn't let me be an actor, you know, and I'm so talented. I've got his voice down pat, don't I?'

'Yes, you do. How can you remember him so well?'

'Easy. Home movies, dozens and dozens of them. Mommy never stopped playing them, over and over. Like the photographs—she put a new picture of Daddy on his wall every September 11, so I had to look at him every day of my life. Perfect Daddy. Graduating from Columbia. Skiing down Whisder. Tennis club champion. And she'd remind me, too, lest I forgot. "Be good, Harry," she'd say. "Remember if it weren't for you, Daddy would be with us now."'

'Why blame you?' It made sense for Penelope to hate Lucie, but her own son?

'Because I got sick with whooping cough, Daddy stayed in New York so he wouldn't catch it from me. And he died. My fault.'

What a bully, a monster, Penelope had been. 'Fate took him, not you.'

'Fate be damned. Mommy lost the best years of her life. *You* took them. And then she died. Tit for tat. You have to die, too. But not before you've suffered, shared all our pain.'

Lucie pushed down her horror. How could he be so callous? 'Did you strangle Trim?'

He thrust his face into hers, and she turned from his acrid breath. 'Of course. When you told me how special he was to you, I decided he'd have to go. He had strong claws: . . . it took several goes before I captured him. My regret was not being there when you found him.'

Don't think about it. Stay focused. 'Tell me more about your mother.'

He wagged his finger. 'Oh no, you can't catch me out. I know that little trick—keep the madman talking until help arrives.' He raised his eyebrows as if she were a simpleton, and her heart banged in double time. 'There is no white knight on his way to rescue you. I've got you where I want you.' He blinked several times. Trickles of sweat snaked into his eyebrows. 'It's your turn now.'

She grasped for a lifeline. 'But you love me, Jonathan. We're going to get married, remember?'

'I told you I was a brilliant actor. You believed my little charades. Oh, how crazy you got when those gifts arrived. I had you guessing, didn't I?' He giggled.

'You were very clever.'

'It was all in your letters, all the clues I needed.' He perched on a bar stool, flipping through the ink-covered writing paper. 'Here . . . *I love, love, love my red stilettos! You are such a darling!* He pulled out another. '*Don Giovanni and Dom P. Together with you, that made my three favourite men all in one night. I am sooo spoiled!* Jonathan sarcastically mimicked her girlish delight. 'You even blathered on about never eating tofu, oysters or rice pudding. Was that some stupid private joke?'

What an idiot she'd been; how easy her letters had made it for Jonathan to reel her in.

'I watched you slide downhill, drinking and failing at work. Going insane because you thought your dear Martin had returned from the dead.' A vein throbbed at his temple. 'You romantic fool.'

'You thought I was preg—'

'No, I'd poisoned you—only a little. I mixed eye drops with a powdered wild mushroom and dropped it in your food. The eye drops gave you fever, and the mushroom made you throw up. Like when Mister Puggles died from rat pellets. Daddy blamed me for that. He got very, very cross. I was five, and I figured if rats liked poison, then perhaps our dog would. I tried other things, too, at school. Worms in a boy's bologna sandwich. A maggoty egg. Gasoline in a drink bottle.' Jonathan smiled. 'I got suspended for that one. We didn't see so much of Daddy after that, just some weekends and a few holidays now and then. He wanted me to go to some sort of boarding school for bad boys, but Mommy insisted she'd stay in Boston and homeschool me.'

So, a bully—not a solitary, nerdy kid. Everything he'd told her, lies. *Placate him.* 'That was kind of her.' Lucie's mind reeled that he'd poisoned her, then insisted on nursing her. 'Were you trying to kill me?'

'It was a test. I'd thought I might kill you that way, but I wanted to punish you a little longer. It was such fun getting revenge. Your face when I asked if you could be having a child reminded me of Mommy. She loved to tell me how she'd vomited for nine months, how foul I'd made her body. The agony of morning sickness was worse than any other pain—worse than childbirth, even, she said.'

'Did you ever miss your father?'

Jonathan turned away. 'We must never be anything other than loyal to his memory. We only remember him as the wonderful man ripped from us by cruel fate.'

Lucie eyed his back: tensed shoulders and rigid neck. 'But you loved him?'

'I hated him.' Abruptly Jonathan whipped around, his face twisted. 'He only cared for himself.' He slid his hands down her sides, into her jacket pockets. 'Aha.' To her despair, he took her phone. Shoved it into his waistband. 'Naughty girl.' He undid his tie and pulled it off. 'That's enough talk. I've other business to attend to.'

'Where are you going?' she asked, her pulse speeding up.

He rammed the tie into her mouth. 'You don't listen, do you? I told you, you have to experience real pain, just like Mommy and me.' He knotted the tie behind her head. 'You're going to sit here while I deal with your precious Everett.'

Lucie tried to protest, but was prevented by the tie biting into the sides of her mouth.

He emptied her handbag. Took her wallet and keys. Threw them, together with her phone, into his backpack. 'Not that I need your keys—I had one cut months ago. I found all sorts of interesting things here to play around with.'

Of course: Martin's note in the shoebox, and the Longines watch in the red stiletto. The sparrow? Maybe other surprises', too, as yet undiscovered.

He wiped the blade of a paring knife up and down his jacket sleeve, then held it up to the light and pointed it at her. 'I sharpened this the way Mommy taught me.' He giggled again. 'Sharp enough to slice the hair from your scalp.'

The knife hovered inches from her chest as she gaped at him, transfixed. He grabbed a handful of her hair; gave a painful tug. They eyed each other, tense, before he lunged in one swift motion. She flinched. The knife pierced the lycra of her leggings. He laughed as he cut through the fabric to her knees, nicking her thighs. A few drops of blood oozed from the pitted holes, while her legs trembled.

'The time for talk is over,' he said, letting go of her hair. He swept everything from the table into his backpack, flung it over his shoulder and gave her a jubilant grin. 'I'll be back soon, and then we can have some real fun.'

She glared at him but could only make unintelligible sounds. He kept on grinning.

And then the doorbell rang.

He calmly held his ground, not turning around, his back to the front door. 'We won't answer that.'

Lucie's heart was thumping as she stared, numb with shock, at her blood-smeared thighs. Then, through the doorway, she looked over Jonathan's shoulder and down the hall. The bell rang again, followed by a gentle rapping. She begged to a God she didn't believe in that whoever waited in the mews wouldn't give up, would realise something was wrong. She tried in desperation to free her hands, but they just grated against the rope; she'd only rub them raw if she continued.

Her mouth chafed at the edges. Jonathan, silent as a statue, wary as a bird of prey, held her in his sights. She kept her gaze unwavering as an unseen hand pushed the front door ajar. *How the. . . ?* Then she remembered: in her panic to find—or escape—from 'Martin' she can't have closed it. Fingers appeared around the jamb, followed by a head; never had she been so happy to see, of all people, Charles F-S.

'Anyone home?' he called out, lumbering down the hall. 'Lucinda? It's me, Charles. I come bearing gifts.'

Jonathan's eyes widened, and he spun around. 'What the hell? How did he get in?' He ripped open his backpack and took out the paring knife, still wet with her blood.

Charles's expression turned from benign to outraged when he saw Jonathan lunging in his direction, and Lucie in the background, gagged and tied to the chair. 'What have you done to her, you scum?'

Unable to control her rising panic, she watched, powerless to act.

Everett, dazed and panting, stumbled from the living room, clutching his stomach, shirt ripped and blood on his cheek. Jonathan two-stepped to avoid crashing into him, then stabbed him in the arm; Everett hollered, collapsed and slid down the wall. Charles advanced, swinging a champagne bottle, but Jonathan headbutted him and made a dash for the stairs.

Everett flung out his leg, and Jonathan tripped, toppling over. With a grunt of pain, Everett grabbed his ankle to hold him down, while Jonathan kicked out his free leg in wild strikes.

Charles staggered over and brought the champagne bottle down on Jonathan's head. He slumped forward, silenced and inert.

'Can you sit on him?' Charles asked Everett. 'I'll see to Lucie and find something to tie him up.'

Everett nodded. Maintaining a grip on his arm to stem the blood, he crawled on top of Jonathan.

Charles stepped over the prone body and moved swiftly to the kitchen. He freed Lucie's mouth and unknotted the ropes around her wrists. Her arms were stiff and numb from being locked tight. 'I'll get you water. And something to wash off that blood.'

'Don't bother. Please.' Her voice rasped. 'We have to call the police.' The rope around her waist dropped to the ground, then Charles ripped the masking tape from her ankles. She attempted to stand, but her legs gave way.

'Stay there,' he commanded. He took a bottle of water from the fridge, opened it, and gave it to her with one hand while rifling through the drawers. 'Any rope, my dear?'

Taking a large gulp, she pointed to the counter. 'In his backpack. And my phone.'

Charles passed the phone to her, then scooped up a roll of masking tape and two coils of rope. 'Perfect.'

She stared at the remaining screwdriver and several knives. Her stomach churned.

After taking another slug of water she lurched, dizzy, to where Everett sat sprawled across Jonathan's back. 'Oh, thank God,' he said, you're okay.' His face contorted with pain and relief.

'Can you speak to the police?' She pressed 999 and passed him her phone.

He gripped it under his chin and, in breathy gasps, gave instructions.

Charles was holding down Jonathan's legs. 'Feet first. You up for it?' Nodding, she wrapped masking tape around his ankles. Charles took a length of rope and, in two nifty movements, tied it around Jonathan's mouth.

Jonathan stirred. Groaned. Squirmed to free his body.

'Here.' Charles whipped a polka-dot handkerchief from his breast pocket and threw it to Lucie. 'Help him.' He pointed at Everett. 'By the way, I'm Charles Fensham-Smith.'

Everett grimaced. 'Everett Black.'

If the situation hadn't been so dire, Lucie might have laughed, but she focused on tying the handkerchief around Everett's arm to staunch the blood flow.

'Thanks,' he murmured, and rolled off Jonathan.

Lucie tried to pull Jonathan's arms from under his body, but he was coming around; he thrashed and made incoherent protests. Charles slammed the champagne bottle down on his funny bone, and he yelped. Then Charles yanked his right elbow from under his prone body, bent it behind his back and held it fast.

Everett kicked his shoulder. 'I owe you one, mate.'

Jonathan cried out as Charles twisted his left arm behind his back. While Charles and Everett pressed his hands together, Lucie wound the rope around his crossed wrists as tight as possible. He wriggled and moaned.

'I hope it bloody well hurts,' she said.

A loud knocking on the front door made all three jump.

A stentorious voice boomed, '*Police.*'

Charles straightened his tie, smoothed back his hair and stood. Three police officers barged into the hallway, summed up the situation and began bringing order to the chaos that confronted them.

A policewoman, blonde with a commanding presence, took charge. 'Cuff him.'

While she spoke into her walkie-talkie, asking for back-up and an ambulance, her male colleagues pulled Jonathan to his feet and sat him on the bottom stair, propped against the wall. His eyes, wild and angry, flashed above the rope gag. But where Lucie expected to see fear, there was triumph.

The older officer—overweight, expression hardened by experience—untied Jonathan and clamped handcuffs around his wrists. A young constable, face blighted with acne, removed the rope from his mouth. 'Name?'

Jonathan sneered. 'Jonathan Atkins. These people have unlawfully kidnap—'

Also known as Harrison Cornish,' said Lucie.

He groaned, his bravado diminished. 'No, that's not true, I made it up.' He sounded like a whimpering child.

When Lucie gasped, the policewoman laid a cool hand on her arm. 'Don't fret. We'll be taking statements from everyone.'

While the younger policeman read Jonathan his rights, he kept interrupting, saying they had it all wrong. 'This woman,' he said, glaring at Lucie, 'is my fiancée.' With a tilt of his head, he indicated Everett. 'She is being duped by that man, who is an imposter.'

'You can give your statement at the station,' the officer said.

'You're arresting the wrong man,' Jonathan insisted.

The officer didn't reply.

'Lucie, tell them,' Jonathan pleaded.

Shaking her head, she remained mute. The whole story would come out soon enough: Harry and his repressed anger at his father; his history of bullying. His need to inflict punishment on scapegoats—her, Everett—for his unhappy life. His controlling mother.

He kept yelling at Lucie, but she refused to acknowledge him. At last, back-up arrived in the form of a detective and her partner, and the officers dragged him away.

'Bitch,' he spat over his shoulder.

LONDON

The paramedics declared that Everett's wounds weren't life-threatening. Nevertheless they stretchered him and took him to Charing Cross Hospital overnight so he could be assessed for any internal injuries. Lucie walked beside him to the ambulance, aware of eyes peeking from behind curtains and, across the street, the inquisitive stare of Mabel.

Lucie laid a hand on his forehead. 'As soon as I'm done here, I'll come to the hospital.'

'You don't have to,' he said with a weak grin. 'As long as you fill in the gaps for me when I'm discharged. I still don't get what this whole thing was about.'

'You being here saved my life.' Later, she would find a proper way to thank him for following his gut and taking the initiative to fly over. And she'd explain about Jonathan. 'No arguments—I'll see you soon.'

As the paramedics hoisted the stretcher into the back of the ambulance, Lucie blew Everett a kiss. She rubbed her hands up and down her arms; a wind had started to get up, and she still wore her gym clothes. After raising a hand to Mabel, she returned to the warmth of the cottage.

Inside, she sat down at the dining table with Charles, and they gave their details and explained events to DCI Windgarth, a gray-haired woman with kind eyes. Her partner—a studious, solemn man—took notes. Eventually he read back their statements, bland and matter-of-fact after the afternoon's bedlam, which Lucie and Charles dutifully signed.

Formalities completed, Windgarth approached Lucie and knelt in front of her, keeping her voice low. 'I'm sorry, but we'll need your clothes for evidence, and also have the police doctor examine you and take photos of any injuries you sustained. Are you up to it?'

She didn't have a choice, did she? 'Of course.'

'Thanks. He's waiting outside. I'll ask him to see you in your bedroom.'

'What happens next?'

'At a guess, Jonathan will be charged with assault and kidnapping, possibly attempted murder. It depends which charges have the best chance of sticking.'

'Will he get bail?'

The officer hesitated. 'I can't say. It depends what level of risk we think he poses.'

Lucie's skin tingled. Surely he wouldn't be allowed to roam the streets.

Windgarth patted her knee. 'Get your locks changed. To be on the safe side.'

After the detectives and police doctor departed, an unreal atmosphere lingered of a drama come and gone. On the surface, everything looked just as it had before.

Lucie found Charles slumped in the armchair—stunned and exhausted into silence—and she flopped onto the sofa without a word. The carriage clock on the mantelpiece chimed seven o'clock, rousing them.

Charles stretched his legs. 'We need a drink,' he said. 'Well, I need a drink. Lucinda?'

She'd rather he left, but after his heroic efforts she couldn't throw him out. 'I'll find a bottle of something.' She gave a wry smile. 'If they hadn't taken the champagne as evidence, we could have opened that.'

He slapped his hands on his knees. 'Perhaps not the right occasion.' He cleared his throat. 'I was dropping it off as a thank-you. For all your hard work of late.'

She doubted it—to keep her sweet, more like—but she'd allow him the fib. 'Well, it certainly got put to good use. Jonathan will have a whopping bump on his head.'

'No less than he deserves.' Charles peered at her from under hooded eyes. 'You've been through quite an ordeal, my dear.'

'Could we not talk about it, please?'

'Of course, of course. Crass of me.' He strummed his fingers on his trousers. 'Nice fellow, that Everett. Serious, is it?'

She ignored the question. 'Actually, I need to go and see him at the hospital.' She pushed her weary body off the sofa. 'Forgive me if we call it day here.'

If she hadn't been so wiped out, she would have laughed at his expression of embarrassed horror. He was clearly formulating a polite English riposte. Then he checked his watch. 'Goodness, look at the hour. Much as I'd love to join you for a drink, it's late—and, frankly, I've had enough excitement for one evening. I think I'll be on my way.'

She didn't demur and led him to the front door. 'Thank you, Charles, for turning up when you did.'

He took her by the shoulders and, to her awkward dismay, kissed her on both cheeks. 'Happy to be of assistance, my dear.' He straightened his tie. 'But when everything dies down and your Australian friend goes home, let's have that glass of champagne.

And maybe a bite of dinner? I think it's, ah, time to talk about a little matter of equity partnership?' His eyes sparkled.

'You're incorrigible.' With a small shove, she pushed him out the door. 'I'll see you in the office. In a few days.' After she'd dealt with the aftermath, farewelled Everett, and recovered her equilibrium.

Everett's bed had been curtained off, giving him a degree of privacy. Blood cleaned up, he looked considerably better than when he'd left her house, although bruising had appeared around his left eye and cheekbone. His cuts were taped with gauze, and he had a bandage around his upper arm. Lucie tiptoed over and sat in the visitor chair. He stirred, opened his eyes and smiled when he saw her.

'How are you feeling?' she asked.

'Bruised and battered and drugged.' He shuffled up the pillows, wincing. 'Bastard threw me a mean kick in the kidneys.' He peered at her. 'You okay?'

'Processing it.' She didn't tell him how the sound of Jonathan's manic giggle ticked incessantly, a metronome in her head. *Hehe. Hehe.* How she'd spent the cab ride gnawing on why she'd given him consideration as a boyfriend. With all her legal training, and her antenna always on high alert for half-truths and obfuscation, she'd been a fool not seeing through him. Maybe she'd seen a spark of Martin in him. Maybe she'd been flattered by his youth and persistence. Maybe she'd used him to fill a gap in her otherwise negligible London social life.

'We got off lightly,' said Everett. 'It's frightening to think how close that madman came to dealing us real harm.'

She clasped her hands tight together in her lap. 'And if the law plays its part, he should end up in jail for a very long time.'

'Thank God for Charles showing up when he did.'

'As if his ego wasn't already big enough, now he can brag to the legal community about how courageous he was.' She fell silent. 'He pretty much confirmed an equity stake.'

Everett momentarily closed his eyes. 'You deserve it. Well done.'

'I may not take it.'

His face lit up.

'I need time. All this . . . *havoc* . . . is making me reassess what's important, what comes first. I think I'll take a few weeks' break. Clear my head.'

'If you—' He stopped. 'If I get the all-clear, I'm leaving midweek.'

Unsaid words hung between them. The way ahead would unfold in its own time.

She rested her hand on his arm. 'I'm still computing everything that's happened, and most of it I want to put behind me.'

The nurse popped her head through the curtains. 'I need to change his bandages.' She gave Lucie a meaningful look.

'I'll be back in the morning.' Lucie kissed the top of his head and stifled a yawn. Her body felt like a dead weight. As she waved Everett goodnight, she heard a small warning voice in her brain: *Whatever you decide, don't live to regret your choices.*

LONDON

Lucie took a taxi from Charing Cross Hospital that delivered her to the cottage shortly before ten. Icy gusts of howling wind swept down the mews, the temperature near freezing. Glad to be indoors, she slammed the front door against the weather, flipped on the light and turned up the central heating. After setting her bag on the hall table, she extracted her phone and took it off silent. Damn—she'd missed a call half an hour ago from a mobile number she didn't recognise. Despite the hospital's assurances Everett would sleep like a baby until morning and be discharged by nine, she panicked and dialled her voicemail, fearing internal injuries, unstoppable bleeding, bruised kidneys.

The grandmotherly tone of DCI Windgarth greeted her: After some deliberation, formal charges have been laid against Harrison Cornish. However, as he has no previous convictions, he's been released on bail, with a summons to appear at his first court date. His bail conditions include not contacting you, relinquishing his passport, and reporting to the station twice a week. Please call me as soon as you get this message, and I will run through the charges and tell you next steps.'

Despite being delivered in such a calm, soothing way, the news came as a thump to Lucie's guts. She'd hoped Jonathan would be under lock and key at Her Majesty's pleasure until his trial.

Hehe. Hehe. Was he still laughing at her? At his cleverness? *Hehe. Hehe.*

A blast of wind buffeted the cottage as the storm gathered momentum. Startled, she took a few quick steps back down the hallway to double-lock the front door before removing her coat. As an extra precaution, she secured the safety chain; she'd never bothered with it before, but Jonathan might still have a copy of her key . . . In fact, she should go to a hotel for the night. She'd book a room near the hospital; all she needed was clean underwear and change of clothes.

Then she remembered that first envelope lying innocently on her hall mat: *At last, I've found you . . .* She should give it to the police as evidence, as it was the only card she'd received that hadn't been typed. Jonathan's handwriting might help put him away.

When she searched the hall table drawer, she found only the unopened box from Antiques & Everything, a few old receipts, and Christmas cards. *Odd.* She was certain it was there—she'd seen it that morning when she'd put the dummy pen in the drawer, and had made a mental note to show it to Everett. Jonathan must have distracted Everett and stolen it when he'd arrived.

Her hand trembled as a more sinister option occurred to her: had Jonathan come here tonight, straight from the police station, while she visited Everett? The idea of him back in the cottage, nosing through her possessions, was hideous.

She scanned the hallway. All the doors were shut, just as she'd left them. What if he were still here? Menacing shadows danced up the stairwell, and her legs began to shake. She clutched the hall table and listened. Outside, rain beat down on the cobblestones, and traffic rumbled in the distance; inside, her breath whistled down her nostrils, and she swallowed her fear. A faint *ting-ting* sounded from the carriage clock in the living room as the quarter-hour chimed. She glanced up at the ceiling: no footsteps overhead, no creaks, no signs of another's presence.

'Is anyone here?' she called out in a tentative voice. No answer. What did she expect? She waited a few moments, collecting her thoughts. If Jonathan were in the house, intent on harming her, wouldn't he have pounced by now? But she couldn't be sure—he might be playing cat and mouse, waiting to trap her upstairs.

She put her phone back on silent and, praying the police woman hadn't yet gone to bed, quickly typed: *I'm at home. I think Jonathan may be in the house.*

The reply was instant: *I'm sending someone. Do nothing.*

Maybe two minutes, maybe ten passed by. Lucie remained motionless, dry mouthed, filtering the night-time noises. A siren grew louder as it came closer, the car speeding down the mews. The wailing stopped. There was a loud *rat-tat* on her door, and a man called out, *'Police.* Are you there, Lucie?'

She hastened to undo the safety chain and unlock the door. A burly uniformed copper blocked the entry, his middle-aged bulk a comforting ballast, leaving her feeling silly for being a bother. 'I'm sorry . . . It may be nothing . . . I'm probably overreacting.' Her voice came in breathy gasps.

He gave an avuncular smile. 'Nevertheless, we'll check. PC Stevens, upstairs. I'll look around down here.'

A younger, thinner policeman wearing thick-rimmed glasses appeared from behind him and slipped past Lucie. She hovered in the hallway while they searched the house. Lights turned on, cupboard doors opened and closed, heavy boots trod each room. Finally they reappeared.

'All clear, ma'am,' the older man said. 'But I'm going to leave PC Stevens here on watch outside—DCI Windgarth's orders.'

Stevens, who looked no more than twenty, gave her a reassuring grin, and she smiled back in relief. 'Thank you.' All the windows faced onto the mews, and she'd feel safe knowing the front door and upstairs balcony were under guard.

Before Stevens ventured back out into the night, he advised he'd be right opposite under the streetlamp, with her house and the mews in full view. 'You go back inside and stay warm,' he said.

'Can I make you a hot drink?' she asked. 'Coffee? Hot chocolate?'

'I've a thermos. My mum always sends me on night shift with homemade soup.' He buttoned up his reflective waterproof jacket and patted the outer pocket.

'I don't envy you spending the night being pummelled by this storm. Are you sure you wouldn't rather be inside?'

For a moment, he wavered. 'I've my orders.'

'And I'm very, very grateful. It's good to know you're here.' His mum should be proud of him.

'It's my duty.' He nodded to her, raised his collar and stepped out into the rain-drenched mews. As he crossed the cobblestones, she was glad to see that the wall towering behind the streetlight would offer him some shelter. She once again double-locked the door and attached the safety chain.

With a yawn, she heard her body beg for the relief of a good night's rest. Aching for her bed with its fluffed-up duvet and duck-down pillows, she made her way upstairs.

Stevens had switched on the bedside light, and she saw he'd taken away the tray of congealed mugs of tea. What a nice, thoughtful lad. On remote control, she undressed, pulled on a t-shirt and bed shorts, brushed her teeth and set her phone alarm for 7 A.M. Before she slid between the sheets, she peeked through the curtains: Stevens, water dripping from his peaked cap, stood facing her front door. He looked up, wiping his rain-splattered glasses with his sleeve, and she gave him a small wave.

After turning out the light, she waited for sleep to overtake her. The windows rattled in the wind. Footsteps, heavy, walked at a fast click down the mews and stopped. A short conversation followed, a mumbled exchange, presumably between the officer and a neighbour. Large drops of rain pelted the glass as the gale intensified. She rolled over and burrowed further beneath the bedclothes until exhaustion shut down her feverish mind.

A flash of lightning through a gap in the curtains and an almost simultaneous crack of thunder roused her from deep sleep. Low bangs and thuds reverberated all around; no doubt, tree branches dropping onto the cobblestones or bashing against walls. The noises sounded so eerily close, they could almost have been coming from inside the house. Another burst of light flickered, strobe-like, across the bed, and she wrapped the duvet tight around her shoulders, waiting for the thunder to follow.

She couldn't let PC Stevens keep suffering out in this storm—he must be soaked to the skin. What would his mum think of her? She'd insist he come inside and sit by the front door; at least he'd be dry. She pulled on her dressing-gown and drew apart the curtains. The streetlamp cast a faint glow through her bedroom. The rain lashed at the balcony doors, and she peered through the mottled drips of water but saw no sign of Stevens. He was probably doing a regular check of the area, so she surveyed the mews to see which way he'd gone. As her eyes adjusted to looking through the rain-soaked glass, she noticed a large bundle at the base of the streetlamp, like a bag of rubbish. She opened the door a few inches, stepped onto the drenched balcony and leant over the railing.

Not a black-and-yellow bag. A body in a high-vis jacket. Stevens. The streetlight beamed on his face: his glasses dangled from one ear, and a dark patch spread from under his head. His eyes were wide open, glazed with horror.

She clapped a hand over her mouth to keep from screaming. Giddy, rain dripping from her hair, she stepped back inside and bolted the balcony door. Nothing could be done for Stevens, poor boy; her first priority must be to alert the police. This had to be the work of Jonathan.

A loud banging started up from below. Once. Twice. Three times. She stood, muscles rigid, brain whirling. She'd locked the front door; secured it with the safety chain. There was no way anyone could break in. She held her breath for several seconds. Deep silence surrounded her.

Just when she thought he'd given up, came the familiar sound of a key in the lock. Thank God she'd put the security latch across. But then a grating sound, metal on metal; squeaky, back and forth. He was sawing through the chain. A thump as the front door swung against the wall, another as it slammed shut.

A second of silence, then quiet footsteps. Her heart galloped.

Blood rushing to her head, she looked wildly around. Panic fluttered in her gut—no time now to call the police. The only escape was onto the tiny Juliet balcony; the sole exit, a fall onto the uneven cobblestones. Although that might be preferable to whatever punishment Jonathan had planned.

Then she recalled the canister of defence spray, which after purchasing she'd quickly dismissed as ridiculous. Who would have time to open their bag, find the spray and conk out an attacker? She'd thrown it into the bedside drawer, intending to responsibly recycle it as the instructions suggested.

She tiptoed to the side of the bed. Pulled out the drawer, ever so slowly, terrified it might scrape. Trying to stop her hands from shaking, she felt around with light fingertips. A watch. A tube. A packet of tissues. *Aha.* The can. Between thumb and forefinger, she lifted it out.

A noise stopped her—not outside, from the storm, but closer. She slipped into bed, keeping her hands above the covers, and clutched the spray at her side. Shut her eyes, feigning sleep. With careful fingers she fumbled for the depressor in the lid, hoping activation was by firm pressure.

A creak on the stairs. Her heart was pounding. A slow squeak. The doorhandle twisted, and the door glided over the carpet with a soft swoosh. Footsteps approached the bed. One, two, three, four, five. The sound of heavy breathing filled the air.

Lucie's chest constricted. Her breath escaped in tight bursts of terror. She gripped the can harder.

'Lucie.'

Her body broke out in a sweat as a cold edge of steel pressed against her face. A sharp point traced a line on her cheek. Blood trickled across her skin.

'I'm back to finish off what Harry failed.'

A woman's voice. A voice she recognised.

Lucie opened her *eyes*. Out of the grimy half-darkness, a threatening form bore down on her, head to toe in black, a balaclava over the face. 'Sonya?'

A long knife glinted in Sonya's hand, droplets of blood running down the shaft to her wrist—Lucie's blood, or from PC Stevens? Another flare of lightning illuminated the room. Sonya's eyes shone from within circles of black fabric. 'No, you fool. I'm Penelope.'

'But . . . Penelope's dead.'

Sonya snorted. 'Fake news.'

Lucie's mind somersaulted, unable to fathom the truth. 'You look nothing like her.' The unhealthily thin widow in the magazine photos couldn't have transformed into this musclebound woman.

'Steroids and botox. Hair dye.'

Possibly . . . 'You can't be. I saw the death certificate.' *Keep her talking.*

'Harry's work. He went to med school for a year, before he failed his exams and I made him study finance instead. He learnt a few useful tricks, though. Forgery. Poisons.' She placed a knee on Lucie's chest. 'But he was never as clever as me. Because the

thing is, Penelope doesn't exist. So when they find your body—
and that copper's in the street—with Harrison out on bail, who
will they come looking for? Who's got motive?'

'He'll tell the police you did it. Of course he will.'

'Get real. I'm *dead!* She pressed her knee in harder. 'And right
now he's at Charing Cross Hospital, waiting for my go-ahead.
Once the police follow the trail of blood, *Everett's blood,* they'll
add two and two together and come up with Harrison Cornish,
serial murderer. Who knows, they may even investigate my death
and arrest him for that, too.'

Lucie struggled to follow her logic, consumed with fear for
Everett. 'You're crazy. Everett's in a ward—there are security
guards everywhere, nurses, doctors—'

'Doctors . . . yes.' A lilt of subtle threat.

Oh God. Lucie closed her eyes against the horror of it. 'No.'

'Harrison will make a very plausible doctor, won't he?'

Lucie pictured Jonathan stabbing Everett—or strangling him,
like Trim. *Focus. Think.* You've thought it all out, haven't you? Every
little detail. You're leaving nothing to chance.' *Keep her talking.*

'Don't you want to know why?'

Like mother, like son: she wanted to show off her cleverness,
be admired. 'Yes, yes.' Lucie huffed out the words, lungs constricted by the weight on her chest. *Someone will stumble across PC
Steven's body. Keep her talking.*

'The two of you ruined my life. Martin wanted Harry insti-
tutionalised—put in an *institution.* I couldn't have that. People
would think me a bad mother. I'm a *good* mother. I've always kept
him close, never let him from my sight. And because I was guard-
ing Harry, Martin died.'

Lucie frowned. 'Martin just didn't want to catch whooping
cough.'

'A trumped-up excuse because you had bewitched him. If it
wasn't for Harry, Martin would still be alive. If it wasn't for you,

I'd still be happily married. Ever since I found out about you, I began plotting how to commit the perfect murder. And then one day Harry, that stupid boy, told me he'd rather be an actor than an accountant. That's when it came to me—he'd torment you, as I'd been tormented.'

'Jonathan—Harry—said it was his idea to impersonate his father.'

In the pitch-dark, Lucie could see the glint of Sonya's eyes. 'Nothing was Harry's idea. I pulled all the strings. But I had to remain invisible for it to work, and he knew that. Because when he murdered you, the police would come up with Jonathan Atkins as a suspect. But Jonathan would be nowhere to be found, while Harry would be reunited with his mother.'

'Well, you had me fooled.'

'It wasn't difficult. Harry hates you. He hates his father, too. But he loves me. Whatever I instructed, he did. I'd let him know when you'd be out of the house. He left that bird in your room, you know, for a bit of fun—that time I told you I kept birds, I could tell you were scared of them.'

Lucie swallowed back nausea. 'What else?'

'Little things. When to drop poison in your food. When to have sex. What to do when you asked to go to his flat.'

Lucie strained to hear any activity in the mews—a car being garaged, a taxi, footsteps—but there was nothing except the wind and rain lashing the trees, and she stifled the image of PC Stevens's inert body.

'It all would have worked out so beautifully. We had you convinced Martin was alive. We had you terrified someone wanted to do you ill. Except for the unexpected presence of your Australian friend, you'd be in the mortuary now. So it's all your fault Everett has to suffer, too.' Her voice hardened. 'Take that knowledge to your grave.'

Lucie tightened her grip on the spray can.

Perhaps sensing the movement, Sonya raised the knife, backed off the bed and stood over Lucie, arm aloft. Then she lunged forward.

Raising the can, Lucie pressed the nozzle. Purple liquid squirted into Sonya's eyes.

Sonya shrieked. Lurched sideways. Stumbled against the chest of drawers. The knife clattered from her hand and spun across the room. Lucie leapt from the bed, dousing her with another spray. Blinded, Sonya writhed on the floor. '*You evil bitch*,' she screamed.

Lucie threw the can aside, and took two steps back. Without taking her eyes off Sonya, she reached under the bed and pulled out a barbell, the one Sonya had recommended she buy. She raised its seven kilos high above her head.

Sonya gazed up, her blank stare never faltering as the barbell crashed down, cracking her skull.

Lucie fell to her knees and watched blood soak into the carpet. Sonya's body twitched. A gurgle. A rattling sigh.

Silence fell, cloaking the dimly lit room. On hands and knees Lucie crawled to Sonya. Summoning her strength, she rolled her onto her side, and felt in the back pocket of her jeans. Nothing.

Kneeling in the blood, Lucie flattened her hands against Sonya's back and gave another shove. Sonya tipped over further, trapping her arms. In the other back pocket, Lucie found her phone. At a press of the home button, the screen lit up. She pressed again. *Press screen to open.* She pressed once more. *Try again.* She crawled around Sonya, yanked out her right arm and pressed her index finger to the home button, but the screen stubbornly remained the same. Middle finger, no luck.

Tears threatened to overwhelm her. *Keep going.*

When she tried Sonya's thumb, a screen of icons appeared. Thank God. In the Messages app, Harrison's texts headed the list.

Fingers trembling, Lucie typed, *Change of plan. Not safe. Leave hospital. Go home.*

Within seconds, his reply came. *Why?*

Don't argue. Just leave. Now.

OK Mommy. And a smiley face.

By the light of Sonya's phone, Lucie located her own on the bedside table. Scrolled to find Everett's number. Sent: *Are you okay?*

It couldn't have been more than a few seconds, but the wait was excruciating. She clutched the phone to her chest and stared at Sonya's body. *I killed her. Martin's wife.* Lucie shuddered.

And then the ping came. *Dozing off.*

Tremors of relief shook her. But could she trust Jonathan to obey his mother's command? Everett must be alerted. *Jonathan at hospital. Tell someone. I'm calling for help.*

Without waiting for his response, she dialled 999 and fought back the urge to throw up. Fierce, out-of-control spasms coursed through her.

A calm operator asked, 'Emergency. Which service do you require—fire, police or ambulance?'

'Police.' Lucie slumped against the bedside table. 'A woman is dead.'

ACKNOWLEDGEMENTS

In my early twenties, I was lucky enough to spend several heady years living in New York in the early 1980s. Almost twenty years later, a few weeks after the events of 9/11, I returned to a much-altered Manhattan. On that trip, I took my children to Ground Zero: cordoned off, smoke and ash still swirling—and we cried as we read the heartwrenching notices about lost loved ones, pinned to the wire fencing. In 2017, during my next visit to New York, I went to the Memorial to pay my respects, and was once again overwhelmed by sadness at the enormity of the disaster; awed at the bravery of the victims and first responders; and struck by how many lives remained touched by the lasting impact of that terrible morning.

Back in my hotel room later that day, the first germ of an idea for a work of fiction took hold, and I began to conjure 'what if?' scenarios. Some months later, seated around the kitchen table with my Penpals writers group—Andrea, Sarah and Jay—the story found shape, and after further brainstorming with my partner (who displayed a knack for the unexpected twist), an outline emerged.

A Voice in The Night could not have seen daylight without the faith of my publisher Barry Scott at Transit Lounge, and the insight and tough guidance of my incredible editor Kate Goldsworthy who challenged me to make the book the best it could be. My thanks also to my agent at NAC Literary, Michael Cybulski and editor Sue Anderson—and especially to Andrea Barton who read each draft, and stayed on the journey every page of the way.

I'm indebted to my wonderful mentor, author Lynn Hightower and all my fellow UCLA students who workshopped, critiqued and gave so generously of their time with detailed feedback. Special thanks go to Mark Hoffman, who painstakingly fact-checked New York locations and corrected my American language missteps.

So many people helped in other ways—John Flockton for psychopath profiling; the readers who gave invaluable feedback (you know who you are), in particular Julia Kelly, Ian Hawthorn and Alex Pope; friends and family who listened to my highs and lows, and offered kind words with a glass of wine; and my high school teacher, Miss Garrood, for giving me a love of the English language.

Finally, a huge thank you to my partner and toughest critic, Brett, who patiently talked over every plot nuance, and steadfastly gave me the space and time to get lost with my imaginary characters; and of course to my children, Will and Tess, for being proud and supportive.

ABOUT THE AUTHOR

Born and raised in the United Kingdom, Sarah Hawthorn lived in Toronto, Dallas, and New York before immigrating to Sydney, Australia. After career jumps from actress to journalist to publicist, she relocated to Bundanoon in New South Wales's beautiful Southern Highlands to pursue her dream of being a full-time novelist. When not writing, Hawthorn enjoys theatre, cooking, and walking her dogs.

OPEN ROAD

INTEGRATED MEDIA

Find a full list of our authors and
titles at www.openroadmedia.com

FOLLOW US
@OpenRoadMedia